LEARNT TO BE CAUTIOUS

JAINA KIRKE

For Troy, whose enthusiasm for my writing sometimes surpasses my own and whose love and support have always encouraged me.

CHAPTER 1

*K*itty Bennet was not quite eighteen and it seemed to her that a new world of opportunity had unfolded before her. With three of her sisters married, Kitty found that she was now the prettiest, liveliest girl left in the house.

No more would she be in Lydia's shadow, whose lead she had always followed into flirtation and adventure. No more would she be snubbed by those who preferred her elder sisters, who always condemned her "wild, unbefitting" behavior. Now only Mary remained, and nobody would care about her. Kitty knew that she was destined to be married before she turned twenty.

Upon this rosy future, however, there was a blemish. Her prospects had not improved as much as she'd hoped with her sister's marriages. Her oldest sister, Jane, had invited her to live with them at Netherfield, and Kitty had leapt at the opportunity. Not only would it get her out from under her father's excessively strict rules, but she fully expected to meet and flirt with every one of Mr. Bingley's single, rich friends. But no such friends had ever materialized. It appeared that most of his friends were already married.

Now, though, there was talk at last of a young man who could be a prospect for her. Her uncle had hired a new clerk—a young, single, handsome new clerk! Aunt Phillips had told Kitty everything, and Kitty begged to be the one to carry the news to her mother. Mrs. Bennet would be beside herself, and this time none of her sisters could take any attention away from her.

Kitty burst into the drawing room at her parent's house at Longbourn, without the slightest regard for the servant trying to announce her.

"Mama!" she cried. "I have such news!"

Not only did her parents and sister Mary rise to meet her, but Jane and Charles Bingley and Maria Lucas, were there as well. Kitty's excitement climbed; she would be able to tell them all, and she knew that at least Jane and Maria would be pleased.

"Oh! Kitty, I am glad you are here," Mrs. Bennet said, setting aside her teacup and hurrying to embrace her daughter. "You are not the only one with news. Jane has come, with an announcement she promises will be exciting!"

Kitty glanced at Jane, who looked as placid as ever, except for a slight blush at her mother's words, and felt a little twinge of despair creeping up under her excitement. "Mine is exciting as well, Mama," she said, but not loudly enough. "I just came from Mrs. Phillips, and—"

"I am sure it can wait, Catherine," her father said, fixing her with a stern look over his cup. Kitty glanced at him and sighed. Ever since Lydia had married, she had found it harder to get away with anything less than perfect obedience to everything he said. And these days, he always seemed to have a new irrational demand. It was only slightly better living with the Bingleys; they were less angry in their discipline, but not much less determined to keep her pleasure to a minimum. At least they let her out of the house to visit her aunt. Mr. Bennet had not even permitted that much.

She sank into a seat on the sofa next to Maria, who gave her only a sympathetic glance.

Mary handed them each a cup of tea, with that precise civility that only she could make so strangely offensive. Kitty took it with a muttered thanks that was largely covered up by Maria's "thank you," and glanced again at her father. He still watched her carefully. Kitty sighed, and looked at Jane instead. *Hurry up, then, and get it over with,* she thought. She should have known that she couldn't have commanded her family's attention so easily.

Jane, seated next to her husband, looked at him with an encouraging smile. He returned it, and stood up. "My dear Jane and I have concluded our search—we have found an estate to purchase, and in fact, I completed the deal last Thursday." He took a deep breath and looked directly at his mother-in-law. "It is, however, rather far from here; in fact, in Lancashire."

Mrs. Bennet gave a wail of despair. "Lancashire! My dearest Jane! So far! How can you leave me without one married daughter nearby to comfort me?"

Kitty snorted. If her mother would only listen a moment to *her* news, she would not be so despondent. Mr. Warde was not likely to take his wife very far from Meryton! But her father shot her a warning glance, and she knew better than to try to mention it yet. "I am very happy for you, Jane," she said, shrinking back in her seat.

Jane smiled and reached across to Kitty, taking her hands. "Thank you, Kitty. I know that you have become accustomed to living with Mr. Bingley and I, and we would wish to have you live with us again— but I think, when we have gone away, it would be better for you to remain here until we are quite settled. That is, of course, unless you have an opportunity to visit elsewhere!"

"Thank you." Kitty said. But she scowled. She would not be pleased to be back at Longbourn, where her mother kept far less fashionable company than the Bingleys and her father was always ready to pounce on her for everything she did. And she never received any invitations to go to London with anybody. But then, if she wanted to have a chance at attracting Mr. Warde, she had to remain in the area.

But in Lancashire she could meet anybody! How could she hope to determine which of her choices would mostly likely lead to the greatest chance of making a gentleman fall madly in love with her? Here she had the man, but there—so much possibility!

Her unenthusiastic reaction to Jane's news sent the course of conversation away from her. Mrs. Bennet thanked Jane profusely and accepted the invitation on Kitty's behalf, but Kitty wasn't really listening. She wondered whether she would be able to get away any time soon. Maybe she could go back to her aunt and arrange to meet this Mr. Warde before anyone else. What would her mother say to that!

"Oh, Kitty, did you not also have some news?" Jane asked after a few minutes, pulling Kitty back out of her thoughts.

Kitty did not want to give her news now, after all that; it certainly would not get the attention it deserved. But Maria was already spurring her on and everyone looked at her expectantly.

Kitty sighed, and stood. She would give it her best, but all the joy had gone out of the announcement. "Uncle Phillips has hired a new clerk. His name is Mr. Warde. And, Mama, she says that he is young, and eager to make a name for himself, and very handsome—and single." Her father merely rolled his eyes to the ceiling at this news, but Mrs. Bennet could be counted on to react appropriately.

"Kitty! That is excellent news! Oh, my dear, we shall have to meet him as soon as may be! Did you find out from your aunt when he is to arrive?"

"He has arrived in town already; yesterday, I believe. But only Mr. Phillips has seen him."

"Well! You will speak to your aunt again, and see if she can introduce us?"

"Of course, Mama. She promised she would, as soon as she is able."

"How wonderful! I am very glad that we will not have to rely on your father to make the introduction." Mr. Bennet ignored that statement and the glare that accompanied it, but Mrs. Bennet didn't give him any chance to defend himself. "Oh, Jane, it seems as though it were only yesterday when we were wondering how we would ever be able to meet our dear Mr. Bingley, and now look at the two of you!" And she went off in another paroxysm of grief over their decision to leave her. Kitty scowled.

"I would have thought that this development would bring you more joy, Kitty," Mr. Bennet said, with that teasing glint in his eye she hated so much. "Do you not expect to like Mr. Warde? That would be a singular occurrence. I am certain there has never yet been a young man in the neighborhood you have not broken your heart over."

"Of course I expect to like him; he is very handsome, my aunt says." She did not know how to answer the rest of his speech.

"Ah, yes. Of course, he will not wear a red coat."

Kitty only shrugged. There seemed little chance of her ever marrying an officer now, and had her mother not also said she once preferred a red coat? She did not seem to have mourned the loss when she married Mr. Bennet.

"Well, my dear, I can only hope that your sister's scheme to have you join her in Lancashire does not conflict with your wedding." He chuckled at his joke and turned away, leaving Kitty to stew in her growing frustration.

On any other day, her news would have been the talk of the household for a week, at least. But not today, oh no. Today, perfect Jane had to come to visit and announce that she planned to leave. Well, Kitty thought scornfully, it would be a greater surprise if she stayed! Meryton was small and unfashionable, and if Kitty had enough money to go somewhere more exciting, she would leave, too.

But a new single man in the region, now, that was *not* expected, and much more exciting. Kitty had begun to wonder whether she would ever have the chance to meet a young man who wasn't already spoken for. Of course, she thought that if Jane or Elizabeth would only take her to London, she might be able to meet someone, but they had both been married for several months and had not made a whisper of doing that for her. So Kitty knew that she would have to shift for herself if she ever wanted to be married, and Mr. Warde was the best chance at that she'd had in a very long time. She would go after him with every bit of strength she had, and she would get herself a husband no matter what. Jane could move anywhere she liked—to America, if she wished. It hardly mattered. Kitty would be married!

CHAPTER 2

onday provided Kitty with her first sign of hope. She had caught a glimpse of Mr. Warde at church, and from what she could see, he was every inch as handsome as she had expected. But he departed directly after the service, so Kitty had not been able to manage an introduction then.

Monday provided her the opportunity she would need. Mrs. Phillips called with the news that she had not only met Mr. Warde, but had actually managed to secure his promise that he would come for supper and cards on Friday. Her visit to Netherfield was to invite the Bingleys and Kitty to this same gathering. Mrs. Bennet had already accepted eagerly, and although Mr. Bingley had a prior engagement, Jane accepted for her sister and herself.

Kitty arrived at her aunt's house that Friday evening with every hope fully excited. How long it had been since she had met any single men! And Mr. Warde would be there already, as she had purposely delayed to ensure that they would be late in stopping at Longbourn to pick up her mother and sister. She was very sure that they would be able to make the most effective entrance if everyone was watching them. Jane and Mary ignored her eager chatter in the carriage, but Mrs. Bennet picked up her enthusiasm about meeting Mr. Warde and

Kitty felt that her mother would be an excellent ally in her matrimonial aspirations.

A small party greeted them on their arrival, but it was a cheerful one. Encouragingly, few other single young ladies had come, and Kitty's hopes rose further when she saw Mr. Warde standing at the back of the room. Surely his twinkling eyes indicated a temperament to match her own.

Mrs. Phillips called him over to introduce him to her family. He examined them each in turn as he approached, and Kitty felt proud of her appearance beside Mary. She couldn't compete with Jane, or Lydia, or even Lizzy, but at least with Mary she was always sure of looking better by comparison.

He greeted them all warmly, and Kitty thrilled to her toes at the sound of his rich voice. The man could read aloud from Fordyce and make it interesting, just by virtue of those deep tones!

"How do you like working for Mr. Phillips?" she asked him, taking a half step toward him and dropping her voice so he would have to lean in to hear her clearly.

He did lean in, and rewarded her with a smile. "I like it very much. Your uncle is an excellent teacher." Kitty blushed, pleased. Complimenting her uncle already was a sure sign of his interest. A promising beginning!

She started to ask him about his preference for parties like this one before Mary interrupted. "What do you do for leisure, Mr. Warde?" Before he could answer, she added, "Reading is a favorite pastime of mine."

"Oh, yes, I do enjoy reading."

Excitement and interest animated Mary's face. "Do you? What are your favorite books?"

Kitty rolled her eyes. Reading! What a wretched conversation to begin at a party like this! Did Mary really think he cared?

But he answered politely and somehow (Kitty could not entirely perceive how it came about) he soon offered Mary his arm and led her into the room. Never mind that, as the elder sister, Mary was entitled to his first attention. Kitty felt slighted, and it stung. What had she done wrong? Things had started off so well. Had she said something wrong? Did she not look as pretty as she'd thought? Oh, what she wouldn't have given to have Lydia help her dress again!

She followed behind them as he led Mary into the room, but he took her to a sofa that did not admit any possibility of a third. Kitty could see no way to rescue him from Mary's miserable conversation. And Mrs. Bennet sealed his fate when she called Kitty over to settle some point of argument with Mrs. Phillips, that apparently Jane could not or would not address.

But at least her aunt could be relied upon to turn the conversation to Mr. Warde; she was always eager to show off whatever she knew of her connections.

"Well, Kitty, what do you think of him?" she soon asked, glancing over at the sofa where he and Mary were talking.

"He is every inch as handsome as you said," Kitty said eagerly. "But what is he like? Poor man! I am sorry that he felt it necessary to attend Mary instead of me. I imagine he is repenting of it now!" She glanced over at them again, and this time caught his eye as he looked at her. She blushed and smiled, and he nodded his head ever so slightly. Kitty smiled more. They had established quite a connection on so short an acquaintance, she thought. It really was a pity that Mary had gotten in the way.

"I have found him to be quite a gentleman," Mrs. Phillips said. "He would do very well for one of you girls, I am sure. Nothing like some other young men we have entertained here in the past!" She glanced at Mrs. Bennet, who nodded an understanding that Kitty felt reasonably sure she did not possess, for Kitty herself had no idea which young men her aunt could mean. She had quite enjoyed the company of all the gentlemen her aunt had introduced her to, even though she had never been their first choice.

With Mary, there was certainly no danger of Kitty being passed over once more. She glanced at her sister again, and again caught Mr. Warde's eye. They exchanged the same gestures as before, and Kitty's heart soared. It would not be long now before he found a way to shake Mary off and come to talk with her instead. And then, who knew? Kitty felt that she was very ready to be fallen in love with.

She quickly took inventory of her appearance to be sure that everything was in order. Brown curls arranged carefully about her face, white gown smoothed and pulled and pinched to show off anything that would entice a man while remaining appropriately modest—yes, the special care she had taken in dressing that evening was sure to do her some good.

"Do you think that he might want to come to dinner some night?" Mrs. Bennet asked.

"I am sure he would not be opposed! How very kind of you!" Mrs. Phillips looked over at the other two and beamed. "He certainly seems to be getting along well with Mary."

This startled Kitty. Did he? Were his frequent glances at her not evidence to the contrary? She looked back at them again but this time his gaze remained fixed on Mary. Maybe her aunt saw something she did not. But Mary! Impossible! She had nothing that would attract any man. It was ridiculous. "I do not think it is that so much as he is too polite to break away from her," she said. "I have caught him looking at me several times tonight."

Mrs. Phillips smiled and patted her hand. "Well, between the two of you, I am not surprised that he is having trouble deciding where to bestow his attention. You are both lovely girls, are you not?"

Kitty looked to her mother, who, she knew, thought very little of Mary's beauty. But Mrs. Bennet said, "Yes, both of them have turned out very well this evening. I am very glad to see Mary continuing to put herself forward. For such a long time she tried to stand out by playing music. But that is not as conducive to attracting a man as is speaking to him, I believe. Why, that is how my other daughters caught their men, is it not?" She and Mrs. Phillips shared a comfortable chuckle and ignored Jane's quiet protest.

Kitty sighed, trying to push down the stab of self-doubt that had risen thanks to her mother's comments. She had never been much for Mary's kind of conversation on the best day, and she was fairly certain that nothing could induce her to enjoy sitting with a man and blinking her eyes at him the way Mary was doing with Mr. Warde. If that was the way to attract a man, could she ever hope to win someone herself? Luckily, she recollected quickly that it was not the way Lydia had attracted her husband. There were other methods much better suited to Kitty's temperament.

"Do you think Mary might play a jig so we could dance?" she wondered.

"Leave Mary be for now. There are hardly enough couples here for dancing at any rate, and she seems to be quite content where she is," Mrs. Bennet said. "But look, Maria Lucas is come and you've not spoken to her at all! Go and sit with your friend, and leave us old married ladies to ourselves." She patted Kitty's hand fondly and Kitty was dismissed with her second sting of the night. "Old married women" indeed! Kitty was not single by her own choice, and if she was not counted among the married women yet, she hoped she soon would be.

And how could her mother not see the reality of the situation? Could she really have missed how uncomfortable Mr. Warde must be, and how badly Kitty longed to rescue him? But she could not see a way to manage it. She sighed and went to Maria, who was deep in conversation with the Meredith girls.

"Oh! Kitty! I thought you would never join us!" Maria said as Kitty approached. "We were talking of Mr. Warde, of course. Blanche says she has never seen anyone so disinclined to talk of pleasant things!"

"Really?" Kitty asked, startled again.

Blanche nodded eagerly, leaning forward with a conspiratorial glance toward the object of her exclusive knowledge. "Yes, I talked him when he first arrived. He was not interested in anything about the neighborhood, or the assembly next month, or any interesting news. The only questions he asked me were about the situation of my family and the kinds of books I read. But when I told him that I am currently reading *The Monk* he actually sneered, and turned away! I though it was very rude of him. And what kind of insipid man doesn't read novels anyway? I think he and Mary will be very happy together." She laughed.

Kitty glanced back at them, surprised at this news. Mr. Warde did not look very interested in what Mary had to say; he kept scanning the room and when he caught her looking at him, he always bowed his head most gallantly. Besides, what man so handsome could bear to be as dull as Blanche seemed to think him? Surely there must have been some mistake. Kitty herself had been stupefied by Blanche's conversation enough times she could easily believe that Mr. Warde had only been trying to escape her.

"Well," she said, "I can't believe anyone would voluntarily sit and talk to Mary for that long. She must be keeping up a pretty steady stream to keep him so captive that he cannot excuse himself. I am sure he would be very pleasant if we could talk with him about something that interested him—we only need to find out what that might be!"

"And do you think you will be the one to discover it?" Maria asked, and sniggered.

"Why should I not be? Do you think it is more likely to be Mary?"

The girls shook their heads, giggling, but Maria looked skeptical. "I do not think it is likely to be any of us. Mr. Warde has only ever demonstrated interest in one thing, from what little I have seen, and that is your uncle's business. He may be handsome, but, Kitty, I really do not think he's a very interesting man."

"I suppose I shall have to determine that for myself, if I can ever free him from my sister," Kitty said.

She did not have the chance, however. Mary monopolized him for most of the night, and the few times when he was available, someone else snatched his attention away before Kitty had a chance. By the end of the night, Kitty was impatient to get home. Her dress was not nearly as pretty as she had thought it, and when Maria spilled tea on it Kitty could not hide the dirty stain that trickled down the side. Moreover, her eyes felt dry, and her head was beginning to ache. After all the promise that the evening had seemed to hold before they had arrived, Kitty rather wanted to cry.

On the way back to Longbourn, Mary actually struck up a conversation about Mr. Warde. "I found him to be very well-informed, and we agreed on a great many things," she said, smoothing her skirts in a manner that struck Kitty as being excessively self-satisfied. "I was very pleased to be able to talk to him this evening."

Kitty rolled her eyes. "Did you bore him to death talking about Fordyce, or music?"

"For your information, Mr. Warde was very interested in what I read, as well as what I play. He said he would like to hear me play for him some time, and I hope to have the opportunity to do so. I found him a very pleasing companion. I doubt you would have liked him so well. He does not share any of your interests—he does not care for dancing, or gossip, or useless flirtation. He is a very sober and intelligent man."

"He did look at me an awful lot," Kitty said, unwilling to ignore her only triumph.

Mary smiled and gave a little shrug. "Yes, he did ask me why you kept trying to catch his eye. He seemed most bemused by it."

This did not fit with Kitty's understanding of their interaction at all. "Maybe he found you a bore, and was looking for an excuse to come talk to me. Did he not look as though he was not entirely attending to Mary, Mama?"

"Oh, Lord, I beg you would not ask me; I haven't the smallest idea of what he was doing. I was much too engaged by my conversation with Mrs. Phillips to think of a little thing like that. I am sure he found you both very charming."

Kitty scowled and resisted the urge to kick her sister. She knew Mary could not really understand what had happened with Mr. Warde, but she did not know how to demonstrate it. One thing was clear, however: if Kitty wanted to get Mr. Warde to fall in love with her, she would have to do it without Mary in the way.

CHAPTER 3

*A*ccordingly, the next chance she had to go to Meryton, Kitty planned to go out by herself and see if Mrs. Phillips would be able to orchestrate a *tête-à-tête* with Mr. Warde. She regretted that she had been forced to wait so long, as Jane found reason after reason why she could not spare Kitty for days at a time. But she had been unable to manufacture any more reasons for today, and Kitty was free to go into town if she liked. She was already at the outskirts of Meryton when Mary came puffing up before her, looking slightly out of sorts.

"What on earth do you think you're doing?" Kitty asked, with a bit more scorn in her voice than she meant.

"I am going to Miller's, of course. I have word that some new music I ordered has arrived, and I am going to pick it up. If you are going there as well, I should be glad of your company."

Kitty scowled. "I'm going to call on our aunt. I suppose you may come along if you wish." She could not think of a good reason to convince Mary to go back, and she knew Mary would never listen if she gave her true reason for going. She rolled her eyes. Now she would have to figure out a way to get rid of her sister.

She fretted about it as they walked, and her worries were only increased as they went through town, for who should happen to come out of Mr. Phillips' offices as they passed, but Mr. Warde himself. Kitty bit back a groan. Her plans were certainly ruined.

She would have to salvage the situation as best she could. She certainly would not want to leave poor Mr. Warde alone with Mary again. She took a deep breath and steeled herself for the battle ahead. Mr. Warde approached them with a reserved smile, and bowed. "Miss Bennet, Miss Catherine. What brings you to town today?"

"I have some new music waiting for me at Mr. Miller's. My sister means to visit our aunt, I believe," Mary said before Kitty could speak. Kitty glanced at her, startled by her less-than-subtle hint, but neither Mary nor Mr. Warde made any acknowledgement of the dismissal.

Mr. Warde bowed. "I am on my way to Miller's myself, to pick something up for your uncle. May I join you?" He offered his arm to Mary, who took it eagerly. Turning to Kitty, he offered the other arm. "Miss Catherine, will you join us as well, or would you prefer to go to your aunt directly?"

Kitty took his arm with a smile and thanks, but her heart sank when she remembered Mary on his other arm. She fell in step alongside them, seething. But he was only being polite, and Kitty figured she could play at that game too.

"So, Mr. Warde, how are you liking Meryton?" she asked before Mary could speak.

"I like it very well. So far, everyone has been very obliging and has done much to help me feel as though I am at home here." He glanced at Mary as he said this, and Kitty couldn't help smirking. She could well imagine what he'd experienced. Mary was not known for her hospitality or friendliness.

"And have you found much to amuse yourself, outside of your work? It is a pity there are not often balls, and our next assembly is not for some time yet, I believe. Are you very fond of dancing?"

"Not everyone is as determined to dance as you are, Kitty," Mary said before Mr. Warde could respond. "Some of us prefer rational conversation."

"Bah! Conversation may have its place, but not at a ball."

"I am not a particularly great dancer," said Mr. Warde with a small smile, "but I will concede that balls are not particularly conducive to conversation, even when one is not in the set."

Kitty shook her head and smiled—he could flirt, after all! *You see, Mary,* she thought triumphantly, *this is how it is done.* "Oh, certainly, but dancing is such lively entertainment, and allows you to enjoy music and exercise at the same time."

"I will grant that it does have that efficient attraction," Mr. Warde said, with a small smile and bow. The conversation lapsed; Kitty waited for him to say more, but to her dismay, Mary soon asked him about some book she knew him to be reading, which Kitty had never even heard of. Their conversation turned down paths Kitty could not follow. And it continued until they reached Miller's and were forced to pause to speak to the clerk, leaving Kitty to stand awkwardly behind as they completed their transactions. She glared at Mary's back.

Kitty felt that she had made some progress, but not enough. She would never get a good opportunity to fall in love with Mr. Warde with her sister always in the way. But how to get rid of Mary? Mr. Warde had proven himself to be polite enough that he would not appreciate Kitty if she dismissed Mary the way she really wanted to.

She brooded in a corner of the shop, pretending to be admiring the lace on display. Some of it was uncommonly pretty, although Kitty had already spent too much of her allowance to be able to get any. Mary and Mr. Warde had stayed at the counter, and were chatting quietly while they waited for their things. Mr. Warde kept glancing at the shopkeeper every few moments, but Mary's attention was fixed on him. Kitty frowned. How could Mary not see that Mr. Warde did not care about whatever she was droning on about? She shook her head. She would have to come to his rescue.

She hurried back to them, trying not to look rushed, and smiled brightly at Mr. Warde. "Did they have everything you need, Sir?"

He raised one eyebrow and glanced at Mary, and Kitty hid a smile. Clearly her sister had not thought to ask after his success! "Yes, I believe so. Although I am distressed for your sister's sake; they seem to have misplaced one of her new music sheets, and they are now beginning to wonder whether they ever had it."

"Oh! Well, I suppose it is fortunate that Mary has so much other music with which to divert herself while she waits," Kitty said. Why did he insist on dragging Mary into this? Of course she found something to nag about. She always did when she came to Miller's. "But I suppose my uncle will be grateful that your business was not affected by the same error."

"I am sure he will, though he will undoubtedly be more distressed by the situation of his niece." That had to be sarcasm, Kitty knew. No one who had known Uncle Phillips for more than a day could suppose that he would be more upset by his niece missing a piece of music than by a disruption to his business.

"Kitty, there is no reason you should wait for me. Go ahead to call on our aunt; she will certainly be expecting you and it would not do to keep her waiting."

"Yes, indeed. I can wait with Miss Bennet and escort her there when this matter is resolved. There is no reason to fear for her."

Kitty did not fear for Mary's safety or comfort or anything else, but this resolution had so far taken root in their minds that they were walking her to the door as they spoke and deposited Kitty (rather unceremoniously, she thought) on the road outside, then took their leave of her.

Miserably dissatisfied, she stood staring at the shop for several moments. What had she done wrong? Oh, how this made her miss Lydia! Had her younger sister been there, she would have been doing all she could to attract Mr. Warde to them, rather than trying to stop him from ever saying anything interesting. Especially now that she did not have her own marriageability to worry about, Lydia would have been the perfect companion.

She glanced back at the shop, but could not see her sister through the window and the other people collected inside. It was hopeless to try going back in. She turned on her heel and marched rather viciously toward her aunt's house.

Most puzzling of all, Mr. Warde seemed more oblivious than Mary to what Kitty wanted. Had he not caught any of the hints she had sent his way? She had not been brazen, exactly, but neither had she been particularly subtle.

But then, they had never actually managed to have a real conversation, because Mary kept butting in where she was not wanted.

It wasn't until she stood at her aunt's door that she realized what Mary was doing, and with that realization came a snort of derision. She thought she was flirting with Mr. Warde herself! That did explain her dogged determination to get in the way. Kitty was just going to have to try harder to get him alone.

CHAPTER 4

$\mathcal{K}$itty tried her luck in Meryton the next day. She didn't have a plan, nor did she know whether she would be able to find Mr. Warde free when he appeared to be so diligent in his work, but she imagined that he might be eager enough to see her that he would be willing to leave it for a while. Surely her uncle might spare him for a short time in service of his niece.

Her uncle's offices were bustling when she arrived, and, not having any business inside, she hesitated to go in. She wandered around Meryton for a while, wondering what to do next, hoping that she would run across him on an errand or something, before finally deciding that she might at least go call on her aunt and see if she would be willing to help.

Mrs. Phillips, always glad to receive her, ushered her into the sitting room with a smile. When gossip and greetings had exchanged hands, she asked what brought Kitty to visit.

"My sister rather monopolized Mr. Warde yesterday," Kitty said, "but I thought you might have an idea about giving me a chance to meet him today, and know him better."

Mrs. Phillips paused for a moment. "Well, Mr. Phillips did leave some of his paperwork here this morning when he left. I could have you deliver it to him, and bring something to eat for the rest of the office as well. I know that Mr. Smythe and Mr. Burns will be glad of it, and I imagine that Mr. Warde will be too. It would give you an excuse to go and see him, and while he is eating you may play hostess, and demonstrate to him how good you are."

Kitty agreed readily, and when the time came, happily hurried away burdened with a small luncheon for all of them. The men who were working welcomed her gladly, but to Kitty's severe disappointment, Mr. Warde was not among them. She handed out the cakes her aunt had given her, and asked her uncle about Mr. Warde.

"Oh, I believe he is still working in the back. Poor man; he's taking the brunt of this increase in business. Good worker, though. I'll go and get him."

"Don't trouble yourself," Kitty said. "I'll go. I know you are all very busy and I do not mean to keep you."

"Thank you, my dear." He gave her a smile, and bowed his head to his work.

Kitty took her basket and wandered into the back, smiling to herself. That couldn't have worked out better if she had planned it. A few minutes entirely alone with Mr. Warde would be just what she needed.

She found him hunched over a table in the back, poring through a pile of documents scattered over it.

"I've brought you something to eat," Kitty said. "My aunt sent something for everyone."

He looked up, squinting at her in the dim light. "Oh? Thank you. You can leave it here." He cleared a space on the table in front of him and patted it.

Kitty took her time pulling the food out of the basket and arranging it on the table. "The others are eating in the front room. Do you not wish to take a few minutes to join them?"

"No, I think I should stay here. I might be at this all day as it is, and I do not particularly wish to have another late night of it." When Kitty continued to stand there, wondering what to say next, he added, "I am most grateful for the sustenance, however." He offered her a warm smile with his thanks, and returned his attention to the papers before him.

"I am sorry to have had so little chance to speak with you yesterday."

"Hm? Oh, yes. I was glad to be of service to your sister."

"Oh! Yes." She shook her head a little. She had to turn the conversation away from Mary! "I am glad when I can be of service to my aunt, too," she said, more to fill the silence than anything. She winced at her own stupidity.

"Yes... you visit her often, it would seem."

"I enjoy my aunt's company, and she mine. And there is precious little else to do, most days. It can be rather dull, never to leave the house. I much prefer coming into Meryton when I may."

"Well, I am sure she is glad of your company. Is she not expecting you back?"

"I do not imagine so; not for a little while. She sent me with enough food for myself, as well, which I take to mean that she expects me to eat with you." She hesitated, reaching into the basket again. "I could stay with you, if you would like the company."

He looked up from his papers again, eyebrows raised. "Thank you, Miss Bennet, but as you see, I am elbow-deep in work, and I really cannot spare the time." With a half-shrug of one shoulder, he gestured to the stacks of paper around him. "I am sure your aunt would make a better companion than I, at any rate. Thank you for the meal, however. I do appreciate the sustenance." He bowed slightly and returned his attention to his paperwork. Kitty stayed a few more moments, but he made no further acknowledgement of her, and she did not know what else she might say. So, with a small sigh, she packed up her basket and went back out to the main room.

The others were also working as they ate, and Kitty's appetite had vanished, so she left the rest of the food with her uncle and took the empty basket back to her aunt. She hoped that Mrs. Phillips would be able to improve her spirits. How had Mary managed to poison his mind against her so quickly? And how was Kitty ever going to repair the damage Mary had done?

HER CHAT with Mrs. Phillips did do her some good. Convinced that Mr. Warde would come to love Kitty as much as she did, Mrs. Phillips was encouraging and kind. She, too, believed that Mary would not do for him and would do better to bow out now before she got hurt, but she counseled Kitty to let it run its course; if Mary was determined to break her heart, she would do so whether or not Kitty interfered. She suggested that Kitty come back on her own the next day, and meet her in front of Mr. Phillips' business, whither she would find herself obliged to go on an errand of some importance, just about the time that Mr. Warde usually left. That would provide Kitty ample excuse to encounter Mr. Warde again, but without Mary or distractions from work, and she would finally be able to take some time to get him to fall in love with her without anything getting in the way.

With this scheme Kitty readily agreed, and the next morning escaped in secret to Meryton.

As she hurried toward the town, however, a sniffle from the hedgerow gave her pause.

"Who's there?" she called.

From the bushes crawled the son of one of her father's tenants, a little boy of about six, wiping his eyes and nose on his sleeve.

"Goodness!" Kitty said, crouching before him. "Whatever is the matter?"

In hesitant sentences, punctuated heavily by sniffles and hiccups, the child explained that he had lost the parcel his mother had entrusted him to deliver into town. Kitty, heartily sorry to see any adorable little thing cry so much, agreed to help him search for it.

Fortunately, it did not take long, as the parcel manifested itself halfway up a tree that the child had attempted to climb, and Kitty could just reach it.

"Here we are," she said merrily, plucking it from its resting place. "Never fear, there's nothing wrong with it!" She returned it to its small owner, who clutched it gratefully to his breast.

"Thank you, Miss! Mama would have been so mad if I lost it."

Kitty patted his arm. "Well, let this be a lesson to you, then. When your mother sends you on an errand, see that you complete it first, before you start climbing tempting trees." She smiled. "I know the desire to play first, but you've seen how that may end! Go on, now. Your mother will be wondering what's keeping you."

She sent him on his way with another reassuring pat and went on to town, thinking of how she would tell Mr. Warde the story, and how he might admire her for it.

But on her arrival at her uncle's business, her aunt's demeanor stopped her short in terror. Something was wrong.

"Kitty! My dear! Oh, child, I had hoped you would not come!"

"What? Aunt Phillips, whatever is the matter?" Kitty ran to her, hands held out.

"He is not here, my dear—Mr. Warde left this morning for Longbourn!"

CHAPTER 5

*K*itty's heart leapt and sank at the same time, creating a very uncomfortable sensation. "What? Gone to Longbourn! Why?"

"Your uncle said he asked permission to have the morning off so he could bring some sheet of music to your sister. I suppose the shop got it sorted after she'd left. But he's been gone for some time; did you not happen to see him on your way here? I thought, since you pass by the office..."

Kitty thought of the little boy and his parcel, sending her heart straight to her stomach. "No, I stopped to help little Johnny Martin find something he'd lost. Oh, aunt, do you think I might catch him if I go there now?"

"I do not know, but you must try. Hurry, my dear!" Her aunt kissed her cheek and Kitty turned and fled. She ran a little way, but she knew that her father would disapprove if she arrived out of breath and flushed, which would delay her from seeing Mr. Warde. She forced herself to slow down. Perhaps if she did not meet him at Longbourn she might meet him on the road.

Kitty struggled to pace herself and resist her near-frantic eagerness to be there, and she managed to arrive with an appropriately composed expression. But it was all for naught.

"Kitty, my dear! It is a shame you did not call earlier. You have just missed Mr. Warde! He left not ten minutes ago," said Mrs. Bennet when Kitty entered the room. Kitty's shoulders slumped.

"Did he? Oh, I am so sorry to have missed him!"

Mary, who had already retreated to her pianoforte with her new music, began to play, and Kitty scowled.

"Yes," Mrs. Bennet said, "he came to give Mary the music she could not get yesterday. I think it was very good of him to do so, was it not?"

"Yes, very good." Kitty barely listened to what her mother said, distracted by Mary's terrible playing and her worries about Mr. Warde. "Did he give any other reason why he had come?"

"No, but he did regret that he could not stay longer; it seems that Mr. Phillips had not given him long to run his errand. I did imagine that he might be hoping to see you, my dear, and I hinted that you were staying at Netherfield at present."

Relief forced a small smile to her lips. "Did you? I am all the more sorry to have missed him, then. Do you think he will be able to come to Netherfield? I must tell him how disappointed I am that I was so close to seeing him and could not."

"I invited him to a family dinner some night this week, and he accepted, but said he was not sure of his schedule yet. He promised to send word when he knew which day would be best, which I appreciate very much. You should come, too."

"Oh, yes," Kitty said. This news mollified her somewhat; he wanted the chance to make it up to her, of course. It would be too bad that Mary could not be got rid of for the dinner, but Kitty would simply have to find a way to ensure that she sat next to him, and was as charming as she could be.

WHEN SHE SPOKE to Mrs. Phillips a few days later, however, Kitty's confidence took a blow. She asked her aunt how she thought things were going with Mr. Warde, and Mrs. Phillips developed a sudden interest in looking at anything that was not her niece.

"Oh! I... that is to say, I do not know... oh, Kitty, I am sorry, my dear."

Kitty frowned. "Aunt?"

"I spoke with Mr. Warde briefly yesterday, when he returned from Longbourn, and he seemed not to be disappointed to have missed you, as far as I could tell. In fact, I believe that he went with the purpose of seeing your sister Mary."

"Mary! Impossible! What man would want anything to do with her?"

"I do not know about that—Mary is not as outgoing as you are, but of course, she is very clever, and very thoughtful—and perhaps Mr. Warde would prefer that to your exuberance and beauty. But that hardly seems like any gentleman, I know. Perhaps I was mistaken."

"It is only because he knows Mary so much better than he knows me," Kitty said, "and that is because he has never spoken more than three words with me without Mary being there to interrupt and commandeer his attention. I have no doubt that she wants to attract him, but I am sure that he is only being polite in conversing with her as regularly as he does."

"That may be true; and of course you have seen them together more often than I have," Mrs. Phillips said. "So perhaps you are right; perhaps the best thing to do is to try to talk to him without Mary there, and give him the chance to see your charms." She smiled and patted Kitty's shoulder.

"Do you think I might see him today?" asked Kitty.

"Not today, I fear, but see if you can talk to him this Sunday at church. It will ensure you have a topic to start with; you can discuss the service."

But Mr. Warde was not at church on Sunday. He had, it appeared, something of a cold, and had remained home in bed so as to have the best chance of being recovered by Monday. Kitty felt for him—spring colds were a source of immense frustration to her, too—and took the opportunity to have some beef tea sent over to him, with her good wishes for his recovery. It was all she could do, and she hoped it would be enough.

SEVERAL DAYS LATER, Kitty sat in the drawing room at Netherfield with Jane, stabbing her needle listlessly at her work. There had to be some other way she could see Mr. Warde again. But what?

Her musings were interrupted by the arrival of the post, and with it two letters for her. One came from Lydia, the other from Elizabeth, and Kitty broke the first open eagerly.

MY DEAR KITTY,

I simply cannot tell you how busy I have been lately! La, but such is the life of a married woman. My Wickham and I go out nearly every night, or entertain if we do not go out, and so we have been driven quite to the brink with all our comings and goings! I do love entertaining, and we have such merry card-parties. And the other evening, my husband won us enough to buy me a new dress, and I am simply wild with excitement over it.

Truly, you must come and see us soon! My father must give over eventually. There are balls and parties all the time and more officers to flirt with than ever there were at Meryton. They are such dears, too, and do enjoy a good flirtation! You must come and see them soon, for I have told most of them all about you, and they are quite wild to meet you. Write soon and say when I might expect you, so I can be sure to have a room for you. I shall have you a husband before the summer is out!

And tell Mama that if she might spare the brooch she mentioned in her last letter to send it with you; I am sure she will know what I meant.

ALL THOUGHTS of Mr. Warde vanished. Kitty dropped the letter on her lap and looked up at Jane. "Lydia has invited me to come and stay with her this summer! Oh, I should dearly love to go."

Jane laid her own letter in her lap and looked at Kitty with a measured calmness. "I do not imagine that Papa will permit it; but you should read your letter from Elizabeth before you make any decisions. You may wish to rethink your plans then."

Frowning, she picked up Elizabeth's letter and skimmed it until she found the portion Jane must have meant.

MISS DARCY HAS ASKED an old friend of hers to Pemberley for a few weeks this spring, and I think it would be very good for you to come to Pemberley at the same time. I know that Meryton society is not all you wish it to be, and I think that you will find more opportunities for good company here. Jane tells me that she does not anticipate being able to chaperone or entertain you very much during the move, and as I am under no such constraint, now seems to be the right time to bring you to Pemberley.

I have written our father for his permission as well, and he has granted it; now it remains only for you to accept, if you like. I do believe that you will like Miss Darcy very well, and Pemberley has enough charms to keep you amused for as long as you wish to stay.

"OH," she said, and put the letter down. Pemberley was certainly the grander establishment, and Elizabeth might give her more than Lydia could do; Kitty might get a new gown or two out of the visit, between Elizabeth and their mother. But she and Lizzy had never got along especially well and Lydia would be sure to introduce her to more interesting people, and allow her more freedom. Besides, Mr. Darcy frightened her, and Mr. Wickham charmed her.

Jane looked up and smiled. "You see; you have a greater opportunity before you than what Lydia may offer. I think you should go to Pemberley. I am sure you will love it there, and you will have the opportunity to make more friends than you have had so far. Lizzy tells me that Miss Darcy will have a friend of hers to stay at the same time, and I am sure the three of you will get along very well."

Frustration welled in Kitty's heart. "Lizzy is not likely to take me anywhere nearly as interesting as Lydia would," she said, choosing each word carefully. It was always difficult to tell what would work on Jane.

"Lydia does not have the resources to take you to the kinds of places that a young lady might meet with an eligible gentleman. Besides, you know Papa would never consent to your going."

Kitty could not deny it, much as she wished to. Her father had so far forbidden Kitty's favorable reply to every one of Lydia's invitations, and there had been many. "But why not? Lydia is a married woman, and have you not said yourself that I have improved of late?"

"You have improved, dear, but I don't have any idea of Lydia's having done the same, and you know that she would be as irresponsible toward you as Mrs. Forster was to her."

Kitty held back a snort. She was counting on Lydia being exactly as lenient as Mrs. Forster! She ached for a romance of her own, and what was more romantic than a whirlwind courtship, or even an elopement? And Newcastle was much closer to Scotland, so if she did need to elope, she would not have the trouble getting there that Lydia had faced. It would be perfect.

Kitty privately resolved that she would make a case to her father as soon as could be.

HE WAS NOT SWAYED, however, when she went to him the next day.

"Absolutely not."

"But, Papa—"

"Kitty, I know very few ways of explaining this to you so that you will understand, that I have not already used. You will follow Lydia into all manner of trouble if I let you visit her, and I do not intend to have another debacle on my hands like the last one. You may go to Pemberley, if you choose it, but you will not go to Newcastle, or anywhere else under Lydia's guidance, while I have any say in the matter."

Tears burned at the back of her eyes, but before she could protest again, he continued, "Elizabeth is offering your a much greater opportunity than Lydia, you know. Go to Pemberley, and for heaven's sake try to comport yourself well enough that she doesn't send you home before you've been there a week."

"I don't wish to go anywhere, if I can't go to Newcastle."

Mr. Bennet shook his head and stood up to leave. "Very well, then, stay here, where your best hope for marriage is your uncle's under-clerk! That will make a fine match for you, won't it."

Kitty brushed past him and hurried to find her things. What kind of a match would she find at Pemberley, anyway, with Mr. Darcy there to frighten everyone away? And what exactly did her father mean, suggesting that Mr. Warde would be such a poor match?

She didn't know on which point she would prove him wrong, but she was determined that she would prove him wrong on one of them.

CHAPTER 6

$\mathcal{M}$uch as Kitty wished she was immune to her father's cutting remarks, she was still unsettled by his scornful words, especially about Mr. Warde. Was he really such a bad match for her? True, he was not as rich as Mr. Darcy, or even Mr. Bingley. And he was less charming than Mr. Wickham. She would rank lowest of all her sisters if she married him, except for Mary, of course. But he was handsome, and secure in his station—she would be no worse off than Aunt Phillips, and that would not be so bad, would it? Besides, her only object at present was to make him fall in love with her. She didn't have to accept him if he proposed. But it would certainly be nice to know that someone actually could love her, and very romantic to thing she had broken someone's heart, like a true heroine.

Fortunately, her mother's dinner was fast approaching, and Kitty intended to take full advantage of the opportunity it presented. It had somewhat widened in scope, becoming a small dinner-party rather than the family dinner that Mrs. Bennet had initially proposed. Kitty expected that to work in her favor. She would have an easier time distracting Mary with someone else if there were more people there.

Mr. Warde was deep in conversation with Mr. Phillips when Kitty arrived with Jane. Before she could come up with a plan to approach them, Blanche stopped her and wanted to chat. It was nearly impossible to break away from Blanche Meredith, the tiresome bore. Worse, Mary suffered no such impediment and went directly toward Mr. Warde, who soon noticed her and detached himself from his conversation to greet her. Kitty seethed, and wondered whether she ought to go try to interrupt and rescue him. But then Maria Lucas arrived, giving her the perfect opportunity to sneak away, and she had no trouble taking advantage.

As she drew near to her sister she could hear their conversation; Mary was prattling about the music he had brought her. Kitty scoffed under her breath. Who on earth cared about Mary's terrible taste in music? There wasn't much point in allowing that conversation to go on any longer. Mr. Warde would probably thank her for rescuing him from such tedium.

"Hello Mr. Warde; how are you this evening?" she asked cheerily. "Has my sister talked your ears off yet? I'm sure you must find her a bore by now."

He looked over at her with less eagerness than Kitty would have liked. "Miss Catherine. Good evening. Your sister has been telling me how she is getting on with the music I brought her. Since I asked her about it, you cannot truly imagine that I am bored."

"I wish you would call me Miss Kitty; everyone does, and it feels so dreadfully formal when you call me Catherine, as though we hardly know each other."

He raised one eyebrow and glanced at Mary, whose expression bore a striking resemblance to the one she wore when Kitty tried to play the pianoforte. "Forgive me, Miss Catherine, but we do hardly know one another, do we not?"

Kitty shrugged, smiling. "I suppose you could make that argument now, but surely it will not be long before it is entirely unnecessary. There is a simple solution to your dilemma: simply take the time to know me better." She adjusted her stance to show off her figure in a more flattering light.

"Kitty, Mr. Warde and I were talking; it is very rude of you to interrupt unless you had something particular to say."

There were many particular things Kitty wished to say to her sister, about taking a hint, and letting others ever get a word in, and monopolizing handsome young men, but she said none of them. Instead, she smiled. "I only hoped to become better acquainted with Mr. Warde; you and he have spent so much time talking together that I feel quite left out."

"Forgive me, Miss Catherine," said Mr. Warde, "but I was not under the impression that you and I would have very much to say to one another. You have introduced no topic of conversation thus far but my boredom, and I have assured you that it is not at issue."

Stung, Kitty took half a step back. She realized too late that their conversation had drawn the attention of most of the room; only the giggles around her alerted her to the situation. She looked between Mary and Mr. Warde with a growing sense of desperation. What would Lydia say? She did not know—could not think. "That is only because thus far we have not spoken more than ten words to each other!"

"Ten words is enough in some cases. I am aware of your preference for dancing, and fashion. As I have absolutely nothing to say to either interest, and since you have demonstrated no knowledge of my own interests, it seems to me that there is no reason for us ever to embark on a more intimate acquaintance than we currently enjoy." He bowed slightly and turned away, Mary following his lead with a self-satisfied smirk.

Kitty stood very still, her stomach tying itself into knots. It was not that he did not know her—he did not *like* her! Was she so terrible as that? Worse, she could feel the gazes upon her, almost hear the gossip that even now would be racing through their acquaintance, that Kitty Bennet had made a fool of herself to a man who preferred her sister— the plain, insipid, obnoxious Mary! Her face burned and her breathing grew more frantic. She had to find Jane. They could go home. They would have to go home.

She scanned the room. But instead of Jane, her mother hurried toward her.

"Kitty! My dear Kitty!" Mrs. Bennet took Kitty's arm and led her to a chair where she could sit. "Oh, my poor dear," she fussed. "I am sure no one would have imagined—how he could be so rude—to prefer Mary, though! Well, for her sake, I hope he offers for her—I am sure no one else will—but for yours..."

Kitty's stomach gave a funny jolt at that thought. If he made an offer to Mary, of course Mary would accept. And that would mean that he would be her brother. How could she stand it! And for Mary to find someone to marry her before she did! It was impossible, plainly. Kitty could not hope to find anyone if Mary found a husband first. Her sisters might all have been more beautiful and accomplished and flirtatious than she, but not Mary. They might all have been married before her, but never Mary. If any Bennet sister was going to be an old maid, it would be Mary, not Kitty.

"Mama, I want to go back to Netherfield," Kitty whispered. "Please."

Mrs. Bennet glanced over at Mary, who still chatted quietly with Mr. Warde and, Kitty thought, looked abominably self-satisfied. "I will talk to Jane," she said after a moment's deliberation.

She vanished to find Mrs. Bingley, leaving Kitty to the scrutiny of the room. Kitty wished desperately to vanish from their view; she knew they were all laughing at her and she could not bear to sit there and let them stare at her.

But it did not last forever, and Jane came back with the news that she would take Kitty home. Kitty felt so relieved to go home that she did not bother to be offended that Mary would have more time with *him*. She didn't let herself think about it; she only followed her sister out to their carriage and rode home in silence.

Tomorrow, when she felt better, she would confront Mr. Warde. There had to be some kind of misunderstanding, surely—and if not, he owed her an apology.

THERE WERE two problems with Kitty's plan: how to find Mr. Warde, and once she found him, how to get an opportunity to speak to him. Mary would be watching her closely, of course, and it appeared that

Mr. Warde was not very interested in speaking to her at all, which would not help matters. Jane could not be counted on for anything, and Kitty did not think it would be wise to go back into town.

She spent the next three weeks in agony. She only saw him in passing, when she went into town, and he barely condescended to bow to her. She was furious with him for the slight, and with herself for having formed any designs on a mere under-clerk, and with everyone else for encouraging the match between him and Mary. So when he arrived at Longbourn three weeks later, while she and Jane were there visiting, she could only think of proving to him that he had missed something exceptional in her.

She tried to catch his eye, but he looked only at Mary. She opened her mouth to speak, but before she could get a word out, Jane asked him how his work was coming on.

"Very well, thank you. Mr. Phillips is entrusting me with more every day, and I believe that he is pleased with my progress."

"Did you—" Kitty began.

"Has he talked to you about partnership?" Mary asked, as though she hadn't noticed Kitty's words.

Kitty didn't hear his response, too busy was she trying to find a pause in the conversation. It never came; no one paid her the smallest attention. She might as well have not been there altogether. Kitty began to feel rather frantic. All she wanted was an apology. Was that so much to ask?

Eventually, the conversation wobbled, faltered, and ceased altogether. They sat in the parlor awkwardly together, looking around at each other, and Kitty suddenly remembered a certain visit of Mr. Bingley's. Mrs. Bennet had not yet winked at anyone, but that was probably only a matter of time.

"Have you had much chance to practice your new music since we last spoke, Miss Bennet?" he asked, glancing around the room.

"Yes, a little; I took your advice, and am rather pleased with the result. Would you like to see?"

He said that he would, and Mary hurried away to collect the music sheets that she had been scribbling on.

Kitty saw her chance. "Mr. Warde," she said, and flinched when everyone looked at her with a severity completely unwarranted by the situation. She cleared her throat and tried again, her confidence shaking as much as her hands. "I wanted to say... that is... I am sorry for making you uncomfortable, the other night." He opened his mouth as though he wished to reply but Kitty was already too far in to allow him to interrupt her. "I do not entirely understand how I made you uncomfortable, when we have barely spoken to each other, but it seems that I have done so, and I am sorry. But pray, tell me, what did I do to you to deserve such treatment?"

"Kitty!" exclaimed Jane. Mr. Bennet coughed, poorly covering a laugh.

"I cannot believe you would accuse Mr. Warde of mistreatment!" Mary said, bustling back over to his side. She thrust the music sheets at him, and turned to glare at her sister. "He does not need your harassment, Kitty, and if you need to know the reason why he said what he did, you may wish to investigate your own behavior toward him."

"I have done nothing that warranted a public set-down!" Kitty exclaimed.

"If you have not done it before, you are doing it now! Go away and leave us be, if you cannot be civil."

Kitty wanted to stand her ground. She did. But her mother stood up next and grabbed her arm, and nearly dragged her from the room, with Jane following and already quietly trying to calm her mother, and she found that she did not have the energy to resist. Mr. Bennet excused himself behind them, and Kitty knew, with a sinking feeling, what was going on inside the room they'd all vacated.

Jane took her home immediately, and Kitty did not argue. She said nothing as they went to the carriage, and Jane must have sensed that she did not want company, for she honored Kitty's silence. Kitty did not think she could bear even sympathetic comments at this point. How on earth could any man choose Mary over her? What had she done so wrong that she could not attract the attention of such a handsome man, but Mary could? Which was worse, that she had failed to attract him or that Mary had succeeded?

She didn't see any reason to avoid the trip to Pemberley now. As miserable as it would be to go live under the scrutiny of Mr. Darcy and Lizzy, it would be worse to stay here and live through Mary and her mother planning a wedding, and she would never convince her father to let her go to Newcastle now. The arguments that were sure to arise were already giving her a headache just thinking about them.

To Pemberley she would go, then.

She heard her mother's joyful cries ringing through the house as they pulled away, and knew she had made the right choice.

CHAPTER 7

*K*itty announced her intention on the next day. She scowled at the knowing smirk that her father gave her.

"Excellent," he said. "I have been thinking of visiting Pemberley myself; you can come with me."

Kitty rolled her eyes. Did he ever tire of joking with her?

But he looked quite serious. And quite like he was anxious to be amused at her reaction.

Mr. Bennet, travel? And with her? She wanted nothing more than to get away from him, and the rest of the family, not to have him come be disapproving over everything she did in Derbyshire as well as in Hertfordshire! She had to force her mouth closed to hide her shock.

He chuckled and patted her hand. "I did not imagine that you would be especially well pleased with the arrangement, but nevertheless, I am going. I have already written to Lizzy to tell her that I would be sending you to her, and I do not imagine that she will mind if I come along."

In vain did Kitty endeavor to dissuade him. He was absolutely decided upon his course. He hadn't seen his favorite daughter since her wedding; he would find more intelligent conversation at Pemberley; he had exhausted his own library and wished to enjoy

Mr. Darcy's—nothing she put forth went unanswered. She was at length obliged to resign herself to the inevitable and submit to his going.

In a little more than a week, they left for Pemberley. The morning of their departure was grey and cold for May, and Kitty shivered as she waited in the hall for the carriage to come around, wondering whether she had really made the right choice. Her mother's delight and her sister's gloating were unbearable, but would she really be any happier surrounded by people who were richer, prettier, and happier than she?

Mr. Bennet remained silent through their preparations to leave, which did not increase her hopes for an enjoyable journey, and Mrs. Bennet fluttered nervously about them both, worrying about every possible eventuality which might prevent their safe arrival at Pemberley. By the time they actually managed to climb in the carriage, Kitty foresaw that she would not enjoy herself any more at her second eldest sister's house than she had at Netherfield, if even that much. She wondered idly if Miss Darcy or her friend were much for trimming bonnets, or whether they might lend her some of their dresses to wear, or make over. There seemed little chance for better entertainment than that, for unsociable Mr. Darcy would inevitably avoid going anywhere interesting. She sighed heavily. A long journey stood before her and she stood to gain nothing from it.

Her father did nothing to help. He buried his head in a book which he had brought along, apparently for this very purpose. Kitty rather envied his ability to sit and read for the whole of their journey. She suffered from terrible sickness whenever she tried to read in a moving carriage, and she did not have a novel with her anyway. Instead, she looked out the window and tried to envision what the next few months might hold. With her father there, all she saw was days of miserable boredom listening to other people play music better than she could and talk about people she didn't know. If she was very lucky, that would be the worst of it.

She tried to close her eyes and doze off, but Mr. Bennet's occasional snorts of laughter seemed intentionally timed to make that impossible. She would be dead of boredom and irritation before they even reached Derbyshire.

She had never been half so far from home as Pemberley, and wondered briefly whether she might at least find some interesting places to explore around the estate or the nearby town. Travel for its own sake had never really appealed to her, no matter the current fad for it. But she couldn't help being a little bit curious, knowing that she would be somewhere entirely new. Whether or not she would be able to explore it much remained to be seen. Her father did not object to her going into Meryton, but only, as she had heard him tell her mother, because "there is little enough trouble she could possibly get into with so many people about who know her, and with whom she must continue on good terms if she wishes to remain in society. That should keep her in check."

She scoffed a little, under her breath, causing her father to glance up at her. "Did you say something, Kitty?"

"No, Papa, nothing."

He shrugged one shoulder and went back to his book. Kitty went back to staring out the window, biting back a heavy sigh.

By their second day of travel, her boredom overcame common sense and her desperation drove her to foolishness. "Papa?" As soon as the word left her lips, she regretted it.

He started, nearly dropped his book, and looked at her with such surprise that she immediately wished she could take back even the thought of speaking with him. After several moments of strained silence, he finally said, "Kitty, did you mean to attract my attention, or were the long hours of idleness finally too much for your wits to handle?" She blushed, wishing she hadn't said anything and entirely unsure of how to respond to his sarcasm. He continued. "Come, come, child; your mother would have been talking my ear off this entire journey. I have been unaccustomed to such silence. If you would like to speak, you are welcome to do so; and I promise to give you as much attention as I would give to her."

Kitty sank back into her seat, desperate for something to say that would redeem herself a little bit in her father's eyes. "I... I only wished... that is..." She panicked, having completely forgotten whatever half-formed question she had been working towards, and said in a rush, "I only wished to know how much longer before we must change horses again."

His sarcastic eyebrow reached for his ever-retreating hairline. Kitty avoided wincing at it, but only just. "I believe that we have some time to go, yet. Do you need to stop and stretch your legs? I believe it is safe to stop here for a few moments if you need it. There are, as far as I know, no highwaymen on this stretch of road."

Kitty had not thought of the risk of highwaymen, and though some of her novels featured rather fascinating men of that profession, she found that she was not very keen on encountering one outside the pages of a book. She informed her father, with as much dignity as she could manage, that she would be quite able to wait until they stopped again for the horses. He only smirked, and Kitty strained her mind for a safe way to change the subject.

"When we arrive there, do you imagine there will be any dancing?" That was probably not the safest choice she could have made, in fact. Why must she always realize these things when it was just too late?

He sighed and turned his open book over his knee to keep his place. "I do not imagine there will be any dancing for the majority of your stay there, or any flirtation, or any frivolity at all if I can help it. I am not taking you to your sister that you might make as ridiculous a spectacle of yourself at Pemberley as you are suffered to do at Longbourn, Catherine."

This stung, probably more than he intended, and Kitty's throat tightened. "I have no intention of making a spectacle of any sort, Papa, and I never had."

"You did an admirable job of persuading me otherwise," Mr. Bennet said, half under his breath. He shook his head and glanced at her. "Nevertheless, now is as good a time as any to have this conversation. I will not have you behaving at Pemberley as you usually behave at home. You will not leave the house unescorted, and you will need to find something more productive to fill your days than searching out new ways to make young men irritated with you. I have asked Elizabeth to limit the number of social outings, which she will be happy to do, I am sure, and I hope that you will take this opportunity to find a way to better yourself."

Kitty's heart sank further with every word. "Papa, I do not—"

"Do not argue with me on this, Kitty. I will not hear it. My mind is made up. I will not have another Lydia on my hands."

"Lydia managed to find a husband all right," Kitty said, unable to keep her voice from rising.

"Lydia managed to entrap herself with a scandalous rake whose only mistake in choosing her was getting caught. She is not an example to follow. She is a lesson to learn from. The only reason she managed to escape from that ordeal with her reputation even mostly intact is because Mr. Darcy is a damned fool in love."

"But—" That sounded nothing like the portrait Lydia had painted of her marriage.

"No, Kitty. I will not be gainsaid."

"What will I do with myself? You have left me nothing to entertain myself!"

"You could try learning how to be a rational human being," Mr. Bennet said, in a tone which suggested that he did not truly anticipate her taking him seriously. "Or finding some way of occupying your time that is not so wholly dependent on the willingness of others to humor your foolishness."

Kitty knew her father's opinion of her. She knew that he considered her to be stupid, and thoughtless, and shameless. But this—this casting it up before her and laughing at her, without allowing her any means of escape, still felt like he was grinding her into the dirt with his boot-heel, and Kitty had no one else there to deflect his wit toward. Helpless frustration swelled in her breast, and her eyes burned with unshed tears. She knew it would only make matters worse, but she could not help herself. He had pushed her too far.

"I hate you," she whispered. The tears flooded her eyes however much she tried to fight them back. "You are the worst, cruelest, most hateful man I have ever known, and I wish to God that I had been born to anyone else!"

"Well, if you had, you would probably hate him just as much, so you will forgive me if I do not trouble myself overmuch about it," Mr. Bennet said with a shrug. He lifted his book from his knee and began to read again.

Kitty could only stare at him and will the tears to leave her alone. She was losing that battle, as well, and they began to fall down her cheeks. She could not allow herself to lose her composure completely, and prove her father right! It took all her effort to hold back the rest.

How could he? He did not know her. He had never taken the trouble to know her.

And she could never hope to get out from under his roof unless she could find a husband. Which she could never hope to do if she followed his stupid rules. There was no hope for her. And no choice; she would have to disobey him just to get away from him.

Her stomach clenched tightly and she pressed her hands against it, willing herself to calm down. It was no good. She felt like a tea kettle forgotten on the fire, all steam and boiling water looking for a way to get out and scald someone, and it was everything she could do to hold it at bay.

She looked back at the window of the carriage, but she couldn't see anything. The rain had gotten heavier, and her vision was fogged with tears.

CHAPTER 8

They endured a long, silent journey the rest of the way to Pemberley. Mr. Bennet did not seem to notice that Kitty refused to speak to him, which took some of her vindictive pleasure out of the exercise, but she maintained her silence the rest of the trip, even at the inns and turnpikes. She did not need to talk to him to show him that he was wrong about her.

They arrived at last, however, and pulled into the drive in reasonably good time. The staff were lined up outside to receive them, and Elizabeth and Mr. Darcy were waiting as well. She smiled a little bit. At least Elizabeth looked happy to see her.

Mr. Bennet took his time putting away his book and finding his walking stick, and Kitty scowled, knowing that he was testing her patience on purpose. She did not want to try to brush past him and risk his wrath over some silly mistake. She meant to start this visit out well.

He climbed out of the carriage and turned to help Kitty out, but she did not want to allow him the satisfaction of being of help to her, any more than she wanted to give him the satisfaction of speaking to him. She grabbed the sides of the carriage and stepped forward.

As her foot hit the rail, though, she lost her grip on the side of the carriage and fell, tumbling inelegantly downward. Her foot caught in the rail of the step on the way down and with a stomach-rending jolt, it twisted around somehow. She caught herself by her hands on the gravel drive, and hung suspended with her foot still trapped in the rail. A few seconds passed before the pain hit her, and she cried out.

"Kitty!" Elizabeth cried, running over to try to help her up. "Are you all right?"

Kitty couldn't quite find the words to respond to her sister's question. She opened her eyes and glanced at her ankle. She was reasonably certain that it should not be that size. Oh, what her father must be thinking now! So much for proving how little she needed him!

"Lizzy..." She had to squeeze her eyes shut again. "Ouch!"

Mr. Darcy came and knelt at her other side. "See if you can get her foot free, Elizabeth," he said quietly. "I will have to carry her into the house." He turned back to someone behind him; a servant, Kitty assumed. "Is her chamber ready now?"

Kitty did not hear the response, as Elizabeth had grabbed her foot and pulled it free of the carriage step, and Kitty gasped as the pain shot up her whole frame.

"Good. I will take her there. Send someone for the surgeon." Vaguely, Kitty wondered whether her injury really warranted a call from a surgeon, but she was not about to object to anything Mr. Darcy said.

"Yes, Sir."

"All right, Kitty," he said, and put his hand on her shoulder. "I am going to lift you up, and carry you to a place where you can lie down. I am going to do my best to be careful, but it might hurt a bit."

She bit her lip and nodded.

"Can you put your arms about my neck?"

Opening one eye, she did as she was asked. He put his arms around her gingerly and lifted her up. It did not hurt as much as she feared it would, but she could not allow herself to open her eyes again or think very hard about what was happening. It took everything she had to keep from being overwhelmed by the jolting.

The walk to her chamber seemed to take weeks, and the only thing that kept her from crying out at every step was Lizzy's constant stream of apologies to her, and directions to the staff. It gave her something to focus on, but she had to fight to keep her mind on her sister's voice. At last, Mr. Darcy stopped moving.

"I'm going to set you on the bed, now. I recommend holding your leg up so it does not hit the bed."

She did as he suggested and he lowered her down to the bed. Kitty slowly opened her eyes and glanced around the room. It was a bright, cheerful apartment, much bigger than Kitty's room at home, and if she had come to it under less painful circumstances she would probably have been enchanted by it. The bed even had rich yellow brocade curtains on the canopy. Kitty loved yellow.

Mr. Darcy turned to his wife and murmured something in her ear. She nodded, and he patted her shoulder and left. Lizzy sat down on the edge of the bed.

"The surgeon is on his way here, Kitty. Let me help you get your shoes off and get as comfortable as you can, so we can be ready for him when he arrives, all right?"

Kitty wanted to nod, but she couldn't quite move her head. The thought of trying to move the shoe terrified her, even though she could feel her ankle swelling against it painfully. "Do we have to?" she managed to whisper.

"I am afraid so," Lizzy said with an apologetic smile. "You do not have to do anything if you do not want to, though. I will take care of it if you want to lie back for a moment, and then we can worry about your coat and your bonnet."

This plan did not much appeal to Kitty, and suddenly she began to wonder whether she would be happier if she took off the boot herself. But Lizzy had already started unlacing it, and Kitty leaned back against the headboard and squeezed her eyes shut in anticipation of the coming pain.

Every touch Lizzy made to it was agony, and she twisted her hands up in the comforter and focused everything she could on not crying out. If Lizzy would just leave it alone, she could survive the dull ache, but this—this had to be the sort of pain that killed people.

"Almost there," Lizzy said soothingly. "Your foot has swelled up so much that it will be difficult to get off, but I think we can do it without having to cut the shoe." Kitty could only nod.

When Lizzy started to pull on the shoe, Kitty couldn't stop herself from screaming. It felt like Lizzy was trying to pull off her whole leg, and it did not seem to be helping at all. "Stop, stop!" Kitty cried. "Let me do it!"

"Are you sure?" Lizzy looked at her doubtfully.

"Yes! It can't possibly be any worse than you doing it," Kitty snapped.

"Very well." Lizzy stood up and took a step back to give Kitty room to work.

With an angry groan, Kitty forced herself to sit up the rest of the way and take stock of the situation. Her boot was partway off, but not far enough to be able to get it any further off without hurting herself. She wondered for a moment whether it would really be better to cut it off after all. But she really did like those boots. Lydia had so envied their bright buckles! She took a deep breath. If she kept thinking about it, she would never be able to do it. She took a tight grasp and a deep breath, and closed her eyes. Then she yanked.

For a second she felt nauseated and lightheaded and wondered whether she was going to faint—glad that she was already sitting on a bed. But she managed to keep conscious. She flung the boot weakly to the floor and nearly collapsed back onto the bed.

Lizzy came back to her side in an instant. "Oh Kitty," she said, shaking her head. "Would you like me to do the rest?"

Kitty did not open her eyes; she only nodded. Lizzy set about taking off the rest of her outer things.

"All right. Would you like to get under the blankets until the surgeon gets here and can take a look at it?"

Kitty shook her head.

"We should probably put some pillows under your ankle; it will help keep the swelling in check. Let me get it for you."

Kitty did not respond to that, but she tried to brace herself for the pain. Her ankle had progressed to a dull throbbing now, but she could sense that moving it would be agony.

"Are you ready?"

"No, but go ahead," Kitty said. She lifted her leg a little way to ease the transition and regretted it immediately, and even more so when Lizzy picked it up at the knee and guided it onto the stack of pillows she had made. Kitty winced and sucked her breath in through her teeth, but did not trust herself to say anything. Thankfully, it was over quickly.

Lizzy sat back down at the edge of the bed. "Now, we only need to wait for the surgeon. Would you like me to stay with you?"

"Yes, please."

The shadow of a smile flitted across Lizzy's face. "Very well. Shall I tell you about the others who are staying with us at Pemberley?"

"There are others?" Kitty wondered.

"Yes, three. Mr. Darcy's cousin, Colonel Fitzwilliam; the colonel's friend, Mr. Knott, and a friend of Georgiana's, Miss Pratt."

Two gentlemen! Kitty could hardly believe her luck. She would not be able to dance with any of them with her ankle like this. How unfair!

"What are the gentlemen like? Are the unmarried?"

Lizzy shook her head, but her smile grew. "They are both very good gentlemen, as far as I know, but I should warn you that neither of them is here to search for a wife, and they are not very likely to be interested in you. I did not invite you here to introduce you to them. Besides, the Colonel has no fortune, and neither has Mr. Knott, to speak of; he is a clergyman and has come here in search of a situation. They will neither of them be able to afford to marry without some regard to money, and you have none to offer."

"And the lady?"

"I do not know her at all, but she and Miss Darcy were good friends when they were younger, and they have not seen each other in a very long time. She is only recently arrived home from school, I understand."

Kitty did not know what she could say to that, so she only

shrugged and looked around the room. Now that she had more attention to give it, she could see Elizabeth's touches here and there, in the new wash-stand and the smart little wardrobe.

"Do you like the room?" Elizabeth asked.

"Yes, it is very pretty."

"I thought it most suited your tastes. Miss Darcy's chambers are not too far from here; I hope you and she will become friends. I think she is a delightful person."

Kitty did not really think she would find Miss Darcy so appealing, but she agreed to appease her sister. She did not know whether or not she would be able to find a way to keep herself occupied without someone to distract her, anyway, since clearly she would not be walking for a while. She was relieved when the surgeon came.

He was a friendly man and quite gentle with Kitty, but that did not mean that his ministrations hurt less; and, he insisted on leeching her ankle, which she found disgusting no matter how necessary it was. But the leeches did manage to get the swelling down, and by the time he left she felt a bit more comfortable. When Elizabeth left her alone to rest, she had no trouble falling asleep.

SHE AWOKE to her throbbing ankle, and noted with distaste that the swelling had increased a little as she slept, and she had somehow managed to knock it off its pillow tower. It appeared to be later in the day, and as she pulled the bell-cord by her bed to call for someone to help her, she couldn't help wondering what she would do with the remainder of her day. Her plan had been to go into the nearby village of Lambton and explore, but if she couldn't walk, she couldn't do that. She could hardly bear the thought of spending a quiet evening in company with the Darcys and her father, and even if those other young men were there, she would not be able to impress them very easily when she couldn't even stand under her own power. And two young ladies who were already friends with each other weren't likely to want much to do with her.

Instead of a servant, Elizabeth came in. "Did you sleep well, dear?" she asked.

"As well as I could, given the circumstances," Kitty said. "Where is everyone?"

"Papa has retreated to the library, and I believe Mr. Darcy is with him. I shouldn't be surprised if we do not see either of them until dinner this evening." She smiled and shook her head fondly. "Miss Darcy, Miss Pratt, and Mr. Knott were with me in the music room. Should you like to join us?"

"I suppose so." Kitty's heart sank a little. Miss Darcy and Miss Pratt were already showing off their superior skills to the gentlemen, no doubt, and the gentlemen hadn't even had a chance to meet her. At home, she knew that she could hold any man's attention (except for Mr. Warde, but she dismissed that thought quickly). Here... she would be the poorest girl present, and injured as well. What would they care for her, who could not amuse them in any way? She was not confident enough in her own charms to believe that any of them would care for her over the celebrated Miss Darcy, or anyone Miss Darcy chose as a friend.

"I will have my girl help you dress; she is the most gentle thing, and she will be very careful of you. When you are done, she will have someone come to carry you down to us. Mr. Darcy believes he might have a cane somewhere for you, if you prefer, but I think this evening you will be happier if you do not attempt to walk on your ankle at all."

"Thank you, Lizzy." Elizabeth left Kitty in the hands of her maid, who was every bit as gentle as she'd promised. It wasn't long at all before Kitty, freshly dressed, felt much more refreshed than she had thought she could be. By the time the footman came to carry her down, she felt as though she might be equal to keep from entirely embarrassing herself in company.

CHAPTER 9

*I*n the music room she found Elizabeth, the two young ladies, and two young men who must be the ones Elizabeth mentioned. They rose when she came in and were very solicitous after her well-being, and were indeed introduced to her as Mr. Knott and Colonel Fitzwilliam. The taller, pale lady was Miss Darcy, and the one with the deep brown hair and reddish complexion was her friend Miss Pratt.

Miss Darcy was as beautiful as Kitty had heard that she would be. Beside her, Kitty felt dowdy and terribly backward, and her injury only made matters worse. Miss Darcy would have descended from a gig twice as precarious as her father's carriage, and made it look as easy as gliding across the room. No wonder Lizzy liked her so well! She was perfect.

Miss Pratt immediately established herself as friendly and talkative. Kitty's tongue tied itself into a knot as soon as she tried to greet them, and she could have sworn that she saw a laugh in Miss Pratt's eyes. She did not wish to dwell on that reality. Miss Pratt and Miss Darcy had been sitting together on a sofa, but moved to nearby chairs so Kitty would have somewhere to sit where she could put her foot up. She wished they hadn't, and her face burned as she thanked them. Her tongue still hadn't found itself, and she sounded like an idiot.

Mr. Knott was tall, and seemed all angles and awkwardness, although he had a very kind face. He smiled warmly at Kitty, asked after her well-being, and seemed genuinely concerned with her response, but not exceptionally conversational. Besides, he was a clergyman, and therefore uninteresting. Colonel Fitzwilliam, on the other hand, was everything gentlemanly and friendly, and very jovial with her to take her mind off her injury. Even though he did not wear his red coat, Kitty liked him immensely. She imagined that he might even look something close to handsome if he donned his uniform. And as to fortune, well, perhaps her wealthy brothers would be willing to contribute something to her portion if it meant she would be able to marry a man she truly loved. She felt suddenly much less hopeless.

"Well, Miss Bennet," said the Colonel as she settled her ankle atop its tower of cushions and arranged her skirt around it, "I suppose you are immensely disappointed that you will not be able to attend the assembly tomorrow evening."

Kitty's heart dropped. "There is to be an assembly tomorrow evening? Oh, Colonel! How dreadful!"

"Aye, there is indeed, and we had planned to surprise you and take you to it, had we not, Mrs. Darcy?"

"We had discussed it," Elizabeth said with a halfhearted smile, "but I was by no means resolved to do it. I think it will be better for Kitty to have a chance to adjust to life at Pemberley before we provide the excitement of a public gathering, and though I am very sorry that the choice should be made for us in such a manner, I do not pretend to regret this result."

The hesitation in her sister's voice did not escape Kitty, but as it did not matter whether Elizabeth would have told her about the assembly, or allowed her to go, she did not dwell on that aspect. "I am exceedingly sorry that I should have injured myself at all, but to have missed an assembly because of it is absolutely dreadful!"

"Do not fret, Miss Bennet," Miss Darcy said softly. "We will find plenty of other ways to amuse ourselves. Perhaps I could read to you?

51

I have been reading some very good novels lately and I think you would enjoy them very much. Miss Pratt and I have just begun *The Absentee*."

Kitty had not heard of *The Absentee*. Still, a novel of any kind was a good prospect, although this did very little to redeem the loss of the assembly. She tried to let it cheer her and push the assembly from her thoughts.

"Do you know, I have been wanting to read that myself," Mr. Knott said. "Would you object to my joining you, and reading with you?"

"We could take turns with it," Miss Darcy said. "Miss Pratt and I were talking of reading it aloud anyhow, rather than trading the book back and forth."

Kitty frowned, less certain that she would like that. She was no great reader, and reading out loud did her no favors. "Thank you, but I am not certain I could focus on the page for long enough to read it aloud," she said. There were, perhaps, some benefits to being an invalid.

"Never mind that; the rest of us will take turns reading it to you, and you only need to sit back and listen. That will help you to keep your mind off your ankle anyway, and we can talk over what we have read afterwards, and make prodigious fun of the fools in the story, for they always are immense fools, I find," said Miss Pratt, laughing.

Kitty couldn't help smiling at Miss Pratt. Her laugh was delightful. "That sounds lovely," she said.

THE FOLLOWING DAY WAS, accordingly, not nearly as miserable as Kitty feared it would be. Miss Darcy gave her one of her old bonnets and asked her to trim it new for her while they read, having been informed by Elizabeth that this was a pastime which Kitty enjoyed and was reasonably good at, and they spent a good portion of the morning reading *The Absentee* together. Kitty quickly learned that she liked Mr. Knott's reading best. He did different voices for every character and often had them laughing till their sides hurt, regardless of the story's tone.

Elizabeth came in partway through a chapter, and Kitty was sad to have to stop. But her disappointment vanished at her sister's announcement.

"There is another gentleman who will be joining us in the next few days. His name is Mr. Johns, and his family has owned Edgepark, a small estate nearby, for many generations. However, it is in need of serious repairs, which he has chosen to undertake, and he needs a place to stay until the house is fit to live in. He will probably not be here often, as he will be spending most of his time at Edgepark. I expect that we will see him only for dinner in the evenings, if that."

"My brother agreed to this?" Miss Darcy asked, frowning. "That doesn't sound like him."

"He was the one who proposed it, in fact. Edgepark has been all but a ruin for a very long time. If Mr. Johns is interested in restoring it, Mr. Darcy is happy to encourage him to do so."

Kitty made a little face. "Restoring a ruin sounds like an awful lot of work."

"Yes; aren't you glad we don't have to do it?" said Miss Pratt, laughing. Kitty laughed with her.

"I think it is a very good thing. It is never good for a place to fall into disrepair, and it will greatly benefit the village to have someone established there again," Elizabeth said.

"And the gentleman who chooses to take on such a task cannot be unwilling to work on improving the whole region, if necessary, and not just the house," Mr. Knott added. "Everyone will benefit from his interest. When does he arrive?"

"He intends to come on Tuesday or Wednesday."

Kitty was happy to spend the rest of the morning speculating about the newcomer, and she and Miss Pratt, who showed a similar inclination, found themselves sitting together and wondering over him.

"Do you imagine he is handsome?" Kitty asked.

"Who knows? He might be old and ugly, and married already. Mrs. Darcy did not seem to know much about him."

"Except that he's a good man for coming in and repairing that house."

Miss Pratt shook her head. "I don't see what the fuss is about that. It's probably good that he wants to fix the house, of course, and I would dearly love to see how he finishes it! Can you imagine the fun you would have in decorating an entire house new?"

"How freeing it would be! I believe the only trouble I would have is keeping myself from spending every farthing I have. But is it really possible that no one here knows anything of him?"

"It must be, for I have not found out anything other than that he is coming down from London, which is no great surprise. Where else should he live?"

"He must be very fashionable, if he can live in London and renovate an entire estate."

"And very rich," added Miss Pratt, her eyes growing wide as her smile.

Kitty beamed too. "Fancy if he should fall in love with one of us!"

"It must be you," Miss Pratt said, "for given the choice between us, I think you are the more eligible, assuming that Miss Darcy would not be interested, and I do not believe that she would, somehow."

This brought a frown to Kitty's face. "Why not?"

Miss Pratt leaned in closer and lowered her voice. "I cannot find out that she is at all interested in marrying. I get the impression that she would rather reach her majority, inherit her ridiculously large sum of money, and go on living a single woman forever, entirely self-sufficient."

"Indeed!" Kitty could not believe it; Miss Darcy's fortune was considerable enough that she could afford to be choosy when it came to marriage, but it had never occurred to Kitty that it might be enough to remain unmarried altogether. "Why on earth would she not wish to marry?"

"I do not know! I have hinted and schemed as much as I know how, but so far I have been able to learn nothing. The odd thing is, I do not believe that she is entirely opposed to the idea of matrimony;

she is only convinced that she does not require it. And is quite happy that it should be so."

Kitty shook her head and glanced over to where Miss Darcy sat, quietly talking with Colonel Fitzwilliam. "I cannot understand it, certainly."

"Nor can I, but I have made it a mission of mine to learn to understand, if I might."

"Oh, yes," Kitty said, and added that she might adopt that mission herself.

Miss Pratt looked over at Miss Darcy and the Colonel. "And what do you think of him?" she asked, her voice even lower.

"The Colonel?" Kitty asked, matching her tone. Miss Pratt nodded. "He is very pleasant. But I do wish I could see him in his uniform. He may be more handsome in it."

"I think he is quite handsome enough without it, but I will own, it would add a dash of something essential."

Kitty looked back at him briefly, but her initial impression remained: he was very charming, but not handsome. She looked back at Miss Pratt with her eyebrows raised.

"Do not look at me so! I can well see that you do not like him as well as I do. I suppose I should thank you for that, since it means I will have no competition." She winked.

"Ah." Understanding dawned and Kitty smiled. "In that case, I will do one better for you; I will help you win him, if he can be won."

"Would you indeed? I should be ever so grateful!"

Kitty, feeling all the satisfaction of a person in the position to help a potential new friend, said that she would.

CHAPTER 10

$\mathcal{M}$r. Gregory Johns arrived on Wednesday. Had Kitty been able, she would have stood out with the Darcys to receive him; being forced to wait in the sitting room was a kind of torture she had never before experienced. What would he be like? He must be very well-dressed if he was so rich, and that meant he was probably also handsome, and almost certainly fascinating—and by the time he finally came in to the room, she had about convinced herself that he would be the most incredible man she had ever encountered.

His initial appearance did not disappoint. He arrived in style behind Mr. Knott and Colonel Fitzwilliam, and made the two of them look quite commonplace by comparison. Kitty could not stop staring at him. His blue coat was the height of London fashion, and set off his smooth complexion and shining brown hair to perfection.

"Miss Bennet," he said, his silky voice making her quiver as he bowed over her hand. "It is a pleasure to meet you. Allow me to say that I am very grieved that you should have injured yourself so, for had you not, I would take this opportunity to solicit your hand for a dance this evening, and wheedle someone into playing for us!"

Good Lord, he was exactly what Mr. Warde ought to have been! "Oh!" Kitty said, blushing deeply, "if I could, I would be delighted to accept, but as you see..." She sighed and gestured to her foot, propped up on a stool and a series of cushions and secured under a light blanket.

"Indeed, indeed, you poor thing," Mr. Johns said, and sighed. "We will have to seek other ways to entertain you, then, will we not?"

"Mr. Knott has been reading *The Absentee* to us some mornings, and we mean to resume tomorrow morning," Miss Darcy offered with a shy smile. "Perhaps you would like to join us."

"That sounds delightful, Miss Darcy!" He turned to her and bowed his head, eyes twinkling. "I would be honored to join, if my duties at Edgepark do not call me away."

Kitty saw an opening to regain his attention and seized it. "Yes! My sister told me you were remodeling your house."

"I am indeed. Alas, it is proceeding but slowly, as these things tend to do when one is particularly eager for them to move faster," he said, shaking his head as he took a chair beside her. "But it means I will be able to enjoy your hospitality for that much longer, and in such good company, so I cannot find too many reasons to be downcast about it." This last was addressed to Elizabeth, who accepted it with a graceful nod and the appropriate niceties.

The day passed quickly in such company, particularly as the Colonel and Mr. Johns seemed almost to be in competition to see which of them could be more agreeable to the general company. Kitty chose to believe that they competed for her benefit as an invalid as well as a pretty young lady, and enjoyed it as such. Mr. Johns was very attentive to her, and she did everything she could to deflect Colonel Fitzwilliam to Miss Pratt, and thereby they passed the day as enjoyably as she could have wished.

Dinner itself began with more lively conversation and more laughter than Kitty could have imagined possible at the Darcy home. Even Mr. Darcy, in better spirits than Kitty had ever seen him, was occasionally prevailed upon to add to the jovial conversation, and spent the rest of the meal smiling upon his wife and the others in turns. The only thing that could have made the evening sweeter would be the prospect of an assembly to look forward to and talk about, but even her broken ankle had netted her the sweet attentions of her dinner partner, Mr. Johns, and Kitty could not be that upset about it.

"Are you quite comfortable, Miss Bennet? We can have more cushions fetched for you, if you need them." He appeared to be on the cusp of summoning someone to bring them before she could respond.

She smiled at him. "No, indeed—do not trouble yourself, I beg you. My ankle is well supported and has not bothered me in the slightest."

"If you are certain..."

"Very, thank you." She reached for her wine and took a sip, marveling at the spread before them. She knew that the Darcys were rich, and of course Pemberley was an intimidatingly fine house, but she had not anticipated a meal of this luxury for a family dinner even if they did have company. She saw her favorite hare soup, bottle peas, and at least two different kinds of ragout, and that was just the side of the table where she sat. She remembered her mother supposing that Mr. Darcy must have two or three French cooks, and given the food she had seen so far, she could easily believe it. The whole table was a work of art.

It tasted as good as it smelled, too, and Kitty listened happily to the conversation around her and enjoyed the meal. When Mr. Johns engaged her attention she chatted with him quite amiably about anything that came to her mind, and enjoyed his gallant attentions to her.

How well the evening progressed! If she continued at this rate, she would be engaged to Mr. Johns before she had to return to Longbourn. Wouldn't that just show Mary, and her under-clerk!

When the ladies withdrew, however, Miss Pratt claimed the spot on the sofa beside her and proceeded to abuse her friend for her abominable neglect. "For," said she, "I have not been able to speak three words to the Colonel all evening, and I was counting on you to help me."

Kitty apologized; she had been so focused on Mr. Johns and the pleasure she found in his company that she had quite forgotten about her friend.

"Well, I will require you to repent by helping me when they join us. I mean to persuade Miss Darcy to play a duet with me, and you must ensure that he attends the performance, and my playing particularly."

"When you have finished playing you must come and attend me; I will have him nearby and you can use me as your excuse to talk to him."

Miss Pratt beamed. "That is perfect. Thank you!"

Accordingly, when the gentlemen joined them, Miss Pratt asked Miss Darcy to play with her what they had been practicing, and they moved to the pianoforte. Kitty looked eagerly for an opportunity to engage Colonel Fitzwilliam, but instead of him, or even Mr. Johns (whom Kitty would happily have accepted as a substitute) Mr. Knott came and sat beside her during the performance. The two gentlemen in whom she had the greater interest sat on the opposite side of the room and conversed with Mr. Bennet between songs. Kitty did not know how to engage their attention without being able to stand and walk to them herself, and had nothing to do but cast apologetic glances toward her friend and express her distress by what means she had available to her. It was hardly enough.

To make matters worse, Mr. Knott seemed entirely unaware of her distress. Every time the music paused for a moment, off he went again. "How are you liking Derbyshire, Miss Bennet?" and "What do you like to do with your mornings?" and all manner of innocent-sounding questions in which Kitty perceived malicious intent. Did he not see that she wished to talk to the other gentlemen? She kept looking toward them, but none of them noticed her.

Very well, she would simply have to turn the tables. "Have you known Colonel Fitzwilliam long?"

He looked surprised at her question, and a little bit offended, and Kitty realized belatedly that she had not answered his last question. Well, who cared about the feelings of some clergyman who couldn't even get a living on his own? If he had come only for the living Mr. Darcy had open, he would behave himself around that gentleman's family, no matter what they did.

"Yes, I suppose I have. Several years at this point, anyway," he said.

"We met through a mutual friend, who introduced us just a few months before I finished school."

Kitty nodded, barely listening. She tried to think of how she could turn the conversation into a request to bring him over to her. But Mr. Knott seemed bound to cross her purposes at every turn. "My mother was so proud of the acquaintance—it was the first sign of such social consciousness I had ever seen in her, and it quite took me back. But she, worthy woman that she is, could think of nothing more than my prospects, which I must admit improved on knowing him. I am grateful to have found such a friend."

"He seems to be a very generous friend." She knew she sounded stupid, but she couldn't let him turn the conversation back to himself or his mother. What grown man talks so much of his mother, anyway?

"He is indeed, and very good company, too. When I was last at my family's house..." He entered into some story or other about himself, and his mother, and some favor the Colonel had done for them. Kitty listened for any opportunity to contradict what he said, or ask something that he would have to defer to his friend and call him over for an explanation, but he deflected or answered every inquiry without requiring any assistance at all. By the time he finished with his story, the other ladies had finished playing, and Kitty could do nothing for Miss Pratt except watch helplessly as she was drawn into a conversation with the Darcys.

CHAPTER 11

*M*iss Pratt, as it turned out, did not blame Kitty for the events of that evening, but Mr. Knott. And as the gentlemen did not join them at all the next morning, having gone to view Edgepark together, they were at their leisure to discuss it.

"What did he mean, anyway, by coming and talking to you? Anyone could have guessed that a clergyman would not have been your first object when there were other sources of amusement at hand; and you were not particularly welcoming toward him."

"Perhaps he thought he ought to offer her some companionship, as she was sitting alone," Miss Darcy suggested.

"He ought to have known that he could be but poor comfort."

"I am sure he did not mean any harm by it," Kitty said, "and he was... pleasant, I suppose. Though I would have enjoyed it more if I had not so wished that he were someone else. I do prefer the company of the other gentlemen to his, and it was decidedly miserable to have all my plans so effectively frustrated."

"What were you planning?" Miss Darcy asked.

"Miss Bennet has agreed to help forward my acquaintance with Colonel Fitzwilliam." Miss Pratt picked up her teacup and took a long sip. "And I believe she has every intention of forwarding her own acquaintance with Mr. Johns."

Kitty blushed. "Well, he is very handsome, and if he owns an estate, he must be rather well-off. Particularly because he is doing so much work on it."

"Yes; does anyone know his income?" Neither Miss Darcy nor Kitty did. "It is strange that we know so little of him!"

"I do not believe my brother expected him to spend very much time in our company; he probably did not think it was important to find out."

"I wish he had," Kitty said, "because it would be good for me to know more of him. No matter his income, though, I enjoyed his company, and he was very attentive to me last night."

Miss Darcy gave a start and turned to Miss Pratt. "Wait. Your acquaintance with my cousin? Why, Miss Pratt, are you—" She cut herself off, looking confused.

"Intending to make him fall in love with me?" supplied Miss Pratt, smiling. "Yes, I certainly am, if I can manage it. Should you not like me for a cousin?"

"Of course I will, if you are his choice."

"I hear a 'however' in your voice, my dear." Miss Pratt laughed. "Never mind. If I am his choice, I am sure you will be happy for us, and if I am not, I hope it will not harm our friendship at all."

"No, indeed." She placed her hand over Miss Pratt's and smiled.

"Well, Miss Darcy," Kitty said, eager to restore her place in the conversation, "I have nearly finished with the bonnet; what do you think of it?" She handed it to her and awaited her verdict.

"This is far superior to what it was!" said Miss Darcy. "You have an excellent eye for this kind of work! I would be honored to wear it again."

"If only you could walk, Miss Bennet, I would suggest we go out for a stroll and try it out," said Miss Pratt. "But perhaps we might sit outside to do our work for this morning? It looks beautiful out."

"We do have a little garden seat overlooking the lake, where I have often brought some small piece of work to take some air, but it is rather far for Miss Bennet to try to go on her own." Miss Pratt's hopeful look faded, and Miss Darcy bit her lip and glanced out the window.

After a moment's thought, she amended, "I might be able to persuade my brother to provide us with the gig, if you like. Of course, one of us will have to sit in the groom's chair, but it is not very far, and he can walk behind to attend the horses."

They all agreed, especially Kitty, who missed being out-of-doors.

The sun shone so brightly that for a few minutes she could not look at anything past her toes, and even with her bonnet shielding her eyes, she had to squint to see. But there was a welcoming breeze blowing, and as her eyes slowly adjusted, she could look around and admire the beautiful blues and greens of the day. It really was the perfect summer's day, and Kitty found it so refreshing that she longed to do nothing more than to remain there all day.

Miss Darcy had brought along some of her work, the beginnings of a blanket she was making for the mother of one of Pemberley's tenants. "She is often sickly, and almost always cold, and has only a very thin blanket to cover herself," she explained, and asked if they would like to help.

Miss Pratt declined, preferring to focus only on the conversation, and Kitty followed her lead. To pretty things for herself and her friends, she had no difficulty devoting her time. But there was no fun in a boring, utilitarian blanket. Besides, there was more than enough work for her to do indoors, when they finally had to go back. Kitty did not mean to waste her time on it now.

Miss Pratt told them stories of her acquaintance in London, which was far greater than Kitty could boast in any place, and seemed to be greater than Miss Darcy's, as well. Kitty laughed merrily at them all. Miss Pratt seemed to know a number of people who were always getting into the worst kinds of scrapes, which made for excellent stories, and if they did tend toward the scandalous at times, Kitty did not object. It only made them all the funnier.

One young lady seemed to show up in Miss Pratt's stories oftener than the others—Miss Pratt identified her only as "Camilla, who used to be Miss Irons" and when pressed to explain told her story in thrilling tones. "I do not remember her name now; I know that she is married, but I have not seen her since.

"She went away to visit some uncle, or a relative of that kind; it hardly matters who. I heard there was another gentleman there at that time who went rather wild over her, or so everyone thought, but would not make any motion toward making her an offer. Apparently he was rather a rake, and liked nothing more than to make young ladies fall in love with him. Well, my dear Camilla knew better than to fall for that! She had always vowed that she should never be a laughingstock for anybody. So she found a way to entrap him; I never learnt the details; anyway, next thing you hear, she is married to the man, and quite pleased with herself, too, from all I have been told! I wish I could see her again; I should dearly love to hear more of the story."

"Goodness!" Kitty said, somewhat overawed. "I could never be so bold as that. I wonder that she had the courage to do it!"

"Oh, she was always good for boldness, if for nothing else." Miss Pratt laughed and stood up to shake out her skirts and walk around to Kitty's other side, where Miss Darcy sat, taking in the view as she went. "This is a lovely spot, Miss Darcy. I can see why you come here so often. I declare, I would like it above all things if we could spend every morning out here!"

Miss Darcy smiled a little bit. "Yes, isn't it pretty? When Miss Bennet is able to walk again, we will be able to come out more frequently."

"Well, Miss Bennet, in that case I must implore you to walk again as soon as possible. I will not be happy until we can come here again."

Kitty sighed. "If there is any way to recover faster, I do not know it, but I wish I did, for this is miserably tedious."

"I am sure you will be walking again before you know it," Miss Darcy said, patting her hand.

"Oh, yes—this is nothing to the time my friend Miss Harding broke her leg. It was ten times worse than yours, Miss Bennet, I am sure, and she was in plasters for ages. She missed all the balls for the whole season, and was obliged to turn down I do not know how many invitations because she had to be carried everywhere."

Kitty gasped. "How dreadful!"

"Yes, isn't it?" The flutter of her fan wasn't quite quick enough to hide how she puffed out her chest.

Miss Darcy patted Kitty's knee. "Your injury is not that dire, Miss Bennet. I am sure that you will be recovered before very much longer."

Kitty, whose ankle throbbed at the mere thought of walking on it, did not think she agreed.

THE OUTING PROVIDED a welcome break in their morning routine, but Kitty could not help preferring what happened the next day, when all of the gentlemen—including Mr. Johns—joined them halfway through the morning for more *Absentee* and some conversation, which Kitty enjoyed more than anything. Mr. Johns told them all about Edgepark, describing the improvements to be made, and more exciting, the intention he had of taking them all to tour it as soon as the ladies could go in safety.

"Is it so dangerous now, then?" Kitty asked, feeling a small thrill.

"There are many areas in which the floor has begun to rot, and there is a chance of falling through," Mr. Johns answered, "and unless you know precisely where to step, you are indeed in great danger."

"Oh!" said Kitty. "The house must have been absolutely destroyed!"

"I had heard it was in bad shape," Miss Darcy added, "but nothing had given me the impression that it was as badly off as that. I wonder that you don't have the entire building pulled down and start fresh!"

Colonel Fitzwilliam laughed. "I suggested the same thing when I saw it yesterday, but he is determined, it appears."

"I am indeed. But Mr. Knott agrees that it can be salvaged; I am not alone in my insanity."

"I believe it can, with enough time and money. It is a handsome house, or it used to be. Rather old-fashioned, of course." Mr. Knott shrugged. "But as you are considering altering the face at least, I don't imagine that will matter. Certainly everything else about it will be made new, and probably be quite handsome."

"Do you know fashions in housing?" asked Miss Darcy with genuine curiosity. "I know next to nothing about it, though my brother has some interest in it."

"Yes, well, at one point I expected to inherit an estate of my own, and spent some time researching improvements I might have made to it." He colored a little. "But as that inheritance went elsewhere, all my research turned out to be solely for my own amusement."

"How dreadful for you, to have been robbed of the income you had expected!" said Miss Pratt. She leaned forward. "What happened?"

Mr. Knott's color deepened. "I do not feel myself robbed. A closer relation, who had been presumed dead, was found living, and returned from abroad on learning that he had an inheritance. Fortunately, he was generous enough to offer to send me to school, if I wished, since he was taking the place I had anticipated obtaining."

"How very kind of him," said Miss Darcy.

"Yes, and if he had not, I should not have met Colonel Fitzwilliam, and therefore none of you. So, you see, I am quite in his debt." Mr. Knott smiled around the room, apparently quite content with his lot.

"But to have lost your entire future! Surely you did not view it with such resignation as you do now," Kitty insisted. She could not believe that.

"Why should I not? I am certainly not well-equipped to run an estate the size of Rookwood, and I was relieved when I found that I would not have to. My ambitions have always run toward other things."

"It is not easy to find a position as a clergyman these days," Miss Darcy said quietly.

"No," he agreed, "but I did not say that my ambitions ran toward easier things. Only different ones."

Miss Pratt huffed and rolled her eyes. "I don't see what kind of person could possibly prefer a life in the church to one of ease and comfort on an estate."

"You see one before you, Miss Pratt," Mr. Knott said with a small smile. "I will admit that my mother was very upset on my behalf, and I am certain that she would have rather seen me go to a more illustrious establishment. But she knows my temper, and has since told me that she believes I am better equipped for the path God has set me on."

Miss Darcy smiled. "She sounds very wise."

"She is exceptional in every way."

"You are close, then?" asked Kitty.

"Yes. We were not always—there were many years, when I was younger, that I resented her for certain elements of my childhood which were only partially her fault. But for the last few years, we have reached an understanding and an intimacy that more than makes up for our previous falling-out."

Kitty could not understand that. She liked her mother very well, but she had no desire to increase their intimacy at all. Miss Pratt also seemed uncomfortable with the subject, because she changed it to something else, and the conversation moved on.

THE OTHER GOOD thing that came out of that morning did not reveal itself to her until they were going to dress for dinner, when Miss Darcy found her.

"I have a gift for you," she said, holding something behind her back and smiling shyly.

"Have you? Thank you! But I am sure it is not—"

"Don't be silly! You will be very glad of this." She pulled from behind her back a very elegant, old-fashioned ladies' cane. "This belonged to my great-grandmother. Elizabeth and I were looking for it this morning. It took us longer to find it than we thought it would, but I thought, since you seemed to be so restless without being able to walk under your own power, that a cane might help you get around."

Kitty took it eagerly. "Thank you so much! This is perfect!" She proved her enthusiasm by immediately putting it to use. She stood up, leaning on it heavily, and took a tentative step forward. Everything felt terribly stiff, but it worked. She walked all the way to the window seat with it, though it quite tired her out to do so. "Miss Darcy, I cannot thank you enough!"

"I am very glad you like it," she answered, smiling. "It seemed a shame that you are so completely dependent on others to move you where you wish to go."

"I could not agree more." Kitty wanted nothing more than to spend the rest of the day hobbling about, but after only ten minutes of that her arm shook under the strain of holding her up and she had to stop and rest. But it was an excellent beginning. No longer did she depend upon the whim of whoever happened to be around to help her walk. If she needed to go to a different room, or even to cross the room, she could. The level of freedom that would afford her made her giddy.

She took delight in making her own (slow) way to her room to dress for dinner, and completed her toilette as quickly as possible so she could hobble her way back down to where the others were gathering to go in together. She would be one of the last to arrive, but she would arrive under her own power, and she would happily savor that triumph.

As she passed the salon door, however, she heard something that stopped her where she stood: her own name, from what sounded like Mr. Johns. She couldn't help pressing her ear to the door.

"...not entirely respectable."

"I don't know about that. She's just one of those that gives an unfortunate impression of herself, but she's reasonably pretty, at least," Colonel Fitzwilliam said. "That counts for something, don't you think?"

"Reasonably pretty does precious little good when one is so transparent in one's intentions! Poor thing! I bet she thinks she's a lot of fun," said Mr. Johns. "Maybe she is, but she's not exactly marriage material, what?"

Kitty turned away from the door, fighting the fury that rose within her. Was that his opinion of her? Surely the others would defend her —surely they did not all have such an opinion of her! Surely one of them thought better of her than that. If only someone did, she could get them to help her show Mr. Johns what he did not see. Perhaps someone was defending her even now! She leaned back toward the door and listened carefully again.

"...Here he is now. Darcy, where on earth have you been?" Mr. Johns said.

"My sister wanted me. Apparently she took it upon herself to find a cane that has been in the family some years and give it to Miss Bennet, and she wanted to be sure that I approved." He paused, and Kitty heard glasses clinking. "I can't imagine why she thought I should not. If I had believed we still had that old cane I'd have dug it up myself, but I thought it had been lost years ago. Miss Bennet will be happy to be able to walk on her own again, I am sure."

Mr. Johns answered, "Aye. Tis a pity that she can't dance, with the ball coming up. I am surprised that she hasn't been remarking on it."

"We haven't told her of it, and do not intend to," Mr. Darcy said. "She's distressed enough without having to learn of a ball she would not be able to attend."

"Surely she could go and watch the other dancers, at least?" said Mr. Knott. "There are other amusements to be had at a ball than dancing oneself."

"Mrs. Darcy seems to think that would only make it worse for her. She has never been particularly good at taking pleasure in the delight of others, from what I gather. It would be kinder to just keep her ignorant of the whole proceeding."

This time Kitty really did have quite enough. She crept away from the door, eyes smarting and appetite lost.

Mary would tell her that she deserved it for listening at doors. And she might have been right, but would not it have been better if they had not been discussing her at all? Should they really have been talking about a poor girl in their midst who couldn't even walk, as though she was some kind of joke? And there would be a ball, and she wasn't even supposed to know about it! That stung worst of all. Of course she would rather dance, but she could at least put on a pretty dress and watch the others dance instead, could she not? Besides, was that not her choice to make, not someone else's to make on her behalf? They should at least have asked her!

She turned, intent on finding Elizabeth and demanding to know why she hadn't been told about the ball at all, until she remembered that Elizabeth believed Kitty was ignorant about it, and Kitty would have to confess to eavesdropping on the gentlemen if she did so.

Torn between humiliation and rage, she didn't hear the door open or the approach of someone behind her until he spoke. "Miss Bennet! Walking already, I see?" She recognized his voice instantly: Mr. Johns. Her cheeks warmed.

Kitty could not turn to face him until she had composed herself. "Only with the support of the cane, I'm afraid. I'm not much good yet." She turned around at last but could not meet his eye. How could she, knowing what he thought of her?

"Well, I'm sure you'll be walking on your own again in no time. Dancing, too, and if I don't miss my guess, you're looking forward to that just as much."

"Yes... but it hardly matters. I'm clearly not the kind of girl a man would wish to dance with, anyway. Apparently, I'm not entirely respectable."

His eyes widened the smallest bit, which gave her a little jolt of satisfaction. "I see you heard some of our conversation in there." She nodded, blushing at the memory of their words. "What you must not have heard, however, is that the young lady of whom we spoke was not you, but Miss Pratt?"

Miss Pratt! "I thought... I thought I heard my name..."

"Likely you did, since she has taken such a liking to you. She is the sort of person a girl wants for a friend but a man wants nothing to do with, I think. All her charms are for her own sex only. You, on the other hand, possess the rare and enviable charm of being equally agreeable to both." He smiled, taking a step closer to her. "Do not let the idle conversation of bored men concern you, Miss Bennet. I assure you, there is nothing about you which can invite the kind of censure which Miss Pratt has done."

"Thank you," she said breathlessly. What a man! He found her more charming than Miss Pratt, and more ladylike too. He was so kind to her, and how careful he was to soothe her feelings! Everything promised a perfect romance. She could see that Mr. Johns would be an excellent husband—and here she thought she would have been content with Mr. Warde. How foolish! She knew better now. Nothing could compare to Mr. Johns.

"And when you have recovered enough to dance, whenever that may be," he said, glancing at her cane, "I beg you would reserve your first dance for me. Nothing would give me greater satisfaction."

Kitty curtseyed as well as she could around the cane, her blush now of pleasure. "It is yours, whenever it happens. I will dance with no other."

She was determined that it would be at the ball. It might be a lot of work to be dancing before the ball came, but with such inducement before her, how could she help but succeed?

CHAPTER 12

*K*itty really had no idea how to go about speeding up her recovery. She had a vague idea that if she exercised it more, and stretched her abilities, her ankle would somehow heal faster. And she didn't want to ask anyone for help, for fear that they would ask her why she was working so hard, and she would not have a good answer for them. So she decided to press forward alone.

She arrived in the music room earlier than anyone else for a week to practice. She stayed well clear of the pianoforte and that more cluttered side of the room, but she cleared a little track around the perimeter which gave her pretty good exercise. Her ankle throbbed by the end of these exercises, but she could manage it. Overall, she thought, she progressed quite well, although she had not really set herself any goals by which to measure her progress. Her only real target was to be well enough to dance by the time the ball took place, whenever that might be.

By the end of the week she could hobble along quite nicely with her cane, although she had not yet been brave enough to try walking without it. Today, she planned to figure out how to walk without that assistance if it killed her, although she was fairly confident it would not come to that.

She started small, and took a lap around the room with her cane to get used to the exercise again. Then she decided to start trying to walk without it. She laid the cane gently on the armchair in the corner, and stood balanced on her good foot, trying to decide where she would go. It couldn't be far. Maybe the window nearby? It was probably three steps away. She might be able to make it that far.

She struck out, arms outstretched on either side of her. She moved slowly, all her attention focused on placing her injured foot down in such a way that she would not hurt it. She touched it to the ground, then put a little bit of weight on it. It seemed stiff, but it did not hurt yet. More weight, bit by bit—still no pain. A smile began to break out on her face through lips pursed in concentration. She could do it! Most of her weight was on the ankle and it ached a little, but it was nothing she couldn't handle. She swung her other leg forward quickly and stepped the rest of the way to the window. She had done it!

Of course, it was a far cry from dancing, but it was an excellent beginning. If she could have danced in celebration, she would have, but that would come soon enough. She would be walking by the end of the week, and dancing would surely follow.

She rested against the windowsill for a few minutes, and looked around the room for her next objective. A writing-desk stood on the wall between her window and the next that might be close enough to walk to. It would be pushing it, but after the success she had just experienced, Kitty felt energized and ready to try nearly anything.

A door banged in the hallway, and Kitty turned back to the door to see whether the person would come in and find her. Maybe she should go back to the cane instead, just in case. What if someone found her? But when no more sounds followed, and when there were no signs of anyone at the door, she shook her head and went back to her task.

The writing-desk usually had a chair, but Kitty had removed it at the beginning of the week to make room for her walking. Now she wished she hadn't; she could have positioned it halfway in case she needed it. But never mind that. If she had to, she would lean on the wall. She stepped forward and began her slow progress toward the desk. One step—two, three, four, five—she wasn't so sure she would make it!—six, seven, eight, and she was there! She laughed with joy. She would be dancing yet, and in plenty of time for any ball.

But it had taken a lot more out of her than she expected, and she had to rest before she tried it again. Her ankle was not used to supporting her weight any more and she could feel it straining against the work she had asked of it. She would probably only have one more walk in her that morning.

Could she make it all the way back to her cane in one try? It was easily twice as long as what she had just done, if she went straight there and did not stop at the window again. But it might be possible. She would try it, as soon as she got her strength back.

When her ankle stopped throbbing quite so hard, she forced herself back up. She would not have much time before the others joined her. Feeling rushed and not quite as sturdy as she had felt before, she took her first step forward. Her ankle began to protest the strain. Another step. "Come on," she muttered, "just this one last push and that's all I'll do for the day." Another step. It really was starting to hurt. Another step.

"Kitty!"

Her father's sharp cry startled her so badly that she jumped and let out a yelp, which turned to a gasp when she landed on her ankle wrong and crumpled to the ground. But someone caught her just before she reached it; she looked up and saw a smiling Mr. Johns.

"Oh," she said, feeling stupid. "Thank you." She looked around and saw, to her shame, that nearly everyone was standing around and watching her—only Mr. Darcy was not there.

Her father rushed over to her. "What on earth are you doing?" he demanded, as the two gentlemen helped her right herself.

"I was trying to walk." Tears welled in her eyes, both from the pain of her ankle and the humiliation of getting caught.

"I can see that, but what on earth possessed you to do it alone, without telling anyone? You're not nearly recovered enough for that!"

Mr. Johns stepped back, but still hovered nearby.

Kitty squeezed her eyes shut and the tears began to drop onto her cheeks. Her ankle screamed at her and she could hardly focus on what he was saying. "I just wanted to dance again," she whispered, hardly daring to glance toward Mr. Johns. He smiled a little bit at her, and she felt a little bit encouraged.

"Dance...?" He sighed. "Kitty, there was never any chance that you would have been recovered in time to go to the ball." She opened her eyes in time to see him wince. "You weren't supposed to know about that."

Kitty lowered her eyes again and wiped the tears off her cheeks furiously. Mr. Bennet gazed at her for a few moments. "You already knew, didn't you."

Kitty only sniffed. It didn't matter now whether he knew.

"Oh, Kitty." He sighed and shook his head. He turned to the rest of the party. "May I have a word with my daughter?"

Mr. Johns handed her the cane and bowed, and followed the others out. Kitty glanced back toward her father, feeling a little lightheaded and very, very stupid. But she couldn't meet his eye. He would only be thinking the worst of her.

He paced the room for a few moments, and neither of them spoke. To be sure, excuses and explanations were racing through Kitty's mind, but she couldn't hold on to one long enough to turn it into something worth saying. And Mr. Bennet seemed conflicted with himself.

"Papa," she ventured at last, "I just want to walk under my own power again."

"And to dance with every gentleman in the house," Mr. Bennet said. He rubbed his hand over his face and through his thinning hair. "Or, failing that, fall into their arms, apparently." Kitty blushed, but said nothing. "I do not know what to do with you, Kitty."

"I do wish I could go to the ball," she said, gathering her thoughts and speaking carefully, "but I don't see how that's going to happen. I don't even know when it is... I just overheard some of the gentlemen talking about it, and I thought... if I could get better before it happened, maybe..."

"The ball is next Friday evening. You are not likely to be recovered enough to be able to dance by then."

Kitty looked down at her cane and shook her head. He was right, of course.

"I can completely understand wishing to be able to walk under your own power again, but what I will never understand is your constant need to make a fool of yourself to every young man you meet. Do you think that makes you more attractive to them? Because I can assure you it does not."

"I am not trying to make a fool of myself! I only want to have some fun!"

"My dear child, your version of 'fun' seems to come exclusively at the cost of other people's sanity. And falling on Mr. Johns like that! Are you trying to outdo your sister in stupidity, or scandal?"

Kitty flinched a little at this. Why did he always go out of his way to make her feel like the worst kind of daughter? And she never knew how to respond, so most of the time she did not. She wished she had Lizzy's quick wit. Lizzy always had a gentle retort to their father's quips that turned his pique into amusement. Kitty had never picked up that skill. "I did not know he was there," she said, her voice barely audible even to her. "I had not intended to fall on anyone. I wanted to walk, and you startled me."

"Well, for heaven's sake, next time call someone responsible in to help you. If you had fallen without someone here to catch you, what might have happened?"

"I wouldn't have fallen if you hadn't scared me!"

"Do not take that tone with me, young lady. If you insist on walking, ask your sister to help you. She will, no doubt, be more than willing." He sighed again and walked to the door, pausing just before he reached it. "I'll send the others in." Kitty made no answer, so he left.

So she couldn't go the ball. She had vaguely known it all along, but she hadn't let herself acknowledge it. And she had made some progress, even if her father had come in and messed it all up after. She would just have to find another opportunity to dance with Mr. Johns.

IT WAS ONLY A FEW DAYS, however, before Kitty found that she missed the exercise and sense of progress that her morning attempts at walking provided her, and she resumed her practice. However, she had set herself back quite a bit when she fell, and she spent most of her first day frustrated at the stabbing pain that shot through her at every step. By the time the others joined her, she was more than ready to be done.

The next morning she tried it again, resolved to move more slowly and take better care lest she injure herself yet more. But the pain soon became unbearable, and, expecting to have some time before anyone joined her, she sank into a chair and indulged in a bit of a cry. She was mortified, then, to be joined by Mr. Knott.

"Miss Bennet?"

She wiped at her eyes and sniffed, but she could not hide her distress. He came and sat in the chair beside her, holding out his handkerchief. Kitty, hating herself, her ankle, and every wretched second she had spent trying to walk again, took it and tried to compose herself. Who would be next to walk in? Mr. Johns? Miss Pratt? Her father?

Mr. Knott waited in gentle silence for her to be ready to speak. Finally, she gathered herself enough to apologize. But he stopped her before she could get past two words. "No, there's no need. I have had a broken ankle before. I know how frustrating it is to find yourself completely incapable of doing things you had, to that moment, never considered being deprived of doing. You never appreciate the ability to walk, I've found, until the power of walking is denied you. Suddenly, walking seems to be the most powerful freedom available to man."

She sniffed and smiled a little bit. "Yes. And I miss dancing." She glanced at the door, but so far no one else was coming to join them.

"I would imagine so. Particularly when Miss Darcy and Miss Pratt are able to spend so much time practicing what their dance masters have taught them."

"Do you dance, Mr. Knott?" Kitty asked. She was immediately struck with the memory of Mr. Collins dancing at Netherfield, the last time she had watched a clergyman try to dance, and she could not help envisioning Mr. Knott doing much the same. She bit back a laugh. But then, he had not always meant to be a clergyman; perhaps he was a better dancer.

"Occasionally. I am not the worst dancer in England, I suppose, but I am certainly not the best. I have such trouble keeping all the dances straight, that I often begin doing one and end trying to do something quite different."

Kitty smiled and looked to the door again. Still safe, as far as she could tell. "Do not the leading couple help you to remember which to do?"

"No, though you are not the first person to suggest that they should. Never mind, though. I know enough to fumble my way through a dance, and really, isn't dancing more about getting to know one's partner than perfecting the forms?"

She shrugged. "I suppose, though I am happiest when I can do both. And some gentlemen are miserably dull, but dance very well, which is its own kind of trial."

"That I can well believe," he said, laughing. "Dull individuals are not found only amongst the males of the world, I promise."

"You don't need to tell me that. What do you think we do when we withdraw after dinner? Nothing but sit around and gossip or bore each other to tears. It's frightfully dull." Someone walked past the door, but it was only a servant. When would someone else join them? She had no idea how to talk to Mr. Knott, and as he was not Mr. Johns, she was but little interested in anything he had to say.

He smiled and did not respond, and they sat without saying anything to each other for several minutes. Kitty couldn't think of a single thing to say to him, and she could hardly look at him. Where could the others be?

Then, out of nowhere, he stood up and held out his arm to her. "Maybe I could help you walk. If you lean on me, I can provide you better support, and if you start to fall I would be able to catch you. That way you needn't hurt yourself again, but you can continue to make progress."

Several things entered her head at once. What on earth did he mean by it? Why couldn't Mr. Johns have made her the offer instead? Should she accept? Would her father be angry with her if she did? But to walk again—she needed help, even if it was only someone there to stop her from going too far. "I—I suppose—Mr. Bennet may not—but if he does—"

"I will clear it with him and ensure we are properly chaperoned," he assured her. He glanced behind him. "In fact, I had thought we would be joined soon or I would not have remained unchaperoned with you this long. Shall I go and find the ladies to join you?"

"It is probably close to time to go down to breakfast," Kitty said.

He pulled out his pocket watch and confirmed that she was right. "In that case, allow me to help you down to the breakfast room." He held out his arm again, and this time Kitty accepted his help.

CHAPTER 13

*W*ith Mr. Knott's help, she did make great improvements in walking on her own, but it was not enough to dance by the time of the ball. Kitty did not give up hope completely until that morning, but then even she had to own that she had no hope of dancing that night.

"I still wish to go, however," she said resolutely to her sister.

Elizabeth frowned. "There will be little else to do but watch the others dance," she warned.

"There are usually card tables in another room, are there not? And there will be many people to talk to."

"Most of the young people will be dancing, dear, as you well know."

"Yes, but how am I to meet anyone if I do not go? I could watch them when they dance, and talk with them when they do not. And I could still have the pleasure of seeing my friends well-liked."

Elizabeth did not care for any of Kitty's arguments, but Kitty was determined to wear her down, and she spent the entire morning laying out every reason she could think of for why she should be allowed to go. Finally, her sister agreed to take her along.

"But you must promise to inform me as soon as you begin to feel fatigued. I need to be sure that you are not overtaxing yourself. I want to be sure that you will be well enough to dance at the next ball. And I do not wish you to leave my side unless you are with someone else of our party. I still do not believe that this is a very good idea."

Kitty barely heard these stipulations, but she agreed to them and hobbled as quickly as she could to her room to change. She had not had the chance to get any new dresses made, and her best looked rather shabby when she considered what the other ladies would almost certainly be wearing. But she refused to allow it to matter; she meant to meet as many people as she could, hopefully widening her acquaintance in the area, and opening opportunities for more parties in the future.

But she needn't have worried about her gown. Miss Pratt knocked on her door and came in bearing a silky blue dress that was every bit as elegant as the one she was already wearing.

"Mrs. Darcy said that you probably did not have much to wear," she said, "and I thought, since we are close to the same size, that you could borrow one of mine. It's last year's fashion, I'm afraid, but it's very pretty and I think it would suit your color."

Kitty did not know how to express her joy, but she did her best and thanked Miss Pratt at every moment. When they had gotten her into the dress and pinned it in place, they were both very pleased with how it looked.

"Now, you should take this shawl, and drape it so—" Miss Pratt arranged the fabric carefully—"and you must wear those slippers, and put this in your hair." She produced a little pearl and sapphire comb, and tucked it into Kitty's braid. "There!"

"Oh, how I wish I could dance! How well I look!" said Kitty.

Miss Pratt laughed. "You do look very well, but it is probably better that you can't dance. This dress doesn't fit you well enough to stand up to an evening of dancing without forcing you to run off to re-pin it every time you sit down, and that would be very tedious. But you will look very well tonight, and distract every person you meet into forgetting about your poor ankle altogether."

"Yes," Kitty said mournfully, "up until they ask me to dance, and I must turn everyone away."

"Never mind that; I will not dance either, unless a very *particular* gentleman should ask me." Kitty easily interpreted that even without the significant look which accompanied it and, very sensible of the sacrifice her friend was offering to make, could not be more grateful.

They went down to meet the carriage together. The others were all gathered in the front hall already, waiting for them. They were as complimentary of Kitty's dress as she could have wished, particularly Mr. Johns.

"Miss Bennet, if you could but dance, I would secure your hand for every dance you could spare," he said, bowing over her hand. "Of course, by this point, they would all be snatched up by other young men, and I would have nothing to do but watch from my place in the set, neglecting whichever poor creature I coerced into standing up with me."

She giggled. "I doubt that, sir, but I appreciate the thought."

"Well, we must agree to disagree. At any rate, all I can offer you is my assistance into the carriage, if you will accept it?"

Nothing could be more agreeable to her. She climbed into the carriage with the highest of spirits and the greatest anticipation of the delights of the evening before her.

They arrived slightly late, and the first dance had already begun. Kitty stayed close by Elizabeth's side and eagerly greeted every new acquaintance, and as they made their way into the ballroom she felt that it would have been a pity, indeed, to miss this night. Every face that passed before her was a potential friend; every whispered word a piece of the choicest gossip; every glowing smile a portent of her own happiness to come, even if she could not dance at all.

To further her delight, Kitty found in her sister an excellent chaperone. Mrs. Darcy introduced Kitty to a number of young ladies with whom she was likely to get along, and several gentlemen as well, which gratified Kitty very much. She had a weak sort of pleasure in being obliged to turn down requests to dance on account of her ankle. She entertained some impossible fantasy of some of them being so taken with her that they insisted, on learning of her condition, of sitting down with her for the dances which they would have bestowed on her; but of course that did not happen. Several of them did indeed seem very disappointed to find her unable to honor them, and with that she meant to be content. After all, she had already received the sweetest compliments from the man whose attention mattered the most, hadn't she?

Miss Darcy and Miss Pratt kept to her sides and helped her take some of the weight off her ankle, and when they at last reached a chair into which Kitty could lower herself, they posted themselves beside her and kept up a constant chatter about the dancers going by. Miss Pratt knew more about the individuals than Miss Darcy did, if she knew them at all, but Miss Darcy recognized more of them. Between them both, though, and Elizabeth's interjecting what she knew at times, the first set passed in such enjoyment for Kitty that she hardly remembered to regret her injury.

The Colonel, who had disappeared at some point after their entry, rejoined them shortly before the conclusion of the first set to ask his cousin to dance with him for the next. Kitty thought that was exceptionally good of him since Miss Darcy was so shy, and would be best off beginning with someone who knew how to keep her at ease. But Miss Pratt was not pleased, and Kitty could not blame her for that, either.

"At this rate, I shall *never* be able to dance," she said to Kitty, in a mournful undertone.

"It is only the first full set that we are here," Kitty answered, smiling. "You have the whole ball before you. Stand up with someone else, when you may, and when he sees you going down the line he will likely realize that he wishes to ask you next."

"Do you mean it?" asked Miss Pratt. "I promised you that I would only leave your side to dance with *him*."

"Of course. This is in order that you might dance with him, and anyway, if I cannot have the pleasure of dancing myself, you can afford me the pleasure of watching you dance a set or two over the course of the evening, and one of them is bound to be with him. Then, when you come back to me, we can talk over every moment. You must pay very close attention and promise me that you will remember everything, for the only dancing I shall do tonight is through you."

"Thank you, my dear friend!" And she applied to Elizabeth immediately for an introduction to a suitable partner.

Kitty only sat alone for a few moments, for Mr. Knott soon joined her, offering punch. She would have preferred Mr. Johns, but as he was dancing with a Miss Bell, and Kitty was otherwise quite alone, she did not want to send him away. She accepted the punch gladly and asked him if he did not mean to dance.

"Not for this set, at least," he said. "I observed that your companions have all left you, and I thought you would be happier with some company. It is dreadfully lonely, being entirely alone in a crowd."

Kitty could not deny that she did not prefer to be left alone, particularly at a ball, so she thanked him heartily and sipped her punch. It tasted watered down and too bitter, and she soon lowered the cup to her lap and kept it there. Without the exertion of dancing to raise her thirst, poor punch was not at all pleasing.

She watched Miss Pratt join the set just a few couples down from Miss Darcy and Colonel Fitzwilliam, and she smiled. That would give her friend a good chance to impress him.

"...Mr. Johns, since our arrival?"

Kitty blinked and turned to Mr. Knott. "Forgive me; I missed the first few words of your question. Mr. Johns?"

"Yes; I only asked if you had seen him since we arrived. I think he has vanished entirely."

She shook her head sadly. "I saw him taking his place in the set, but I do not see him now. I was so hoping for the chance to see him dance. Or he could come and talk to me for a time, as you did, if he is not inclined to dance." Elizabeth rejoined them at this point and freed Kitty to look about the room, but she saw no sign of Mr. Johns.

She did not recognize Miss Pratt's partner, but he seemed very attentive to her, and she seemed to be enjoying it. She danced very well: graceful, light, and easy. She would pair the Colonel's gravity beautifully, when they finally were able to dance together. But too quickly, the dancers moved down, and her friends were lost from view. She turned her attention to her sister and Mr. Knott instead, but with inward sighs and regret. If only she could have danced with Mr. Johns!

"And you really did have a cousin come back from the dead just to inherit it!" Elizabeth was saying, her eyes twinkling. "How very novel!"

Mr. Knott laughed. "Yes, exactly! It is not *so* unusual, however, for a man to flee to New York when he feels that it will benefit him, and not *so* unusual for a man to come home on learning unexpectedly that he has a large inheritance waiting for him."

"How did he learn of it?" Kitty asked.

"A friend of the family had travelled to New York on business, and happened to stop for coffee at my cousin's cafe. He recognized him and, in his astonishment, immediately revealed that the inheritance that should be his would soon be settled on me. My cousin took the next ship he could find back to England—going to some trouble, as I understand it, thanks to the war."

"And all this time, you knew nothing of any of it?"

"His ship had gone down in a terrible storm; we had thought that no one aboard had survived the passage. And he never wrote to us to tell us otherwise. We found out afterwards that he believed it was best that way, as it would allow him to make a clean start."

"Why...?"

"He'd had a truly dreadful argument with—well, to own the truth, with his elder brother, who was originally first in line to the inheritance. The family had sided with the brother, and so he took a cue from the parable of the prodigal son, took what money he had coming to him, and fled. He broke his mother's heart in the process, poor woman."

Kitty sighed over the romance of the whole story. Who would have thought that plain, boring Mr. Knott would be connected with such a history?

"And has he now reconciled with the rest of the family?" Elizabeth asked.

"Oh, yes. The old quarrel was immediately forgotten, of course. He has since admitted that he was in the wrong, and too young and full of his own worth to admit it. But he has been established at Rookwood Park for some time now, and is very respectable."

"You must not like him very well," Kitty said. She could imagine how he felt, robbed of his inheritance by so undeserving a cousin, who had run away in such a manner!

"Not like him?" repeated Mr. Knott, one eyebrow raised. "Of course I like him! We were great friends as boys, and if any man is well-suited to running Rookwood, it is he. I daresay he'll do a better job of it than I would have done, so it all turned out for the best in the end."

"But... you were left with nothing, after expecting everything!"

"An education and a good connection are hardly nothing," Elizabeth said firmly.

"And I hardly expected everything. I was first in line for only a month or two." Mr. Knott sipped his punch and shrugged. "Honestly, the church suits me much better."

Elizabeth asked him some question about his education, and the conversation moved on. But Kitty could not help dwelling on Mr. Knott's situation. He had been on the verge of gaining a respectable establishment, and to give it up so cheerfully to this ungrateful prodigal cousin seemed to her to be hardship beyond endurance. Of course he could do nothing about it now—and he was talking to Mrs. Darcy, whose husband had a vicarage to bestow that had just opened up several weeks ago. Perhaps he was only pretending this cheerful resignation for the sake of obtaining that living. But Kitty still believed him ill-used, and she thought it rather disingenuous of him to pretend that he did not feel at least a little bit as though he had been robbed of his rightful place.

And *would* this set never end? How long had they been dancing, anyway? They were still out of sight, and Kitty entertained visions of them both being whisked off by their partners to be romanced all night—visions somewhat checked by her sudden remembrance that Miss Darcy had stood up with Colonel Fitzwilliam, who was of course destined for Miss Pratt.

But what if Miss Pratt fell in love with whatever gentleman she was now dancing with, and left the poor Colonel to nurse a broken heart?

Of course, if that happened, Kitty could step in. Watch Lydia crow over her when Kitty's husband outranked Mr. Wickham, anyway!

But then, what about Mr. Johns? Would she throw him over for an officer, even if it meant less money to live on?

"Lizzy, who is Miss Pratt dancing with?" she asked suddenly. She had to know his name so she could plan accordingly.

Elizabeth looked at her with an expression of astonishment; Mr. Knott muttered something about punch and walked away. Elizabeth leaned in. "Kitty, that was very rude! Mr. Knott was speaking and you interrupted him."

"Was he? I'm sorry—I didn't notice."

"Kitty!"

"Oh, don't look so scandalized. Poor man. I do feel badly for him, of course, and I will apologize when he comes back but I must know everything about Miss Pratt's partner before he returns."

Lizzy sighed. "His name is Mr. Rackham, and he is a friend of Mr. Darcy's from school. He is very gentlemanly, and I believe that his conversation will entertain Miss Pratt, but I do not expect anything to come of the acquaintance because I have reason to believe that his heart is engaged elsewhere. So let's have none of your nonsense about seeing them married before the end of the summer. You are far too much like Mama in that respect."

"But—"

"No. Mr. Rackham is perfectly respectable, and you do not need to think of him any more than that. And when Mr. Knott returns, I will expect you to either listen to him and participate in the conversation, or keep quite silent and not interrupt when others are speaking. You will either mind your manners or I will take you home. Is that quite clear?"

Kitty seethed, but she knew that she must acquiesce. "Yes."

"Thank you."

They sat in silence until Mr. Knott returned with more punch for all of them. Kitty set her old, still-full glass well under her chair, where it would be out of the way and less likely to be kicked over, and forced herself to sip at the fresh cup slowly. She did not even allow herself the tiniest wince at its bitterness. She could feel Elizabeth's gaze on her.

Mr. Rackham and Colonel Fitzwilliam brought the ladies back when the set ended, but both were immediately claimed for the next set, and left Kitty to face the prospect that she was likely to spend the evening listening to her sister and Mr. Knott discuss the most uninteresting subjects imaginable. Suddenly, coming to this ball seemed like it had been a spectacularly bad idea.

One of the gentlemen to whom Elizabeth had introduced her on their arrival walked by, and Kitty thought, for a moment of heart-fluttering hope, that he was coming to talk to her. But he claimed the hand of a young lady sitting nearby whose name Kitty did not know. She could not help watching them darkly as they moved to take their places in the set, particularly when his place turned out to be immediately beside Mr. Johns. It was the only time she saw him that night.

In fact, she saw very little of anyone except her two constant companions. Miss Pratt seemed to take her release for a dance or two to mean the whole evening, and even when Miss Darcy sat with them for a set, she usually talked with someone else, and Kitty could not find a way to interject. By the time the others were ready to go home, Kitty had long repented of her desire to come at all, and wanted nothing more than to get away from all of them.

CHAPTER 14

$\mathcal{T}$he following weeks, which ought to have been filled with joyful reminiscing about the delightful time they'd all had at the ball, passed very slowly for Kitty. To be sure, the others did their share of recollecting every moment of every dance, and Kitty tried to summon enough enthusiasm for their experiences to avoid suspicion, but when she discovered that, not only did Miss Pratt not dance with Colonel Fitzwilliam, but she danced the supper set with Mr. Johns, it was all she could do to feign complacent interest in the matter. She was heartily grateful when the talk of the ball began to wear thin and they moved on to other matters of conversation.

At least the next ball would not see her in the same state as this one had. Kitty was more determined than ever to walk under her own power again, and she improved steadily as she worked at it. Sometimes she had Mr. Knott's help, or that of a servant, but more and more she struck out on her own. Eventually she felt confident enough to cross her room without the aid of her cane, and when she could do that four times together without any pain and very little stiffness, she decided to give up the cane altogether, and very glad she was to be rid of it.

To make the most impact, she determined that the first time

anyone saw her without the cane should be when she came in for dinner. Everyone would already be gathered together, and she took special care in dressing that night to give the best impression. She would be the last one there, which would allow her the most dramatic entrance. A smile spread across her face at the thought of it. How pleased everyone would be for her! Perhaps she could persuade Lizzy to give a ball in her honor, now that she would be able to dance at it. If Mr. Darcy should be in the proper mood, it might be done.

Accordingly she dressed slowly and carefully that evening, and crept to the parlor as quietly as she could, so that when she practically danced into the room it would make the most possible impact. She couldn't help the broad smile that spread across her features, nor did she wish to.

Miss Darcy noticed first. "Why, Miss Bennet, you do not have your cane!" she said, smiling.

Kitty shook her head. "No indeed."

"Are you quite well, then? You can walk under your own power?"

"Yes, look!" She strode across the room in a manner more triumphant than ladylike. "I think I shall not need the cane again."

"Congratulations, Miss Bennet!" said Mr. Knott. "I know that you have put a great deal of effort toward making this possible again."

She curtsied her thanks and turned to the rest of the room; however, the congratulations she received from them was tepid at best and largely distracted. Lizzy was deep in conversation with her husband and her father; Mr. Johns was equally entrenched with Colonel Fitzwilliam and Miss Pratt; and overall her triumphant entry fell a little flat.

"For the next ball," she announced, "I mean to dance every dance, if I can, to make up for the last one."

Miss Pratt did look her way at that, with an approving smile, and Mr. Johns expressed his anticipation of the pleasure which they had been denied last time, with a knowing smile that told Kitty that he had not forgotten his promise to her. But Elizabeth said that she did not know when the next ball would be; indeed, it was very likely that there would not be one for some time, since summer was well at hand, and the weather getting too hot for much dancing.

"In that case, my dear sister, you shall have to hold one yourself," Kitty said eagerly. "How delightful that would be!"

Elizabeth exchanged glances with Mr. Darcy. "Perhaps," she said cooly. "We may discuss it later; for now, we should go in to dinner." Mr. Darcy took his cue perfectly and led them in to the dining room. Kitty's proposal would have to wait.

SHE SAT beside Miss Darcy at dinner, with her father on the other side; not a very agreeable arrangement even if Mr. Johns was across from her. There would be no opportunity to converse with Mr. Johns in anything approaching a free way, with Mr. Bennet right there. Her only refuge for conversation would have to be Miss Darcy. But at least she would likely encourage Kitty, if only about her walking.

Indeed, Miss Darcy was full of delight that Kitty had recovered so well. "And are you quite free of pain?"

"For the most part," Kitty answered. "I have not tested it for long walks, of course."

"Do you think you would be equal to one? Say, perhaps, the distance of that little garden seat we stopped at some weeks ago?"

Kitty toyed with her soup briefly as she considered this. "I think so, for I would be able to sit once I arrived, and recover for the way back. I do not think I would do so well if I had to walk there and back without any rest."

"In that case, how would you like to go on a visit with me?"

"A visit? To whom?"

"One of my brother's tenants—well, I told you about her. The one I made that blanket for. It's finished now, and I need to take it to her. I thought you might like to come with me. The weather has been very fine, and it is a lovely walk. It is very flat and easy, and will be a good test of your ankle; and you will have a chance to get out in the fresh air and enjoy the company of a delightful woman. You will really love

Mrs. Brown. She is a great storyteller, and she is very fond of company."

Kitty blinked and tried to consider this. A walk would probably be just the thing, but with such an end! Some decrepit old woman, whose only solace was in entertaining visitors and telling them stories? She hardly seemed like a person worth visiting. Why, Miss Darcy had even said that she couldn't do simple work any longer. It sounded like the worst kind of bore.

"I do not know," she said slowly.

"Nonsense," said her father. "Forgive me for interrupting, Miss Darcy, but I fear my daughter is being too modest in her estimation of her abilities. Kitty, I think you really must go."

"Papa?" Since when did he care about her making charity visits?

"Now, Kitty, I believe your ankle will hold up to that modest journey."

"I am sure it will," said Miss Darcy eagerly. "And Mrs. Brown will be so pleased to meet you. She has so little in the way of varying company, you see, and she does so love to meet new people."

Kitty searched her memory frantically for an excuse of some kind, but nothing came to mind, and Miss Darcy had already moved on to settling a time. "We cannot go tomorrow, of course, but Wednesday should do very well. If you like, we can go directly after breakfast. I will settle it so that we can arrange for a cart in case the walk proves too much for you."

Kitty could do nothing but accept. She spent the rest of the meal avoiding all conversation, and fighting back the angry flush on her face whenever she thought about Wednesday. How had a night which she had meant to be such a triumph gone off so badly?

After dinner saw no improvement; when the ladies withdrew, Miss Pratt soon joined their conversation, and Miss Darcy extended the invitation to her as well.

"Good heavens! no, I should think not!" was her empathetic reply. Then, as Miss Darcy looked a little bit hurt, she added, "I am entirely useless with invalids and am certain to get in your way. I am quite a disaster at comforting anybody, you know, and I am sure that your venerable old lady will be much happier with only two young women to entertain. I should only get in the way. Besides I really ought to spend that morning practicing my part in that duet, you know. My performance is shamefully backward by comparison to yours."

Kitty watched this prevarication with growing jealousy. How easily Miss Pratt turned aside the invitation which Kitty had been entirely unable to avoid! She was rather offended on Miss Darcy's behalf, though, for Miss Pratt's brusque dismissal had clearly insulted her and she did not know exactly how to respond. Kitty would not have made such a mangle of it, had she been able to find a way to decline. Now she felt obligated to defend a position she herself did not hold, and she found it very uncomfortable.

"Of course we would be glad to have you," she said quickly, "for your liveliness always makes any outing more enjoyable. And I am sure that you can work on your duet tomorrow morning as well as Wednesday."

"If I were wise, I should devote both mornings entirely to my part in the duet and not rise from the pianoforte until my fingers were worn to the bone and I could play it in my sleep," said Miss Pratt, laughing. "But, alas, I do not believe I have quite enough wisdom to induce me to that. I shall have to spend some of tomorrow attending to my correspondence, you know, for I have neglected it shamefully of late. I know you will be quite happy without me; besides, I am sure I am a miserable companion most mornings."

Kitty and Miss Darcy protested that she was not, of course, but before Kitty had done, Miss Darcy had quietly excused herself and gone to speak with her sister. Miss Pratt scooted in closer. "I am *very* sorry for you, my dear Miss Bennet. I saw how they coerced you into agreeing to this outing against your will! I wish I could find a way to rescue you from the chore, also, but I simply cannot think of anything."

"Well, I will enjoy the opportunity for a walk, at least," Kitty said, trying to appear resigned.

"But the errand! What does Miss Darcy mean by inviting you to come with her?"

"Perhaps she finds it as odious as you and I expect to, and wishes for some pleasant company to dull the pain."

Miss Pratt laughed. "I daresay you are right! It is a despicable thing to do, is it not? But I own, I would probably do the same, if I had such a chore before me."

Kitty shifted in her chair uncomfortably. She did not expect that she would find her outing very enjoyable, but it was difficult to sit there and dwell on it with someone who had managed to escape it. She looked over to where Miss Darcy and Lizzy were talking, but she could not bring herself to wholly abandon Miss Pratt. Instead she tried to change the subject.

"How long have you been playing the pianoforte?"

"Not as long as Miss Darcy, certainly," Miss Pratt said with a sigh. "In fact, it was her proficiency, when we were children, that inspired me to take it up. She played ridiculously well for such a young girl, and I was determined to catch up to her. I never had any real chance of that, however. Miss Darcy takes to music like a fish takes to water, and nothing I could have done would have enabled me to catch up to her level of skill. You must be born with it. That will not, however, prevent me from practicing as much as I can! I am determined to make as good a showing of it as I may—especially if it means I can avoid Mrs. Brown!"

"Can you really play for the whole of two mornings?" Kitty pressed. She would not be drawn back in to talking of Mrs. Brown. "I think I should drive myself distracted with the tedium."

"I should imagine that I can manage enough to convince Miss Darcy—and I needn't be practicing while you two are away, if I do not wish to."

No good. Perhaps a different course. "How are things coming along with you and Colonel Fitzwilliam?"

"Oh, I am sure he is enchanted with me," she said with a wave of her hand. "But I do not suppose that I can quite have won him over yet. Still, did you not see him watching me at dinner?"

Kitty owned that she had not, but likely that was because she had not looked at him at all during dinner.

"Oh, well—that is only natural, I suppose, when you had your whole meal spoilt for you with Miss Darcy's stupid plan being forced upon you from all sides. I imagine that you did not even notice Mr. Johns looking at you, did you?"

"No," Kitty said, leaning forward in great interest. "Was he really?"

"Yes! It really is too bad that you won't be able to spend any of Wednesday with him; he said he might not need to go to Edgepark that day and was wondering what he might do with himself."

Kitty sat up straighter, alarmed. "Oh no! Was he? And I missed the opportunity to invite him to do something with us!"

"Yes, but never mind; I am sure Mrs. Brown will be an equally amusing conversational partner, in her way."

No matter what Kitty tried to say to distract her, Miss Pratt always seemed determined to bring every subject back to the odious Mrs. Brown, until Kitty quite hated the old woman. But it was worse when the gentlemen joined them and Mr. Johns actually came over to talk with them.

"Oh! Mr. Johns, you must join me in expressing your pity for this poor girl," Miss Pratt said.

"Why, Miss Bennet, you have not injured your ankle again so soon?" he said, taking the seat beside her. Kitty's heart fluttered from his nearness and her anger at Miss Pratt together.

"No," she said quickly. "My ankle is quite well, thank you."

"It is worse than that," Miss Pratt said. "For, you see, Miss Darcy and Mr. Bennet have conspired together to keep her from us all of Wednesday morning, so that she might visit some old tenant of Mr. Darcy's."

"That does sound like a pitiable fate," he agreed, and looked at Kitty with kind sympathy. "I find nothing so distasteful as spending my mornings affecting concern for those people too poor to be anything other than miserable. I always feel stupid and uncomfortable in their tiny houses, and as soon as I was able to give up the practice, I did so."

Kitty bit back a heavy sigh. "I cannot say that I am looking forward to the visit at all," she admitted. "But I do hope the walk there will be pleasant. It has been such a long time since I have been able to enjoy a walk."

"A walk to such an end sounds like poor compensation indeed," Mr. Johns said. "But as you are committed, I will not venture to think ill of you for trying to make the best of it. I am glad that Miss Darcy did not press us all into going, however."

"Can you imagine the whole party trying to squish ourselves into a tiny little house like that?" Miss Pratt asked, giggling.

Kitty looked back and forth between them and sank back into her chair. What misery Wednesday would bring her!

CHAPTER 15

*K*itty spent all of Wednesday morning sinking under the dread of her upcoming errand, which made her rather dull and stupid company. This would have been unpleasant, but not tragic, had not Mr. Johns been at home and inclined to be sociable with the ladies that morning. He tried several times to engage her in conversation, or a game, only to find her uninteresting enough that he moved on to a new target sooner than Kitty could shake herself out of her mood. That made her bemoan her fate all the more, and darkened her mood another shade. By the time she went to meet Miss Darcy in the courtyard to depart on their errand, she foresaw that nothing about the day could bring her any happiness.

Miss Darcy met her with the blanket neatly folded and tucked under one arm and a heavy basket on the other. She greeted Kitty with a happy smile. "I am so glad you were able to come," she said. "You will love Mrs. Brown, I am sure of it. And, I have a surprise for you!" She gesture to the drive, where a farmer was pulling a wagon around. "Mr. Drury has agreed to take us part of the way, which will spare your ankle. I am sure you will be in no danger of re-injuring yourself now."

Kitty thanked her with as much happiness as she could pretend to feel, and accepted Mr. Drury's help in climbing into the wagon. They set off as soon as Kitty and Miss Darcy were well-settled among the blankets and hay that were spread out for them. Miss Darcy kept up a lively conversation with the farmer, who was bursting with pride over the imminent birth of his first child. His wife had only told him that morning and no man could be prouder or happier. Miss Darcy was delighted for him and eagerly discussed names and futures for the child. Kitty ignored them. She had no real interest in the child; babies were pleasant enough in their place, but this one's place would not be anywhere near her life.

The prospect of their errand rather ruined the loveliness of the day for her. Kitty could not help thinking of how tedious it would be, and how much she would rather be doing nearly anything else. The wagon jolted her about dreadfully, and made her ankle throb. She wished she could have found a way to decline Miss Darcy's invitation, and she wondered again at her father for insisting that she go along. What did he think she would get out of it, anyway?

Kitty had not really been paying any attention to the direction they were going or how long they had been out, and she was actually surprised when they pulled up in front of a neat, if shabby, little house where Mr. Brown (she presumed) was in front of the house, splitting firewood. Miss Darcy leapt down from the cart and, leaving the basket at the gate, ran to greet him.

"Mr. Brown! How are you this morning?" she asked as he set aside his axe. Mr. Drury came around to help Kitty out, and she made it back to the ground without doing further injury to herself.

"Well enough, Miss Darcy, well enough. Mother hasn't made it out of bed yet this morning but she's awake, and I am sure she'd be glad to see you. Do you mind seeing yourself in?"

"Of course not." Miss Darcy turned back to Kitty with a smile. "This is Miss Bennet. She has decided to come along with me today."

She greeted Mr. Brown politely, if distantly, and followed Miss Darcy into the house, blinking in the sudden darkness. As her eyes adjusted, she looked around and saw that the interior of the little cottage matched the exterior well: everything was clean and put away, but it was all shabby and worn. Miss Darcy seemed to see none of it, except for the old woman lying in the bed.

Miss Darcy went straight to her, and held out the blanket with a smile. "Mrs. Brown! I am so glad to see you looking better. Look what we have brought for you!" She unfolded it so that she could display the whole thing.

Mrs. Brown reached toward it and ran her finger along the edges, her eyes filling with tears. "Miss Darcy!" she breathed. "You certainly did not have to do something like this for me!"

"Nonsense," Miss Darcy said cheerfully. "You needed something warmer than this old rag." She gestured to the thin blanket spread out over the bed. "And I had help making it. Mrs. Brown, this is my friend, Miss Catherine Bennet, and she helped me make the blanket for you. Should you like to try it out?" Kitty blushed. She had not helped make it so much as she had sat nearby while Miss Darcy did all the work. What prompted Miss Darcy to lie about it?

Without waiting for an answer, Miss Darcy spread the blanket over the old lady, and gestured for Kitty to help her. Awkwardly, Kitty stumbled over and tugged it down to the corner of the bed. Mrs. Brown was thrilled. "Oh, girls—you lovely, wonderful girls! I am warmer already. Miss Darcy spoils me, you see, Miss Bennet."

Kitty glanced at Miss Darcy. "Yes, I see."

Mrs. Brown patted either side of the bed. "Come and sit with me a spell, if you have the time, and we'll have a good chat. Do you mind getting up some coffee, Miss Darcy?"

"Not at all," she said. "Let me run out and tell Mr. Drury that we are well settled and send him on his way."

"Of course, my dear. Give him my love."

Miss Darcy fairly skipped out of the door, and left Kitty standing awkwardly at the end of the bed. Mrs. Brown patted it again. "Come and sit, and get off your poor foot, dear," she said. "I see you limping on it a bit. What happened to you?"

Kitty coughed and prevaricated but Mrs. Brown would not be put off. Before long Kitty found herself explaining what had happened to her ankle, and what frustrations it had caused her. She kept having to cut herself off because she realized that Mrs. Brown couldn't be expected to understand the life of a young woman of quality. But she couldn't help remarking on the ball at length.

Mrs. Brown showed no symptoms of misunderstanding or boredom, however; she was all sympathy. "I certainly know the trials of a poorly-timed malady. When I was a girl I got sick with the mumps, and couldn't go to a party I particularly wished to go to. I was sweet on a young man who would certainly be there, you see. I was crushed and convinced I'd never have another chance to speak to him. But I saw him again the week after I recovered, and we found ourselves married within the year. Take heart, my dear—the world may conspire against you, but if two people are determined to be together, there ain't nothing in the wide world that will keep them apart."

Kitty did not, in fact, find that to be especially heartening, but she murmured her thanks with half a smile. The mumps indeed!

Miss Darcy returned and made the coffee, and they sat and chatted for an entire half-hour. Kitty was astonished at how much Miss Darcy enjoyed herself. They laughed themselves silly over the stories Mrs. Brown told, and even Kitty found herself smiling at times.

But it was a relief when the time came for them to leave. Kitty took her leave of Mrs. Brown with more cheer than she had yet felt, and followed Miss Darcy outside with a smile threatening to break across her lips.

When they got out in the sun, however, Miss Darcy hefted her basket again and said, "We have another stop to make, if you feel you can manage it. There is a family down the way here with three children, all sick, and now their father is sick as well. I've some food here to bring them, and if I can help them out for a little while it might help them get well faster." She smiled at Kitty, who had to keep herself from scowling back. But she agreed to go, since Miss Darcy had brought the basket this far already. Besides, it made it that much longer before she would have to face the triumph of Miss Pratt, and as much as she was looking forward to the end of this errand, she dreaded her friend's welcome.

They went into the house to find it in complete disarray—nothing like the neat, tidy cottage they had just left—and a woman standing at the stove, crying.

Miss Darcy sprang into action without a second thought. She handed the basket to Kitty, who took it reflexively, and hurried to the poor woman's side. "Oh, Mrs. Stephens, you poor thing! I heard about your family this morning, and I have brought you a nice, hearty dinner to keep you well tonight. Miss Bennet and I are here to help. What can we do for you?"

The perfect balance of concern and industriousness in Miss Darcy's manner worked exactly as it was designed to. Mrs. Stephens straightened herself, turned around, and wiped her sleeve across her face. "Oh, Miss Darcy... thank you... I do not know how we shall manage..."

"One day at a time, the way you always do," Miss Darcy said with a smile. "Come, now, shall we get these things unpacked? I asked Cook to send you whatever she thought you might need, so I am sure we'll find some good things in that basket."

Kitty took her cue and brought the basket to the big table by the fire, and began to pull things out of it. Fresh vegetables, three loaves of bread, and a large tureen of cold soup were duly removed and placed on the table, and she and Miss Darcy arranged them to keep until dinner.

"There," she said, "this will keep you fed for a little while, I think, and in the meantime you can keep up with everything else a bit better. What needs to be done, and how can we help?"

Mrs. Stephens had dried her eyes this time, though she had not stopped expressing her gratitude. She had a list of things she did not know how she would manage to do alone, and between the three of them, they were able to get a good portion of it done. In truth, Kitty did as little as she could, and found her ankle a convenient excuse to avoid doing more, but her friend did not let her remain idle for long.

Miss Darcy loaded up her basket with mending to be done and promised to bring it back in the next day or two, or send it back with someone. She did not imagine she could do it all herself, but with Miss Bennet and Miss Pratt helping, she could manage it. Kitty protested internally at this further incursion on her time, but agreed to help. Confronted with Mrs. Stephens's tear-stained face, she could hardly do otherwise. One had to have *some* heart.

She watched Miss Darcy in some astonishment as she took control of the situation and worked hard. This was a side of her that Kitty had not seen before, nor ever expected to see in anyone, and she found it strangely compelling to watch.

Miss Darcy was arranging for a young man from Pemberley to come and help with some of the more laborious tasks that afternoon, and Kitty listened in with mild interest. A new thought struck her. Would she have the responsibility to do this for her husband's tenants, someday? She wondered whether those tenants might be Mr. Johns'. The possibility made her heart glow.

As they walked back to Pemberley, it dawned on Kitty that Miss Darcy was strangely silent. Kitty could see no reason for it; as far as she could tell, Miss Darcy had actively enjoyed her morning, pleased to have been of help. What could she have to be so cold about now? Was it because Kitty had not been as helpful as she had? But Kitty's ankle was still recovering, and besides, she hadn't wanted to come in the first place!

Even Kitty couldn't be entirely comfortable with such weak excuses. She sighed. "Miss Darcy, I need to apologize. I am sure I was not as helpful as I should have been this morning."

Miss Darcy looked back at her, eyebrows raised, and she did not answer for a few moments. "Thank you, Miss Bennet, for the help you did offer. I know I was not the only one who appreciated it." She smiled a bit, and Kitty understood the matter to be dismissed. They returned to the house in silence, but it seemed to Kitty that neither one of them was entirely satisfied with how their day had gone.

Miss Darcy, eager to get started on their mending right away, had it sent to her sitting room to be ready for them when they had changed from their work clothes. Kitty agreed to meet her there, but with every intention of finding Miss Pratt and enlisting her help in getting out of the work. A person could take only so much in one day, and she had work of her own that she would rather do.

On her way to the sitting room, Kitty met Mr. Johns in the hall. Delighted, she greeted him with more genuine cheerfulness than she'd felt all day.

"Back from your travels already, I see! And now where are you headed so eagerly?" he asked with a little smile at the corner of his mouth.

Kitty told him, and explained about her morning visits, trying to keep her tone neutral. To her surprise, Mr. Johns laughed at her. "So you enjoyed slumming, I see! Well, some girls do like a bit of that, I own. I never could account for it."

That stung. She hadn't enjoyed it, but he had no right to make fun of her for it, even if she had. "I did not say that I enjoyed it. But, I think it a very noble thing to help those who need our aid," she said, and wondered how she had managed to sound so much like Mary.

"I am sure it is, but I never did understand the purpose behind going out yourself, when it does about the same to send a servant with some money, or whatever they need."

Kitty had no response to this and was not clever enough to think of something quickly. Mr. Johns laughed at her again and left her standing in the hallway, rather confused. She hadn't enjoyed it, not really... but it had not been as bad as she'd expected. And Mrs. Brown and Mrs. Stephens were both so grateful for their help. That had to count for something, did it not?

Perhaps she could talk it over with Miss Darcy, and that might help her decide what to do. Of course, Miss Darcy would encourage her to keep going, especially since she had that basket of mending to finish... but perhaps Mr. Johns' argument would make her re-think the matter?

She went on to the sitting room and determined that she would not think more on it until she had talked it over with Miss Darcy and possibly Miss Pratt, anyway.

"You do not look as refreshed from your walk as you were when we parted," Miss Darcy said when Kitty entered the room. "Has the thought of all this work truly stolen your joy?"

Kitty shrugged. "Not exactly, but I met Mr. Johns on my way here."

"That is not the sort of thing that would normally make you so upset."

"He does not exactly approve of the way we spent our morning."

Miss Darcy looked surprised. "Does he not? Well, that is a loss. But do not let his opinion of the activity stop you, Kitty. I know that my brother greatly approves, and Elizabeth has gone with me many times. There are plenty here who do approve."

"But he said that sending a servant with some money would do as well, and I suppose he is right, for a servant could do more useful work than I can, hobbling around like I did all morning." Kitty sighed and fairly flopped into her chair. She halfheartedly flipped through the mending in the basket and tried to find something easy enough to tackle in her present state of mind.

Miss Darcy, who had already selected her piece and was searching for a patch and some thread, set it aside for a moment and took Kitty's hands in hers, meeting and holding her gaze. "He is wrong, Miss Bennet. First, our servants have their own responsibilities, and we depend upon them to keep Pemberley running smoothly so that we can go out and do these things ourselves. Second, there is something that is lost if we do not go ourselves, a personal connection that I would not give up for anything. Do not let Mr. Johns deter you from this course. I saw how much you enjoyed it as we were coming back, and I know that feeling. No man is worth giving that up; that is the reward of true Christian charity and it is a gift from God. Do not let Mr. Johns or anyone else rob you of it." She sat back and shook her head sadly. "No gentleman worth your esteem would ask it of you."

Kitty did not answer, but inwardly she dismissed Miss Darcy's excess of piety. What exactly counted as "worth her esteem" anyway? Mr. Johns was a gentleman, and very attentive to her. She liked talking to him and he certainly sought her out more than any of the others, so he must like her. What else was there?

MISS PRATT finally joined them late that morning, and Miss Darcy soon left to practice her music.

Kitty, unwilling to wait for the awkward interview which must be coming, decided to take control of the conversation before it started. "I actually enjoyed myself this morning. It is a pity you did not come; Mrs. Brown was a very interesting person and I liked her very much. I think you would have liked her too, if you had come."

"Do you?" Her little smile seemed not entirely genuine. "Well, in that case, I am sorry I did not, but I believe you derived more pleasure from it than I would have. I cannot abide such visits." She picked through the basket at Kitty's feet and made a face. "And I suppose this belongs to her?"

"In fact, it belongs to a neighboring family," Kitty said mildly. "I liked them, too."

Miss Pratt did not choose to respond to that, and picked up a piece of work over which she had been toiling for some days. "Did you happen to see Mr. Johns today? I had heard that he was about the house."

"I did, yes," Kitty said, and could not help blushing.

Miss Pratt noticed it and pounced. "Why, Miss Bennet, what is this stain upon those lovely cheeks? What reason have *you* to blush for Mr. Johns?"

"None whatsoever." Kitty focused very hard on the shirt sleeve in her hands.

"But you *wish* you had?" she pressed in a knowing tone.

Kitty made no answer.

"You know, we had decided, a few weeks ago, that if he was going to fall in love with any of us, it must be you. Perhaps we should make that our project for the rest of the week. What do you think?"

"I... think..." What did she think, exactly? She liked him a great deal, and was very much prepared to be fallen in love with. But she didn't know whether she wanted any help, or at least not of the sort that Miss Pratt would provide.

"I think I would like very much to know him better," she said at last.

"Well, then." Miss Pratt looked triumphant and she abandoned her work in favor of the conversation. "I believe that you and I will need a plan, if we are to bring this about." She leaned forward. "Now. Mr. Johns is not here every day, so it is very important that, on the days when he is here, we take full advantage of his presence. We need to put you in the best possible light every time we see him. You should be glowing; you should be lively; you should be the most engaging creature in any room he walks into. But you must not appear to be following him, or desperate in any way; he should feel as though he must win you. Converse with others as much as you do with him; if your conversation is more sparkling when you talk to him than when you are with any other, he will notice. We should have him walk with you as often as we can. Perhaps I shall propose that we all walk out and explore the grounds, now that you are well enough to join a walking party. When you are outside, you can be more intimate."

Kitty put her work aside and leaned in as well. This plan, she could follow, and the prize was so worth working for! In that moment, she knew that she would not return to Longbourn until she was married —or at the very least, engaged. "What about in the evenings? You will have to deflect him toward me."

"I think if you try to send Colonel Fitzwilliam to me, and I try to send Mr. Johns to you, the four of us will end up in company together more often than not, and that cannot fail to be agreeable to us all."

"Do you know how long it will be until Edgepark is ready to be lived in?"

"No, but that is the sort of question you ought to be asking Mr. Johns, anyway. In fact, if you can get him to take you there to see the place, that would be best. See if you can get him to envision you as its mistress while you're there. You should be very eager to keep yourself entirely to him." She smiled and lowered her voice. "If you should happen to find yourself in a less-than-respectable situation with him, do not remark on it; let things happen as they will. I am not saying to compromise yourself with him, of course! But do not be too eager to maintain perfect propriety with him."

Kitty had the most unfortunate impression of Lydia at that

moment, and it almost gave her a start. "I do not know how wise that would be," she said slowly. She wasn't sure how much she should tell Miss Pratt, but she knew that if her father found out that she had been offered such advice, he would be furious, and probably refuse to let her continue their acquaintance.

"I told you, not enough to compromise you! Just enough to show him that your affection for him is stronger than your awareness of your surroundings. If it is done quite innocently, there is nothing the matter with it." She sat back with an air of great satisfaction. "Trust me, Miss Bennet; I have seen this work before, and I am sure it will work for you. We shall both be engaged before the summer is out!"

Kitty could not help being enchanted by that possibility and she strove to overcome her misgivings; when Miss Pratt asked her to "please call me Amy; all my dearest friends do, and we cannot go through this exciting time in our lives together without becoming dearest friends," Kitty was only too happy to reciprocate. After all, Kitty and Amy were a team, united in the common goal of matrimony.

CHAPTER 16

nterlude

WHILE KITTY and Miss Darcy were out on their charitable errand, Elizabeth went to her father in the library. She was looking forward to one of their old chats—if he was in the mood for it. One could never quite tell with him. But Lizzy had always been good at breaking him out of his moods if she needed to.

He looked up at her entrance, and on seeing her, smiled and put his book aside. Elizabeth smiled back; all clear. "Papa. I thought you might want a little chat."

"Ah, my Lizzy! I have missed you." He smiled warmly and patted the chair across from him.

She sat in it and leaned forward, glancing at the book he'd laid aside. "Ovid? Of all the books in my husband's library, you choose one you've read a hundred times before?" She looked at him, eyes narrowed. "What's troubling you?"

Half a smile flitted across his face. "I can't hide from you, can I, my dear."

"You had better not try. What is the matter?"

He looked at her for a long moment, and she knew he was deciding whether to be honest with her. She crossed her arms over her chest and raised an eyebrow at him. Finally, he made up his mind. "Kitty." He sighed heavily and leaned back in his chair. "I have no idea how to keep her safe."

"Safe?"

He nodded. "I had hoped, you know, that removing her from Lydia's influence would keep her from making the same mistakes as her sister, but it appears that I greatly underestimated her silliness. No matter where I take her, she is determined to get herself into trouble."

"Kitty's behavior has not been perfect, by any means," Elizabeth said, selecting each word carefully. "But she has not done anything that makes me fear for her reputation."

"Surely you have noticed her marked interest in Mr. Johns."

She frowned. "Yes, and I wish she would abandon it. I'm not pleased by how that whole situation has gone. We were meant to offer him a bed and a place for his meals while he oversaw the work on his house. I had no idea of his being here so often, or I would have insisted that Mr. Darcy learn more of him before we asked him here." For a moment, she wondered whether she ought to say more—but who better to hear her concerns? Mr. Darcy had heard them all, and shared her opinion. "I am also displeased with Miss Pratt. Poor Miss Darcy has been quite disappointed in her as well, but Kitty has not yet seen through her façade. But what can I do? She has done nothing that warrants such a breach of etiquette as sending her home."

"I do not imagine that Kitty will ever see Miss Pratt for what she really is," he said, shaking his head. "She is far too apt to take people at their word, and follow the worst of them wherever they will go. She has no sense or thought of her own, and she is forever throwing herself after those who would give her neither."

"She is very young, Papa," Elizabeth said, laying a gentle hand on his arm. "It takes time to develop a sense of the duplicity of others, and I know that you well remember the first sting of betrayal from someone you thought was a friend. Give her time."

He shook his head again. "If she keeps on in this way, she may not have time. You did not see how she threw herself at Mr. Warde, completely oblivious to every hint. I had hoped that by taking her away from that, she would improve, but she has only found more opportunity to make poor decisions here. What must I do with her to keep her from making the same choice Lydia did?"

"I don't know." She wished she could say more. She was so proud of him for taking an interest, and trying to do right by his remaining daughters, but what could she advise him to do? Neither of them understood Kitty's motivations well enough to predict her actions. "Perhaps she will improve on her own, if we give her time. It is encouraging that she is out with Miss Darcy today, at least."

"That is only because I forced her to go."

Elizabeth sighed. "Well, perhaps that will be enough to start her down a better path."

KITTY AND AMY were eager to put their plans into action. Together, they schemed to throw Kitty into Mr. Johns's way as often as possible, and as a consequence of that, to bring Amy and Colonel Fitzwilliam together as well. It was not long before Amy observed that they had left Miss Darcy at the mercy of Mr. Knott, and she declared herself perfectly delighted with this result.

"They are rather perfect for each other, in their own way," she mused, "and it would be such fun to watch her brother lose his wits when she declared her intention of marrying someone so little deserving of her consequence! Of course, with her ridiculous inheritance, he would hardly need to take a living, if he did not wish to. I daresay Mr. Darcy would not dare deny him the vicarage if they were to marry, though!"

Kitty could imagine the stormy anger that would overcome Mr. Darcy if his sister were to form such an attachment, and when she was not at risk of being anywhere near him, could imagine it with as much amusement as Amy did. "But do you think she likes him at all?"

"I hardly see how she could not; they are both rather quiet people, and they probably have the same opinions of nearly every person they know. Honestly, in terms of character, I think it would be a very good match. He is much too dull to do for a woman of livelier temperament, and Miss Darcy is so sweet and so affectionate to everyone that she would almost certainly be attractive to him. A woman is not long immune to the charms of a man who is in love with her, I think."

So Miss Darcy was included in their schemes, though Kitty felt, rather uncomfortably, that if she were to find out their plans for her she would be rather offended. Kitty convinced herself that she did not mind; if a happy marriage came out of it, was that not all that would matter? Mr. Darcy would be resigned when he saw how well matched they really were, and the more she and Amy talked of it, the more convinced she was that it would be the best thing for everyone.

It was, however, only incidental to their plans. Their first object was to throw Kitty and Mr. Johns together as much as possible, and accordingly, Amy put their plan into action that evening, by proposing that they all walk out together the next morning and have a picnic brought to them on the top of some picturesque hill.

Elizabeth was enthusiastic about the plan, which Kitty hoped she would be, and readily engaged to help them. By the end of the evening, they had the following day planned out to the satisfaction of all, and Kitty could hardly wait for the day to begin. She was among the first to come down dressed and ready to go, and to her everlasting satisfaction, Mr. Johns was equally early. They had several minutes in the hall together entirely alone, and Kitty was fully prepared to make the most of it.

"I am so glad that you are able to join us today," she told him. "I was afraid that Edgepark would take you away from us again."

"Fortunately for myself as well as for the rest of the party, I do not expect to be needed at Edgepark for a few days yet," he answered. "I am happy to avoid interfering there whenever possible; I find the work very tedious, and would much rather allow the workers to do their job without me constantly being in their way. Besides, the more time I spend there, the more often I change my mind about how I want things to be done, and I am afraid that if I spend too much time at the place it will never be finished."

"That would be a trial," Kitty agreed. "You are much better served to come and relax with us, and trust that your workers have the job well in hand. I am sure that when they are finished, you will be happy with the end result, no matter what it is."

"That is exactly my philosophy on the matter, and I am very glad to hear that you agree with me. There is nothing in the world so gratifying as to hear your own opinions echoed so perfectly from the lips of one who could not have known that you share them—" he took a step closer to her and lowered his voice a great deal—"particularly when they are such enchantingly pretty lips."

Kitty blushed and stammered her thanks, and when the others joined them and they were on their way, had no trouble at all securing his arm for herself.

The day was bright, if a little warmer than was ideal for such an outing, and Kitty felt that the shining sun and singing birds were so cheerful solely because they had seen into her heart and decided to share her happiness with the world.

Perhaps encouraged by her expressed ideas, Mr. Johns continued to talk about Edgepark while they walked, and painted such a picture of the current state of the place, as well as what he meant to do with it, that Kitty felt certain she could visualize it quite clearly. "It sounds like it will be a delightful place," she said with a sigh, thinking of Amy's instructions. "I do wish I could see it."

"Perhaps, when it is safe for a lady to walk around it, I shall take you there. There are one or two spots of which I particularly need a second opinion, and the taste of ladies in general is probably better suited to the object; your taste has already proven close enough to mine that I am sure you would tell me exactly what would suit me best."

"I hope I would," said Kitty warmly, "and I promise that I am completely at your disposal. Name the day and I will go with you to give opinions on whatever you like. Perhaps we could take the whole party, and you will have more opinions than you really know what to do with."

He laughed. "Perhaps we should, and then I can disdain all their opinions in favor of yours."

Kitty glowed, and felt that Amy spoke better than she knew when she predicted their engagement. With such encouragement as this, she would not be surprised if she became engaged within a fortnight!

The prospect which Elizabeth had chosen for their destination did not disappoint; it must have been one of the prettiest places in the park, and at the top of the hill stood a little grouping of garden seats which were arranged to give the best view. The party stopped to rest there and found that an array of cold refreshments had been set out for them. Delight was universally expressed and Kitty took the opportunity to seek out Miss Pratt and exclaim over how well her morning had gone.

"I see that you and Mr. Johns were quite inseparable today," she remarked. "I trust that is a good sign."

"Yes, the best sign," Kitty said eagerly. She recounted the substance of their conversation and watched her friend closely for her reaction. Amy did not disappoint.

"That is very encouraging, indeed! I suspect it will not be long before he is making you an offer. Oh, if only I could say the same!"

"What! You were walking with Colonel Fitzwilliam for a good portion of the morning!"

"Yes," said Amy, shaking her head, "but never alone, and he did not speak to me unless I addressed him first. I do not think I shall have as easy a conquest as you will."

Kitty was very sorry to hear this, and strove to think of ways to help her friend. but very little came to mind. She did not know the Colonel very well, and Amy was so much better at this kind of thing than Kitty.

"Well, perhaps Mr. Johns can think of something," she said at last. "I imagine he would find it great fun to spend the rest of our morning trying to help Colonel Fitzwilliam fall in love with you!"

Amy laughed and patted her hand. "I give you permission to do so, if you must, but do not make it clear to Mr. Johns where my inclination lies, I beg you. What if he should let it slip to the Colonel that I have set my cap at him? There is nothing less appealing to a man than a woman he does not have to win."

"I will pretend it is entirely my own idea," Kitty promised.

CHAPTER 17

*T*he party decided to take the longer path back to the house, and Kitty had more time to plan for her continued triumph with Mr. Johns. Before she could propose her ideas to him, however, Elizabeth joined them, and Kitty did not feel quite as comfortable in involving her sister in the matter as well. She would not approve of Kitty's methods, probably.

Seemingly unaware that Kitty did not in any way desire to be rescued from Mr. Johns's company, Elizabeth skillfully inserted herself into their conversation so thoroughly that she nearly pushed Kitty out of it. Mr. Johns was unfailingly gallant, but the warmth in his address to Kitty had quite vanished, and she was almost relieved when Mr. Knott joined them and she could slip away. Her relief faded to irritation when Elizabeth joined her shortly afterwards.

"Mr. Johns is a very pleasant gentleman," Elizabeth said when they were out of earshot of the others, "but take care, Kitty. You are not doing either of you any favors by being so obvious in your designs."

Kitty winced, only partly because her ankle throbbed a bit when she set it down. She had pushed herself a little too far, it seemed. "I was not trying to be obvious, Lizzy, but how in the world is a girl supposed to make anyone fall in love with her if she cannot encourage his attention?"

"Your goal should not be to make a man fall in love with you, but to be the sort of woman with whom the right man will fall in love," Elizabeth said. "You would do better to err on the side of not showing enough encouragement, than showing too much. You are not of a disposition that makes you very much at risk of showing too little attachment."

This may have been true, but that did not make it sting less, and Kitty did not answer. Elizabeth changed the topic.

When they arrived back at the house, a letter was waiting for Mr. Johns. He took one look at the address, paled very slightly, and excused himself immediately.

Kitty did not know what to make of that, but she would have no opportunity to find out. He announced at dinner that night that he would be departing for Edgepark the following morning, having received in the letter confirmation that it was prepared for habitation.

Something was amiss—Edgepark being ahead of schedule would not have provoked that reaction. But she could think of no way to comment on it without bringing Elizabeth's further censure, and no one else seemed to think anything of it.

She worried about him the whole evening, and it spoiled what should have been an enjoyable night. As she fell asleep, she resolved to seek him out first thing in the morning, and ask him about it. Surely he could confide in her! But by the time she woke the next morning, he was gone.

A WEEK PASSED, and Kitty threw herself into other pursuits, determined to have something to show Mr. Johns if he should come back for her. She picked up whatever work Elizabeth or Miss Darcy needed done, even if it was just mending. Miss Darcy talked of going to visit some of Pemberley's other tenants, who had apparently suffered the same illness that had afflicted the Stephenses, and Kitty actually found herself looking forward to the possibility of those visits. It gave her something to do, and something to keep her mind off of Mr. Johns.

Amy laughed off Kitty's hesitant enthusiasm for Pemberley's tenants, and declined her invitations to join them, but did not say anything against it, either. Kitty decided not to press the matter. Secretly, she liked that she had something to share with Miss Darcy alone. It was much more interesting that way, to have a project she could talk over eagerly with Miss Darcy the way she talked over Colonel Fitzwilliam with Miss Pratt.

Wednesday morning found the whole party gathered in the music room to hear Miss Darcy and Amy play a new duet for them. Kitty had her work with her, having heard the rehearsals often enough that she could divide her attention, but she couldn't focus on her stitches, either. Her gaze kept roaming the room, and her thoughts kept returning to Mr. Johns's sudden departure.

As though her thoughts had summoned him, Mr. Johns joined them partway through the performance, unannounced and unnoticed. When she saw him, Kitty nearly leapt to her feet to greet him, but she remembered her conversation with Lizzy at the last minute, and decided against it. She watched him intently, waiting to see if he would seek her out. But soon she noticed that he did not seek anyone out—he barely met the eyes of those who noticed and greeted him, and he looked decidedly uncomfortable. A little knot started in her stomach.

"What brings you back so soon, Johns? Have you tired of your new house already?" Mr. Darcy asked, a little smile on his face.

Mr. Johns laughed, but it sounded hollow. "No, no, the house is fine. But there is something... well, I'm not as ready to move in there as I thought, I suppose."

"Well, if you need to stay at Pemberley a while longer..." Elizabeth began.

"Oh, no, no... I'm sure I will be quite well there, and you know I can better supervise everything if I am there myself." Kitty did not point out that this directly contradicted his previous statement to her. She wanted nothing more than to go to him and try to cheer him up; this haunted creature was a very different man than the one who had walked and chatted so cheerily with her on their outing a week before. There had to be something else going on, something that Kitty didn't quite understand.

But the others didn't seem to notice anything amiss, or if they did, they didn't say anything about it. They invited him in, and had him sit down, and chatted with him about the weather and the repairs on his house and the whole time he looked like he was on the verge of saying something but never quite got a chance to bring it up. Kitty felt terribly for him. She could see the frustration and desperation mounting.

Before he could finally say whatever he wanted to, the door burst open with a bang and a young, fashionably elegant lady strode into the room with a face like thunder. Mr. Johns stood along with everyone else, and faced her, but he alone had lost all color. "Ah, Camilla. I had thought you were getting yourself settled today."

"I am quite settled, Mr. Johns, thank you." She glared out at everyone, but especially at Kitty and the other young ladies. "Are you going to introduce me?"

"Er. Of course." He introduced them all one by one, Kitty last of all. "This is Mrs. Camilla Johns... my wife."

Kitty sank into her chair, unequal to standing any longer. His wife! She hardly noticed the explosion of exclamations from the others in the room.

Mrs. Johns suffered no such complaint. She sailed over to where Kitty sat, and her expression was anything but friendly. Kitty could not even stand up, she was trembling so much. "So this is the little chit I have heard so much about! Stand up, child, and let me have a good look at the thing my husband has targeted. Good heavens, Gregory, I've seen you do better than this."

Mr. Johns buried his face in his hand and would not look at anyone. Kitty stared up at Mrs. Johns, horrified and completely incapable of standing, or moving at all.

Seemingly ignorant of the expressions of every person in the room, she turned to the rest with a broad smile, that only broadened when she saw Miss Pratt. "Amelia Pratt, of all people! Why, my dear friend, how long it has been since we have seen each other! I daresay you had not even heard that I'd married. Well, this must come as some surprise to you, and I know how well you love a surprise!" She laughed, and Amy did an admirable job of keeping her wits about her; she smiled and bowed her head, and said something perfectly noncommittal, and that was all.

Mrs. Johns turned to the Darcys, who were standing next to each other, Elizabeth's hand firmly on her husband's arm. "I must thank you for the hospitality you have shown to Mr. Johns. I am sure the house would not have progressed so well had he been forced to travel from London all the time!"

"I think you should leave," Elizabeth said in a low voice that Kitty recognized as dangerous.

"Well," said Mrs. Johns, with a nastiness only enhanced by her cheerfulness, "I suppose I should be getting my husband home. He is clearly not well, and we have so much to do to get the house really habitable. Come along, Gregory, dear!"

She sailed out of the room and the rest of them were left staring at Mr. Johns.

"Do you care to explain yourself, sir?" Mr. Darcy said, in a tone that made more than one of them shudder.

Mr. Johns lifted his head and looked around the room. "I never said I was not married," he muttered. But then he squared his shoulders and shot a defiant glare at them all. "Well, and I have done nothing wrong, at that. I thank you for your hospitality to me, of course." He bowed to Elizabeth, who did not return the salute. "But I suppose my wife has my day quite planned out for me. Goodbye." He bowed to them all, and left.

The room resounded with the most uncomfortable silence, and no one could meet Kitty's eyes. A half-strangled giggle escaped Amy, but she clamped her hand over her mouth immediately. The sound struck Kitty like a slap across the face. She felt as though she was burning alive; her whole body must have been blushing. Married! To such a woman, such a cruel, vindictive creature who took pleasure in shaming him, and her, and everyone else; Kitty knew not where to look. How could he be married at all! It had never come up—she had never had any reason to suspect—what must they think of her? Flirting so shamelessly with a married man, bringing scandal and shame beyond what Lydia had done, even; her father would cast her off, her sisters would never speak to her again—she would be cast upon the mercy of the world—not even Lydia would take her in after this. But she couldn't have known!

Kitty sank back against the back of her chair and covered her face with her hands.

After a few tense moments during which she desperately strove not to cry, Mr. Darcy came around to stand before her. Kitty lowered her hands to her lap, but couldn't bring herself to look at him. She couldn't imagine what he could possibly say to her, but it would surely be uncomfortable.

To her everlasting shock, he bent over to look her in the eye, and took her hands. "Miss Bennet, I am immeasurably sorry for this. I should have investigated his character more thoroughly before inviting him to stay at our house, and I most certainly should have taken better steps to protect you. But I promise, I will not allow him in this house again. I will not allow anyone else to cause you such distress." No one else moved. It was as though everyone had been turned to pillars of salt for daring to look at her.

Kitty could hardly think, hardly respond. Shaking, she managed to whisper her thanks, but she couldn't bear to have everyone staring at her like that, and they were sure to hate her. Flirting with a married man! She hated herself as much as they could do.

She wanted to get up and run from them all, but she couldn't seem to stop shaking long enough to stand up.

Elizabeth came to stand beside her husband, who took his wife's hand and pressed it. "Kitty, dear, no one blames you for this," she said, very quietly. "None of us had the smallest suspicion—if we had, we would have let you know of it, I swear. There is no reason why you should feel at all guilty for anything. You could not have known."

Kitty thought this was rather rich, coming from the woman who had lectured her so strictly about her behavior toward Mr. Johns so recently. But she could only whisper her thanks again.

Mr. Knott saw her distress and had pity on her. "I think we should let Miss Bennet alone; she probably needs time to recover her composure, and I am sure we are not helping." He said this, ostensibly, to Miss Darcy, but loudly enough that the whole room could easily hear it. That seemed to bring them to their senses somewhat, and they did not require further prompting to send them along their way. Mr. Knott lingered longest, in fact. When the others had left, he came and stood beside her chair. She stared at him without really seeing anything.

"I notice that you do not have your cane, and you were limping this morning," he said quietly. "I thought perhaps you would like some help walking back to your room. Do you need an arm?"

Kitty wanted nothing more than to thank him and send him away, but truthfully, she was still trembling so much that she probably wouldn't make it to her room without help, and she wanted very much to be there. So she accepted his arm and let him lead her away.

She followed his lead silently, and in his wisdom, he did not speak either. Kitty could not escape the storm of thoughts raging through her mind. What on earth could Mr. Johns possibly have meant by deceiving them all like that? Had he not noticed her expressing her interest in him? He could have told her, if he had told none of the others. She would not have made such a fool of herself if he had. Anger warred in her heart with her shame and mortification.

When she entered her room and flung herself into her chair, a sudden desire seized her to march over to Mr. Johns's house and demand an explanation from him. She deserved it, surely. Not even his wife—such a woman as she!—could deny her that bit of justice. Indeed, Kitty thought, she would very much like an explanation from both of them. What on earth had she been doing with herself all that time, while Mr. Johns was here and going to balls and convincing them all that he was as single as anybody? Hiding away somewhere? Shameful! What kind of miserable creature must she be, that her husband had gone to lengths to conceal her existence from everybody? It was absolutely ridiculous.

But Kitty knew she had no real chance of ever finding anything out, unless she could catch a bit of gossip from one of the servants. Considering that Elizabeth was, even now, almost certainly instructing every one never to bring it up in Kitty's presence, that seemed impossible.

Well, fine. She would forget Mr. Johns, and Mrs. Johns, and the whole sorry business.

Only, now that she knew he was forever out of her reach, she realized how much she had allowed herself to fall in love with him. How could he have done this to her? How could she have let him?

CHAPTER 18

She stayed in her room until dinner, but Elizabeth came and persuaded her to come down for that. "It would look much worse if you did not," she said. "This way you can show everyone that you are as unaffected as you can be, after that initial shock, and that will go a long way to helping things get back to normal."

Kitty did not particularly care if things ever got back to normal, but she did not feel like arguing, and assented without objection. She took no special care of her own appearance, but she came down and tried to smile, and act as though nothing was amiss. The others must have either sensed that they shouldn't speak of it, or Elizabeth had instructed them to leave her alone, for no one mentioned it and if the conversations on other subjects did not seem as comfortable as they ought to be, they were at least cheerful enough to keep her nerves under regulation.

When the ladies withdrew after dinner, however, Amy approached her and Kitty felt sure she was not equal to meeting the look in her friend's eye.

"What a morning!" she murmured, taking Kitty's arm and leading her around the room. "I wonder that you can bring yourself to face being in company at all."

"I am not so affected as that," Kitty insisted. "I liked him very much, but I was not really in love with him, you know." She pushed as much confidence into her voice as she could. She needed Amy to believe that she was not heartbroken.

"Weren't you?"

"No indeed! And I see no reason to dwell on it. We were mistaken in his identity and his character; the best thing to do now is to forget the whole sorry matter and move forward with something else."

"But how he must have been laughing at us this whole time—and at you particularly! I own, it would be a good joke, if you were not so cruelly treated by it." To Kitty's astonishment and mortification, she laughed. "The looks on everyone's faces were priceless! I have never wished so desperately that I could draw, so I might have captured them. I thought Miss Darcy would die of shame, and she did not have half the reason you did. Your defiance to Camilla was spectacular, however. Stone-cold, and would not even give her the courtesy of standing to receive her! Well done, Kitty, well done indeed!"

Kitty did not know which part of this speech to object to first, but Amy misinterpreted her silence.

"Oh, yes, she is the Camilla of whom I told you before. She always was far too high-strung, that girl. And so Mr. Johns is the unfortunate man whom she entrapped into matrimony! Given his look this morning, I believe he has lived to regret it. Well, that does tell me one thing: he is a determined flirt, and not even matrimony can cure him of that. She has the rest of his life to try to mend his ways, I suppose!" She laughed again. "Well, I suppose you'll have nothing to occupy yourself now. You shall have to devote yourself entirely to forwarding my interest with Colonel Fitzwilliam."

She clearly meant it as a joke, but Kitty could not help recoiling at the very idea. She was quite through with making matches, for herself or anyone else. "You had better find out whether he is married too," she said sharply, "before you go any further, or someone else will be laughing at you." She disentangled her arm from Amy's and went to sit with Lizzy and Miss Darcy, where she could at least expect to be left alone.

Thankfully, both Elizabeth and Miss Darcy were happy to protect her from more of Amy's hurtful chatter, and Kitty could keep herself occupied with some of Elizabeth's work while half attending to their conversation. She could not stop herself, however, from thinking over the events of the day and wondering at how quickly her world could go from optimistic to completely hopeless. What on earth would she do with herself now? She had certainly made a mess of things with everyone in the house. She was, in fact, a little bit surprised that her father had not already insisted that he take her home—or maybe he thought that a better punishment would be forcing her to remain here among all the people who had witnessed her shame. She wondered whether the Bingleys were far enough away that she could go to them and be able to start fresh. Would she be forced to be in company with Mr. Johns that far away from Edgepark? She might not ever see him again. That would be preferable. But Mr. Darcy had already promised that he would not be welcome at Pemberley again. Perhaps she would do best to just stay there, and trust that her family would protect her.

Kitty felt a sudden rush of gratitude for her brother-in-law's severe demeanor. She knew that not everyone found him as intimidating as she did, but he was certainly not the sort of man one meddled with, either. If he guaranteed her safety, she would be safe.

WHEN THE GENTLEMEN JOINED THEM, she watched them enter the room with a feeling of detached disgust. She wanted nothing to do with any gentleman at that moment, married or otherwise. She wondered whether it would really be so terrible if she never married.

"Lizzy," she said quietly.

"Yes, dear."

"Do you think... if I never marry anyone, could I come and live with you? I cannot bear the thought of living with the Collinses, but..."

Lizzy laughed a little bit, but gently. "Of course you may, dear, but do not despair of marriage just yet. I know that Mr. Johns has given you a terrible view of men at the moment, and I do not blame you for being disappointed and angry, but not all men are that way."

"That does not matter if I cannot find the ones that aren't," Kitty said.

"And if you do not ever find a man to love you, you will always have a home with us."

"I know how you are feeling, Miss Bennet," Miss Darcy said suddenly. Lizzy looked at her with an expression of surprise, but she nodded once and Lizzy shrugged. Miss Darcy smiled at Kitty. "You are probably doubting me, but perhaps I should tell you my story so that you can better understand."

In a soft undertone, therefore, Miss Darcy laid out a description of her history with Mr. Wickham, to Kitty's growing astonishment. "I truly believed that he cared for me," she concluded with a little sniff. "My poor brother had to prove me wrong by bribing Mr. Wickham to leave me, in front of me. It was the most humiliating, horrid thing I have ever endured." She paused, letting out a shaky breath, and laughed a little bit. "So, you see, I have some idea of what you are feeling—the betrayal, the disbelief, the anger. But it will pass with time, and you will find that you are actually grateful that you went through it, because you will be better at seeing through undeserving men in the future."

Kitty had no idea what to say. By this reckoning, Lydia had married an abysmal specimen of humanity, and Miss Darcy had suffered far more than Kitty.

And she could not help feeling a pang for Lydia. "My poor sister..." she whispered. "What kind of life has she bought for herself? She was so happy to be married first, but to *such* a man!"

Miss Darcy laid her hand on Kitty's. "Yes, I know. But perhaps he might reform, as he has a wife now and must no longer hope to marry a fortune, as he once did."

"How can you say that," cried Kitty, pulling her hand away sharply, "when you and I have immediate proof that there are men in the world who would not hesitate to deceive a lady into thinking whatever she liked of him even if he is already wed to another!"

"Oh, Miss Bennet, I'm sorry—I didn't think of that! But, truly, I do not think that is something Mr. Wickham would do—what would it benefit him? He was not interested in winning hearts as much as in winning a fortune, and without the possibility of marrying a rich woman before him, I do not think he would do as Mr. Johns did—truly I do not—he would have no reason to."

Kitty forgave her right away, but she could not quell her unease so readily. The realization that there was one such man in the world was bad enough, but to know that there might be two, and that her sister might have married one of them...

And the more Kitty thought about her brief acquaintance with Mr. Wickham, and the letters she had received from Lydia since they had been married, she could see that what had formerly cemented their marriage in Kitty's mind as a thing of romance was nothing but a thin veneer of affection: whitewash on a tomb. She shuddered. What had her sister really gotten into with Wickham? What might Kitty have gotten into with Mr. Johns, if it had not been for his awful wife?

"Miss Bennet?"

Kitty smiled a little. "After all that, I think you've well earned the right to call me Kitty."

"Thank you, Kitty—and you must call me Georgiana." She returned the smile, and Kitty relaxed back into her seat the smallest bit. She felt as if she had at least one true friend now, who could actually understand what she felt, and that was something. The awkward glances of the others and the laughing looks of Amy Pratt were, she felt, at least somewhat defended against.

"You know," Georgiana continued after a moment, "I swore never to marry, too, after what happened with Mr. Wickham."

Elizabeth looked up from her work. "Did you indeed? I did not know that."

"Well, I have since changed my mind, of course. But for several months after, I was convinced that I would remain single. I had planned everything—I would live with Mrs. Annesley and purchase a cottage somewhere by the sea, and draw and play music all day."

"You are fortunate that you could afford to do so," Kitty said, "if you wished to."

"I was foolish to think that my brother would not wish me to live with him," Georgiana answered, laughing.

"But you have since decided that you will marry?"

"If I meet someone I wish to marry, I will. I have only decided that I will be very particular about the man I choose to marry, and if he never appears, I will not be disappointed in my life. I have so many sources of happiness, you know, that I do not need to marry to be content."

Kitty felt the implied criticism in this and bristled. "I do not believe that life without marriage can really be satisfactory. But if every man I meet with will be either attracted to one of my sisters or someone else entirely, I shall never have the opportunity to marry no matter what I do."

"Have you not been satisfied with your life so far?"

"Good heavens, no!" Kitty laughed at the very idea. "I have spent my entire life looking for something I shall never have. How dreadful!"

Elizabeth shook her head. "You should not hang your happiness so much on the actions of other people, Kitty. Find ways to be content with yourself, and what you can do."

"For example, you can come with me to the Stephens's again, to return that basket of mending. They will be delighted to see you, I am sure, and very grateful for your efforts on their behalf. I have found that serving them has helped me to begin to overcome my shyness, and taught me to be thankful for what I have." Georgiana held up the handkerchief she was embroidering. "There is no reason, for example, that this should be ornamented, except that it gives me pleasure to have it so, and I am grateful that I am able to make it as pretty as I want it."

Kitty knew she was supposed to feel chastened by this and express her thankfulness for the things she had, but all she could think of was the lonely life ahead of her. Georgiana would marry and leave; Elizabeth and Jane and even Lydia would have children and spend their time and affection on them instead of their spinster sister. She would be abandoned and alone, no matter where she lived. Embroidered handkerchiefs and mending other people's things did not seem like sufficient balm for such wounds.

"I do not believe you have convinced her, Georgie," Elizabeth said, smiling slightly.

"I did not expect to, yet." She laid aside her work and took Kitty's hands. "Your conduct has been much less atrocious than mine was. I fear right now that the wound is too fresh for you to do anything other than ache over it, but I promise, you will find one day soon that things are not so hopeless as you have convinced yourself they must be. In the meantime, I will do whatever I can to ease your mind."

Kitty swallowed back the urge to hug her. "Thank you. I have never had such a friend as you." She pressed Georgiana's hands tightly and forced herself to smile.

CHAPTER 19

When she stood to retire for the evening, the others did their best to pretend as though nothing had changed, but she could see the way they all looked at her. This was not a humiliation to be forgotten in a day. Kitty had a sudden vision of the days stretching before her until they turned into months, always enduring the awkward half-sympathy, half-accusation of her companions, and she had to hold on to the arm of her chair for a moment before she was able to breathe enough to announce her departure and go.

It did not help anything that as she left, her father rose and followed her out. No good could come of this.

Mr. Bennet walked down the hall behind her until they were quite out of earshot of the drawing room, and pulled her aside. "I hope the events of this morning have impressed you with the consequences of your actions," he said, his face shadowed in the dimly-lit passage. "Your behavior is going to lead you to worse infamy than your sister, if you cannot conduct yourself with more propriety."

If only she had more courage, perhaps she could have managed better than her weak response."I did not know he was married. How could I?"

"Whether or not a man is married should not be the deciding

factor in how your behavior to him is judged! You must learn to control yourself. What gentleman would want a wife who can't keep her behavior in check around other men?" He sighed heavily and rubbed his hand over his face. "I do not know what to do with you, child, but it is clear to me that you cannot be left to your own devices or you will end in ruin."

Dread spread through Kitty's stomach like poison through a well. Suddenly, taking her back to Longbourn seemed as though it might be the kindest choice he would consider. What if he thought her so irredeemable that he sent her to live in some quiet country house for the rest of her life, with only some poor, worn-out governess for a companion? She would die of boredom and loneliness! "Papa..."

"Don't interrupt me, Catherine. Lord knows I hate doing this." Another sigh, and Kitty suddenly realized how very old her father looked these days. "From this point forward, until I have satisfied myself on what to do with you, you cannot be left unattended. You are not to leave the house unless Elizabeth or I accompany you. You may not be in company with any gentleman, nor that abominable Miss Pratt, unless you are attentively chaperoned."

Indignation welled up in Kitty. She might deserve some kind of reprimand, but Amy had done nothing wrong to warrant that level of censure. "Miss Pratt—"

He waved her words away. "I know she is the one who put you up to all of this. You are far too apt to take the advice of any young woman who promises you ten seconds of amusement, and you are certain to be amused by only the worst kind of behavior. I suffered you to take far too many liberties when you were under Lydia's influence, but I cannot allow it any more. I ought not to have allowed it then, and I might have saved your sister—that, however, is beside the point."

Kitty thought of Georgiana's history, so recently related to her. She wondered, for the first time, what her father knew of Mr. Wickham's character that she had always been ignorant of.

"You may walk in the garden immediately outside—I expect you to be visible from one of the windows in a public room at all times." He glanced toward the window across the hall from them, which showed little in the dark.

"What of Miss Darcy? I promised her I would go to return the basket of mending we finished."

He hesitated, but shook his head. "You will have to convey your regrets and send the work with her."

"That is unfair! There can be no possible complaint against my doing charity work. What if Elizabeth came with us?"

"Mrs. Darcy has responsibilities of her own and cannot be expected to abandon them to go traipsing about the country with you. I am asking too much of her simply by requesting her help in supervising you while you are in the house. You shouldn't need it, and she shouldn't be burdened with it."

Anger, resentment, and frustration at the excess and irrationality of this punishment welled up within Kitty to the point that she could hardly see. Of course she knew that crying would only lower his opinion of her further. But she had to fight hard to keep the tears at bay. To distract herself, she said, "I know I did not behave toward Mr. Johns the way Jane or Lizzy would have done. I should have been more circumspect in my interest in him. But I do not believe that it was wrong to be interested in him, given the circumstances, and what I knew of him." Then, boldly, "Besides, Miss Pratt encouraged me to do much more than I did, and I refused. I am not wholly without a sense of propriety!"

"That you admit that she encouraged you to behave worse than you did is enough to persuade me that I have done rightly. However, as I will be in company with you regardless, I will be observing you closely. If you can demonstrate consistent good sense, I will think about loosening my rules."

This gave Kitty a small measure of hope, and the burning behind her eyes diminished a little. With Georgiana's help, she could demonstrate as much good sense as her father required of her. "What would you have me do? I will begin immediately."

"I would have you show me that you are possessed of some good sense, as I said."

"But what does that look like? What must I do? How must I behave?" If he could only give her a direction, she could follow it—could do anything he required.

He shook his head. "If you must ask me, then you clearly do not have what I am looking for. When you can show me that you not only know how to behave, but can behave that way, I will grant you more freedom."

Not even remotely satisfied, Kitty cast about desperately for some other argument to make. Her father, however, did not seem inclined to allow her to gather her thoughts, and gestured to the hallway before them. "Shall we? It is time I escorted you to your room."

This was the beginning of a very humiliating practice, Kitty saw clearly. She followed him down the hallway in stony silence, wondering how things could possibly get any worse.

THE NEXT MORNING, her torment began, as she was escorted everywhere by her scowling father. Kitty did not know where to look when he escorted her to the music room, and she was immensely relieved when Elizabeth entered the room shortly after and nodded to Mr. Bennet, giving him the cue to depart. Somehow, it did not seem quite so humiliating to be under Elizabeth's eye. She was able to keep her expression calm when Lizzy came over to her with a sympathetic look, and sat close enough so that only Kitty would be able to hear her.

"How are you doing this morning, Kitty?"

Kitty shrugged. How well could she reasonably be expected to be doing? But her main concern was lifting her father's punishment, not dwelling on Mr. Johns and his ...his wife. In that, Lizzy might be of some help. "I'm very sorry that Papa has decided to be so unreasonable, and that he's dragged you into it. Could you not convince him to be more realistic? I am sure this is unnecessary." She gestured to Lizzy and the door through which their father had left.

"Perhaps it is," Elizabeth said. She glanced at the door and sighed.

"You must know that he his not doing this just to be cruel, Kitty. He wants to protect you."

"Does he indeed? I find that difficult to believe! When has he ever been anything but cruel? He has always belittled me, my whole life. He's always thought that I am stupid and ignorant, you know he has. He's said it often enough. And he is forever making fun of me, and I never know how to answer him. It's all well enough for you. You've always known how to respond, and he's always liked you. He never cared a fig for me."

"Oh, Kitty." Elizabeth put her hand on Kitty's shoulder. She started to say something several times, but she ended up just shaking her head.

"You see," Kitty said. "You know I'm right."

"I suppose. But consider: what have you ever shown him of good sense? Your history has not been such as would encourage him to revise his opinion of you. And you have always been too close to Lydia, and too willing to follow her into trouble. He is only trying to avoid you falling into the hands of another Mr. Wickham."

"And he is so certain that I will! Does he think I've learned nothing from her?" Too late, she realized that her voice was too loud, and Miss Pratt and Miss Darcy had stopped practicing to look at her, and each other. Miss Darcy at least had the decency to blush and put her hands back to her music. Kitty let out a shaky breath and lowered her voice. "If he would only take the time to know me, he would see that I have learned, from Lydia and my own experiences. I am not as stupid as he thinks."

"I know, Kitty. But you must show him, by how you behave. Nothing in your behavior thus far has demonstrated much improvement—you still flirt too readily and put yourself forward to men who aren't worthy of you. And this business with Mr. Johns has frightened him. You must admit, it looks very bad."

"But I did not know he was married! And neither did anyone else."

"True, but think of what might have happened had it escalated any farther! The scandal you would have brought would be beyond even what Lydia did, if he'd gotten his way."

"His way?"

Elizabeth frowned. "Kitty, you must have seen that his design was to... to compromise you, and abandon you. He only wanted to see how far he could take matters before you objected, or were caught."

Kitty had not thought at all of what his motivations might have been, apart from, probably, to forget that he had married such a miserable creature. But there had to be a better explanation than that. He hadn't really wanted to compromise her, had he? He'd never tried to do anything. None of this amounted to anything more than suspicion.

When Kitty didn't answer, Elizabeth continued. "This was a very strange case, I will admit. There is probably little chance that it will ever happen again, but it still frightened Papa. You must understand: he is trying to protect you."

"Well, he's chosen a terrible method." She stood up. "I'm sorry, Lizzy. I need a walk." Before her sister could stand up to join her, she added, "Alone, please. Papa has still permitted me that, if I stay in sight."

Wisely, Elizabeth said nothing as Kitty walked out.

KITTY STORMED out of the house and into the gardens at the south side. Setting out on a likely-looking path, she set a fast pace toward the one place she wanted to go: away. She glared at the sunshine and the serene, well-kept gardens around her as though they had personally offended her, and wished that the day had better adapted itself to her mood. She caught a brief glimpse of the gardener working on one of the side paths, but he scurried away when she stalked into view, clearly not interested in enduring her temper. Well, wasn't that what she wanted, to be left alone?

The more she thought of it, the worse her situation seemed. How could she prove her good sense, anyway, if she was never given an opportunity to exercise any sense at all?

Angry and frustrated, and with tears tightening the back of her throat, Kitty stalked over to a nearby tree and flopped down beneath it. With rather too much force, as it turned out, because she slammed her back into the trunk so hard that she had to bite her lip to keep from shouting. It took several minutes of tightly-clamped lips and awkwardly gripping her shoulder before she could lean back again.

"It is all too unfair!" she moaned. A bird in the tree above her looked down and squawked. Kitty started, then scowled at it. "What? Have you come to lecture me, too? Shoo!"

The bird turned its head to one side and peered at her for a moment, then squawked again and flew away. Kitty glared at the swaying branch it had left, but the brief stab of vindication she'd felt quickly faded back into frustration. "Stupid bird," she said under her breath. Of course she'd scared it off, but that only made her more miserable. Not even the wildlife had any use for her.

She crossed her arms over her chest and sulked. What on earth was she going to do now?

"Why, Miss Bennet, what brings you out here?"

Kitty scrambled to her feet and turned to face the approaching visitor, her surprise and vague sense of shame making her clumsy. "Mr. Knott?"

He smiled broadly and bowed. "Forgive me; I did not mean to startle you. I thought you had seen me coming."

"I... I'm afraid that I was so wrapped up in my own thoughts that I did not see anything," she said, her voice unsteady. She realized she had not returned his bow and dropped a hasty curtsy. She couldn't meet his eyes.

"In that case, perhaps I should leave you to your thoughts; unless you would rather not spend any more time with them. You had a rather thunderous expression on your face." He was still smiling, a little, but his tone expressed compassion and concern. Kitty stared at the ground near his feet. She didn't quite know what to say. When it became clear that she would not respond, he continued, "Or, perhaps you might like to share some of those thoughts with me. I am to be a clergyman after all; I ought to be good at helping people with their problems."

"I very much doubt that you will be able to help me," Kitty said with a brief frown.

"Well, we can't know that until we try, can we? Come, walk with me for a spell and tell me what's troubling you." He gestured to his side and held out his arm. Kitty hesitated. He would not be able to help her, but he might at least be able to sympathize with her. It would be nice to have an ally.

"Very well." She took his arm and followed when he led her back in the direction she'd come.

"Now, Miss Bennet," he said, "is it Mr. Johns?"

"No," she said, and stopped herself so abruptly she nearly stopped walking. He was going to think her a stupid fool and she should not have agreed to speak with him.

"Ah." A pause. Then, he said, "Actually, I don't believe I fully understand. You seemed very upset by him yesterday. And you had every reason to be so."

Kitty bit the inside of her lip. "I am upset with him. But I am more upset with my father; he has refused to allow me out of the house, and what grounds are immediately visible from the house. He believes that it was my fault, and my behavior, which has brought this on."

His lips drew together in a thin line. "Mr. Johns deceived you; that is not your fault. It does not seem to me that your father understands what took place there."

"Yes, and the worst of it is, everything I do seems to solidify his resolve to keep me locked up forever. I do not understand why he should be unfair. I have been out in society for some years now, and there has never been a problem with it before this. But ever since my sister Lydia made such a mess of her courtship, he blamed it all on me and whatever I do makes things worse."

"That is quite a dilemma," he said. He turned them toward a nearby lake. "What have you tried, to help him see your side of things?"

Kitty shook her head. "Everything, almost. I have told him again and again that I am not Lydia, I have reminded him of all the things that she did which I would not, I have tried to follow all the rules he has set me—only I cannot keep them all straight and so I'm afraid I've made a miserable mess of them. But I wish he would see that I am trying, and give me credit for that at least!"

"You wish your efforts to be counted to you as results?" he asked, raising an eyebrow.

"No-o-o, not exactly," she said. "I only wish that he would acknowledge that I am making efforts, and amend his rules accordingly." She took his hand and allowed him to help her over the stream that ran to the lake.

"Ah. So you are bending and he is not."

"Yes, exactly! I do think he could let me go about the house freely, at least. How much trouble can I get into here?" Kitty frowned. "How am I to demonstrate that I can behave myself if he never gives me an opportunity to prove it?"

"I can see how that would be a challenge."

They walked on for some time in silence; Kitty did not know what else to say, though her mind still rolled with indignant thoughts. Mr. Knott seemed content to contemplate the matter on his own. Finally, when they reached the lake, he turned back to her, and let go of her arm. "Well, Miss Bennet, it seems to me that if your father will not give you opportunities to prove your responsibility, you must go out of your way to demonstrate it to him."

"But how? He has forbidden me to go anywhere!" Kitty scowled and turned away. She glanced at a little rock at her feet and, in a fit, scooped it up and threw it with all her might into the lake. It made a most unsatisfactory plunking sound and sank with very little fanfare; hardly the soothing crash she had been hoping for.

"There must be other things you could do, that he has not forbidden to you, and could prove to him that you are not the person he believes you to be." He stepped up beside her and, with a cheeky smile, handed her another, bigger rock. "This one should make a bigger splash, by the way. Much more satisfying."

Kitty looked at him searchingly for a moment, caught off guard. His smile did not waver, and he nodded toward the lake, so she took the rock and threw it after its brother. It did not sail as far, but it did shatter the placid surface of the lake. Unfortunately, it also sent water flying at them with such force that it reached the bank, and her dress, and Mr. Knott's coat. She leapt back, mortified. "Oh, I am so sorry!" she cried.

He laughed and caught her arm. "You've nothing to apologize for! I should be sorry, for I found you the rock. Your choice proved to be the much more sensible one." His eyes lit up with a teasing sparkle. "Perhaps that is where you should begin with your father. When we return you may tell him that you are much more sensible than an ordained man of God when choosing appropriate rocks to throw into lakes. I promise I will act as witness for you. Do you think that will satisfy him?"

Kitty surprised herself by laughing. "Something tells me that it will not, but I thank you for your gallant offer, sir." She glanced back out at the lake. "In the event that it is not successful, however, do you have other suggestions?"

"You might try showing him your good sense through conversation."

She shuddered. "No, I doubt that will go over well. He always knows just what to say to make me feel tongue-tied and stupid. I don't know what to say to him, anyway. He and Lizzy converse comfortably enough, but not the rest of us. He likes Lizzy best."

"Why do you not emulate her?"

"That sounds miserable," she said, making a face. "I cannot become another Lizzy. She is far more clever than I am and she and Papa share the same sense of humor. It is easy for him to love her. I have nothing to offer him and consequently he never cared to try to love me." She shrugged and looked away. "Nor I him, for that matter."

Mr. Knott nodded slowly and began walking along the lake shore, his hands clasped behind his back. Kitty followed behind him. Eventually, he turned his head and spoke to her. "There is not anything you can do to change your father's behavior or preferences, I think?"

"Certainly not that I know of."

"Yes. It is very difficult to convince a man to prefer something he does not wish to like, no matter the inducement. So that leaves you with only one option, as far as I can tell."

"And what is that?"

"Since you cannot change him, you will have to change yourself."

"But I have no desire to change myself!" Kitty stopped following him and folded her arms over her chest. Had she not made that clear? She did not want to be another Lizzy!

Mr. Knott stopped, too, and turned back to her. He came around and stood in front of her, looking her in the eyes. "I know. But we have established that it is impossible for you to change your father. If you wish to change his opinion of you, that leaves only one alternative." His gaze shifted to the house for a moment, then he gave her a reassuring smile. "You do not have to become an exact copy of your sister; I do not imagine your father would appreciate that, anyway. But find a few things that he would like to see, that you think you could do, and pursue those things. I suspect that if you do, it will not be long before he is pleased with the change he sees in you and is willing to make some concessions because of it."

"Why should I have to do all the changing?"

He shrugged. "Because someone has to change first, and it does not look likely that he will. Why should it not be you?" When Kitty did not respond and would not meet his eye, he continued, "He will change, too, of course, if he is able to. But even if he does not, you will have the satisfaction of knowing that it was through no fault of your own that you are still under his rules."

"That sounds miserable, not satisfying," Kitty said, her resentment swelling.

"Perhaps it does, now, but is it not preferable to the state you are in now?"

"I don't see how, for either way I will not be allowed to go anywhere."

He shook his head. "Well, if you are determined to try nothing, I cannot help you. I am sorry for the situation you find yourself in, but if you are not willing to do what it takes to change it, you have no one but yourself to blame."

"And my father."

"Perhaps, perhaps." He turned away, but he only took two steps before he stopped and turned back to her. "I hope you do try, Miss Bennet. There will be other balls, and you would be happier if you may attend them and dance freely."

Kitty thought briefly of the previous ball, at which he did not dance at all. "Would you even go to the next ball?"

His eyes twinkled. "Only if I had some inducement." He bowed. "Would you like me to escort you back to the house, Miss Bennet? I have an appointment with Mr. Darcy to discuss the living he holds, and I should not like to be late."

Kitty hesitated, but only a moment. She allowed him to help her back up to the path and kept her arm in his as they walked, but she paid him no attention. Her mind was entirely engaged with her father.

CHAPTER 20

*M*r. Knott returned her to Pemberley and left her in the foyer to go meet with Mr. Darcy. Unfortunately, at that moment Mr. Bennet emerged from the library, and he did not like what he saw. As soon as Mr. Knott had left, he descended upon Kitty, his face set in lines that did not bode well for her.

"What was that?"

Kitty crossed her arms over her chest. "What do you mean, what was that?"

"Exactly what I said. I just witnessed you walking into this house on the arm of a gentleman, apparently unescorted. What do you mean by that?"

"Nothing. He met me while I was walking in the gardens—in full view of the house, as you insisted!—and offered to escort me back to the house. I accepted his offer. There is nothing wrong with that, is there?" She knew she was not being entirely truthful. She had gone somewhat further than the gardens when she had encountered him, but he didn't need to know that detail.

Mr. Bennet looked at the door through which Mr. Knott had disappeared. "If that were not a respectable man of the clergy, whom I have no reason to doubt, I would be much angrier than I am. As it is, I am not best pleased. Did you hear nothing of my instructions to you?"

"I did not leave the sight of the house! I was well within your rules!"

"I specifically told you that you are not allowed to be in company alone with anyone but Lizzy and me! How do you think I ought to respond to this?"

"By showing some sense and realizing that I have done nothing wrong!" As soon as the words left her mouth, she knew that she would regret them. Her father was turning a most unflattering shade of red.

He did not say anything for several long moments, and if she had not been able to stand there and watch the emotions warring across his face, she would likely have assumed the conversation had ended and left. But she had learned that expression, or, rather, series of expressions, and she knew that to leave would be to multiply his wrath. Worse still, she could see Amy in the hall behind him, watching with wide eyes.

Finally, it came. "Let me be quite clear," he said, every syllable crisp. "You are not to leave the house, by any door, for any reason, without an escort of whom I have personally approved. You are not to step foot outside, or into company with any person not immediately related to you, without my approval and knowledge. You will inform me of your exact whereabouts at every moment, and if I do not know where you are, I will search until I have found you, and not allow you to leave my side until you have learned the severity of my resolve. Do I make myself quite clear?"

Kitty nearly sank into the floor. She knew better than to protest, but it was nearly impossible to grind out her response. "Yes, Sir."

"Very well. Now, let us join the others. I believe we will find them in the music room." He held out his arm to escort her, but she refused to take it. She could still exercise that little bit of rebellion, at least.

Amy ducked into the room ahead of them, and Kitty foresaw the further torment that awaited her with a resigned shake of her head. Amy dropped down beside her as soon as she sat down and picked up a dress to re-trim.

"You poor dear! I heard enough. What an odious punishment! Whom does he think he must protect you from? Does he think Mr. Knott or Colonel Fitzwilliam are hiding secret wives, as well?"

"No; from myself, I suppose."

She laughed. "He doesn't blame you for what happened, surely."

Kitty shook her head, growing angry. "Of course he does. His only other option is blaming *you*, and I am not convinced that he does not, in some measure."

Amy sat back, clearly hurt, and Kitty felt viciously triumphant. It may have been a joke to Amy, but to Kitty it was quite serious, and any true friend would understand that. She pulled her scissors out of her pocket and cut the trim off her dress with what she meant to be an air of nonchalance.

Mr. Knott entered the room at that moment, and judging by the expression on his face, he sensed the tension in the air. "Pardon me," he said. "I think I must be interrupting something."

"No, indeed," Amy said grandly, jumping up from her chair. "You find us all quite bored, and I have been forced to resort to tormenting poor Miss Bennet for lack of something better to do."

His gaze found Kitty's, and she could not hold it. His half-smile mocked her. "Have you indeed? Well, someone ought to come to her rescue. Fortunately, the appointment I had has been postponed, and I am available for rescuing, if Miss Bennet believes it necessary."

"I believe I am beyond rescue," Kitty said. She didn't quite achieve the lighthearted tone she was trying for.

"Surely you do not mean that! No one is beyond redemption entirely until he is dead, and you, Miss Bennet, are not dead, as far as I can tell."

Kitty smiled weakly. "Not yet."

Georgiana took pity on her and interceded. "Were you planning to join us this morning, Mr. Knott?"

"I..." He looked back to Kitty again, and his mouth tightened. "I was, if you will have me. It has been such a long time since I had the pleasure of reading to you, and I thought perhaps that you might wish to find out what happens next in *The Absentee*."

"Yes," said Amy, "we have neglected it shamefully."

In all honesty, Kitty had entirely forgot about the book, but she recognized the attempt he was making to protect her from Amy, and she was grateful to him for it. As Mr. Knott settled in to read, she took up a ruined dress she'd been meaning to mend, and hoped she could make something to cover the mess she had made. But Amy had merely pretended to have any interest in the story, for she sat back down beside Kitty and soon started whispering to her again.

"Do you think your father will allow you to accompany me to town later? I was very much hoping to purchase some new ribbons for this bonnet and I do not think Miss Darcy has anything that will do."

"No, he will not." Kitty glanced over at Georgiana, but Georgiana gazed thoughtfully at Mr. Knott and appeared to be engrossed in the story.

Undaunted, Amy pressed on. "Well, what do you think he *will* permit you? It will be quite dull if we sit here all day."

"Well, that is all he's likely to allow. But you are not obligated to stay with me if you do not like to."

Mr. Bennet stood up and came over to stand beside Kitty, watching her work, and effectively cutting off any further conversation between them. Amy lost heart for the conversation, and Kitty was simultaneously relieved and furious. If only Elizabeth would come back, she would at least be spared this overbearing display of stern discipline. It was punishment, to be sure, but was humiliation really a necessary part of it? Had she not experienced enough of that to last her whole life?

"Forgive me, Mr. Knott, but I did not hear that last. Do you mind going back a page?" she said, glancing up at her father again. She would not give him the satisfaction of knowing how much it affected her, if she could help it.

"Of course, Miss Bennet; is this far enough?" He flipped back and started reading again, and Kitty nodded. She listened intently, determined to forget about her father *and* Amy Pratt.

Mr. Knott read through the end of the chapter, and when he paused to see if the company wished for another, Georgiana spoke up. "Actually, I had hoped that we—the ladies, I mean—could take a basket to another of Pemberley's tenants. It seems that whatever illness afflicted the Stephenses has spread to others, and these have a new baby at home and are struggling to keep a balance." She looked between Kitty and Amy. "What do you think?"

Amy made a face, but before either of them could answer, Mr. Bennet intervened. "Kitty will have to decline, I'm afraid. She is not to leave the house at present." Kitty winced. It was too much to bear; she could feel all their eyes on her. They pitied her, and were surely laughing at her. She stared resolutely at her hands.

A chair scraped and someone stood up; Kitty glanced up to see Mr. Knott standing before her father, his gaze locked firm on him, anger tight around his eyes and reddening his ears. "Mr. Bennet," he said, his gentle tone a poor match for his expression, "I suggest that you consider allowing her to go on this errand. What harm can it do? There are no unknown gentlemen to corrupt her, and only wholesome company to cheer her. It is clear that Miss Bennet regrets her behavior, and wishes to go. I think it speaks very highly of her judgment and character that she does, and sending a young lady on an errand of Christian charity ought to be the kind of thing that punishment is meant to promote. It must benefit her to see others whose lot in life is worse than her own, and to help ease their hardships. It will take her mind off her own situation and teach her to think of others. I believe that her inclination to go does her credit, and should not be discouraged."

Dear Mr. Knott! Kitty had never liked him so well as she did at that moment, and she lifted her head to smile at him.

Mr. Bennet, however, was not impressed. "If I could believe that she cared about charity, I would not hesitate to send her; but as it is, I believe her motivation is much less admirable."

"Well, then, perhaps I might go with them, to supervise her behavior. I am ordained, though I have not yet secured a situation, and in that capacity, I can monitor her behavior if you do not wish to entrust the other young ladies alone with the responsibility."

"I am sure that Kitty will behave beautifully, as she did on our last such errand," Georgiana added quickly, "and if you would like me to provide you with a report of her activity upon her return, I will furnish it faithfully. I am sure I will not need to say anything which will make me blush." She glanced at Kitty with a small, trembling smile.

"Or I could ask Elizabeth to come with us," Kitty added, encouraged by Georgiana's support. "You said yourself that you trusted her to supervise me."

"I already told you that Lizzy does not need to be troubled with your every movement. She has responsibilities of her own."

"You're only saying that because she doesn't agree with this, and she won't be pleased to be asked to go with us only because you have created this rule, and brought her into it." Kitty realized as she said it that she spoke the truth, and Mr. Bennet's momentary confusion confirmed her suspicion. She pressed her advantage. "There will be no reason for me to behave with anything but perfect propriety. I will spend the entire time in the company of Miss Darcy, Mr. Knott, and Miss Pratt, and we will go directly there and directly back."

"Don't drag me into this," Amy said crossly. "You can go on your charity mission if you like, but please remember that I have not consented to go with you, nor do I mean to!"

Kitty thought she ought to have known better than to bring Miss Pratt into the conversation, but she ignored the comment. "And consider, Papa. You encouraged me to join Miss Darcy on her last visit. Why should this one do me less good?"

Mr. Bennet glanced at Miss Pratt, and then at his pocket watch. "How long would it take you to walk there and back, Miss Darcy?"

She thought for a moment. "Less than an hour, if we do not stay long to talk."

"Very well, then. You may go, but only if you promise that you will return to this room within two hours after you leave the house, and if

I hear so much as a whisper of your behavior being the smallest inch out of line, I will be as severe as I am able."

"Oh, thank you!" Kitty jumped to her feet and embraced Georgiana. She bowed to Mr. Knott and then shook his hand, but hastily withdrew it when she realized that her father might think ill of her forwardness. "Thank you. Thank you a thousand times!"

She even kissed her father's cheek in thanks, she was so pleased. "You'll see," she cried as she hurried out of the room to change her dress, "You were not wrong to put your faith in me, Papa!"

THEY WERE outside and on the way to the tenants' house within minutes. Kitty was, in fact, somewhat astonished at how quickly the others were ready to go, but she was grateful to them for their willingness to defend her and put it down to the understanding that they, too, feared that Mr. Bennet would change his mind if they tarried too long. They only stopped to synchronize Georgiana's watch with Mr. Bennet's, to be sure of their time.

Kitty turned to Mr. Knott as soon as they were out of her father's hearing, determined to speak before she forgot her gratitude.

"I am so sorry that we were forced to bring you into this. Thank you for defending me to my father. You see, now, what I am up against. He does not understand my situation or my temperament."

"It is a common failing in a parent," he said. "I confess, it distressed me to see you so upset by his censure. Your behavior toward Mr. Johns was—" he hesitated and frowned, but recovered—"nothing like the sort of behavior that ought to lead to such punishment."

"Truly Kitty," added Georgiana, "you were more in company with him than with the rest of us, and you did not trouble to hide your intentions toward him, but nothing in your conduct would have brought you censure if he had been single as we all thought."

Kitty shook her head. She remembered Elizabeth's reprimand that day of the picnic, and she knew that others, at least, felt that her conduct had at least been partially blameworthy. But she chose instead to voice the question that had been bothering her since yesterday morning. "But what could possibly have prompted him to disguise his marriage to us?"

"We may never know," Mr. Knott said. "It certainly was not the action of an honest man. I am a little bit surprised at Mr. Darcy's inviting him to stay at Pemberley when he knew so little about the man, but Mr. Johns had a very engaging personality, and perhaps he imposed on Mr. Darcy in some way."

"I know my brother would not have exposed us to any risk he thought unacceptable," Georgiana said stiffly.

"You are quite right. Please excuse me."

Kitty glanced at Georgiana's blushing face and thought the kindest thing she could do was to change the subject. "Thank you again, Mr. Knott, for coming with us. I know you probably had other plans for your day."

"Nothing of significance, I assure you. Besides, I am sure the experience will do me some good. I have been too much cooped up indoors of late."

Kitty laughed. "You needn't tell me that! I know only too well what it has been to spend all my time inside, forever wondering whether I will ever have a chance of getting out into the sun again!"

"Forgive me," he said, and blushed. "I forgot that your ankle..."

"Never mind that. I am quite on the mend, and have made it out into the world at last. Let me enjoy the day and the sunshine, and keep me from breaking my ankle again, and all will be forgiven." Kitty waved her hand and laughed again. She glanced at Georgiana, who walked a few paces ahead of them, and wondered whether or not it would be wise to take control of the situation; clearly, Miss Darcy was too shy to walk with them. She was debating within herself how to get them together when Mr. Knott asked a question about the Stephenses which Kitty could easily deflect to her friend.

"I honestly don't know," she said, "but I am sure that Miss Darcy must have an idea of it. Georgiana! How many generations have the Stephenses lived at Pemberley?"

To her relief, the tactic worked, and she came back to walk with them. But she walked on Kitty's other side, rather than taking Mr.

Knott's free arm, which drove Kitty past the edge of frustration. She answered Mr. Knott graciously, however, and to Kitty's delight, the conversation turned to matters of which Kitty could say little, giving them some space to fall in love with each other. But Miss Darcy's good manners would not allow her to be excluded for long and she was eager to find a subject on which Kitty could converse.

When Georgiana expressed her concern that they were excluding her, Kitty replied, "Oh, you needn't worry about me. I am more than content to walk in good company and look at the countryside. There is no place more beautiful in the world, I think. These views are quite spectacular."

Mr. Knott readily agreed, and Kitty felt a little bad for exaggerating her opinion so much. But her spirits were so high that she could not dwell on anything for long, and she felt so pleased with the day and their excursion that she could almost forget about her father.

CHAPTER 21

They arrived with the intent of merely delivering the food and turning directly back. Kitty placed the basket on the table and started to empty it while Georgiana put the things away. Mr. Knott went over to speak with the mother of the family, who lay in bed, holding her infant and coughing. It took no time to get everything put away, and as Mr. Knott prayed quietly with the mother, Georgiana instructed the eldest of the children, a girl of about five, in getting the soup on the fire so it might be heated in time for dinner. They had a little bit of trouble, given the girl's size and that of the pot, but between the two of them they got it in place, and the little girl was elated to be a help to her mother.

As they finished their work, Georgiana checked her watch and shook her head. "We had better hurry if we're going to get back in time. That took longer than I thought it would." She picked up the basket and went to join Mr. Knott at the door, but before Kitty could catch up to them, a scream sounded from the little girl behind her. Kitty whirled to see her clutching her hand to her chest and stamping her feet.

"What happened?" she asked, dropping to her knees before the girl.

The baby was wailing in the bed and the poor mother had all she could do to calm it down.

"Hot! It's hot!"

Kitty gently pulled her arm away enough to see what happened. The girl had touched something hot near the fire and a nasty red burn had spread across her palm. Kitty winced; she had done that herself, once, and knew how badly it hurt. "Oh, you poor dear! Georgiana, is there any flour about?"

Georgiana was already at the cupboard, and found the flour quickly. Kitty took it and tried to get the girl to let her administer it. "It's all right, dear. This will help it feel better, I promise." She grabbed a generous handful of the flour and offered it to her. "You put this on your hand, and then you wrap it in cloth, and that keeps it safe while it gets better, and it takes the hot away."

Sniffing, the girl held out her hand and squeezed her eyes shut while Kitty floured it thoroughly and, without anything else to wrap it in, took off her fichu and wound it gently around the girl's palm. It was an old one of Mary's anyway, and had probably been through Jane and Lizzy before her, so she didn't regret the loss very much.

"Now, doesn't that feel better already?" Another sniff, and a nod. Kitty smiled and stood up, dusting the flour off her skirts and hands. "Good. Make sure you keep that on all day, and you can take it off tomorrow morning if you like. If your hand still hurts, you can put fresh flour on, but be sure to use a scoop to get it out, so you don't make a mess of your mama's flour. All right?"

"Yes'm."

"Are you going to be all right to get dinner on for your family?" Georgiana asked.

The girl nodded, and straightened herself. She wouldn't let a silly burn stop her from getting to act like Mama for a day. By way of proof, she went back to the pot and gave it a good, proud stir.

Kitty couldn't help smiling. "Good girl!" She and Georgiana put the flour away and found an old rag for the little girl. Kitty knelt before her again and held it out. "Now, whenever you need to touch the pot, wrap this around your hand too. The rag will get hot, and your hand will be safe. But move quickly, or else the heat will go through the rag and you'll burn yourself again."

"Like this?" She wound the rag about her fingertips and tapped them gingerly against the side of the pot, then drew her hand away quickly.

"Yes, but you can hold it a little longer than that if you need to. Just no longer than it takes you to count to five. Can you count to five?" The girl demonstrated her ability to do so. "Perfect. That's how long your hand can touch the pot, and only if you have this rag on it. Understood?"

Another nod satisfied Kitty that she'd gotten through, and she joined the others at the door. They took their leave again, and hurried back toward Pemberley.

"How did you know to use flour?" Mr. Knott asked Kitty as they went. Kitty was pleased to detect a bit of admiration in it. It was nice to have someone appreciate her good qualities, at least.

Kitty smiled and shook her head. "I burned my hand in a similar manner when I was a girl, and Mrs. Hill's solution was the flour. My mother was furious when she found out that I had been in the kitchen, getting in the way."

Georgiana checked her watch again. "We had better go faster. We are going to have a difficult time reaching the house within our time after that delay."

Kitty's stomach fell, but she picked up her pace. She'd forgotten about her father briefly, in the excitement, and now she saw the stupidity in that. But she was determined to show him that she could be trusted. If she could only make it back in time!

Mr. Bennet was waiting in the hall for them when they returned, and it only took a glance at his expression for Kitty to know the only time that mattered: they were late. She closed her eyes and waited for the inevitable.

"You are at least a quarter of an hour past your time," he said.

"Their little girl burned herself," Mr. Knott said gently, helping

Kitty to a chair. By the end of their rushed trip home, her ankle had been protesting heavily, and she was forced to lean on him to maintain their pace. "Miss Bennet stopped to help her before we left."

Mr. Bennet's eyes never left Kitty's face, and she had to fight to keep her countenance while she met his gaze. "I'm sorry, Papa—I should have asked for more time in case something happened to delay us."

"Yes." Without looking away from her, he said quietly, "Miss Darcy; Mr. Knott; thank you for bringing her home. If you will give us our privacy, I will see my daughter to her room."

They could do nothing but acquiesce. Georgiana pressed Kitty's hand as she passed, but that was all. She could not help feeling abandoned, and she swallowed hard. It would not do to cry.

"Come along, Kitty." She opened her eyes to see him holding out his arm to her. She took it and stood on her good foot, dreading the walk ahead of her. Resting had only seemed to make her ankle hurt more. She took a step forward and gasped involuntarily, leaning on her father's arm.

"I am very disappointed, Kitty. I had thought that doubling Miss Darcy's estimate would be more than sufficient time to complete your task, but again you have proven that I cannot trust you. And where is your fichu? Have you decided to give over even the appearance of modesty?" Something in his tone made Kitty think that he would not have been satisfied no matter when they'd come back. He would have found something to remark on.

"I gave it to their girl to wrap around her hand. Papa, I couldn't just leave her there with a burned hand..."

"Two hours, Kitty! That should have been more than reasonable to deal with three burned hands, and you only had one!" he snapped. "I am at my wit's end. Each time I try to be reasonable, you disregard the few rules I have given you, and each time you act as though I am a monster for being angry when you disobey. What would you have me do? You will remain in your room for the rest of the day. I will have a tray sent up for your dinner. Perhaps Lizzy will have a better idea of what to do with you tomorrow."

Kitty felt that she should be enraged, and fight him about it. But her ankle hurt so much, and she had a headache from fighting so hard to keep from crying, and she just did not have it in her to do more than allow him to lock her into her room. She collapsed onto her bed and closed her eyes. It seemed as though it would be a very long time before she was free again.

CHAPTER 22

*E*arly the following morning, someone woke Kitty by knocking on her door. When she opened it, Amy snuck in hurriedly and turned to Kitty with a broad smile.

"I came to rescue you. I mean to take a carriage into Lambton today to go shopping, and I want you to come with me!"

Kitty hesitated. If her father found out, he would certainly not approve... but if she did not go with Amy, she was facing a long day of boredom locked up in her room. Besides, there could not be any real harm in going to Lambton to shop, no matter what he thought. She went in to Meryton by herself all the time, back home. This was no different. "Let me find my things, and I will be ready to go directly!"

Amy sat on the bed and watched her gather her outer clothes, merrily chatting about anything that came to mind. She hinted that she had overheard the Darcys trying to talk Mr. Bennet out of his present course, and she suspected that Kitty's imprisonment would not last much longer. But even three more seconds would be intolerable to Kitty, and a trip to Lambton would be just the thing to improve her mood.

Amy had planned everything very well. She took Kitty through back hallways and servant's passages, well out of the way of the library or any other area where they might be seen, and smuggled her into the carriage with the greatest efficiency. Kitty had to laugh at her as she climbed in behind.

"You are quite good at this. Have you had much practice?"

"Not yet, but if I am successful here, perhaps I will make a habit of it."

"I hereby give you leave to practice on me as often as you like." Kitty sighed happily and looked around her. "Is this one of Mr. Darcy's carriages?"

"Yes, he said I could have one to go to town today. Though, I think he expected his sister to join me."

"Why didn't she?"

Amy shrugged. "I don't know. I offered, but she said she wasn't inclined to go, and she was rather offended when I suggested we break you out and take you along. I don't know why, for she is as indignant as the rest of us about your treatment. Do you know, even Mr. Knott is being very cold to your father just now."

"I'm sure Papa doesn't mind in the slightest," Kitty said bitterly.

"No, though I find that to be very strange. What kind of man cares so little for the opinions of those with whom he is living? That seems to be a most uncomfortable way of doing things."

"I think Papa is quite comfortable with making other people uncomfortable. This is rather the best kind of punishment for him; it requires him to do nothing that he does not normally do with his day, and makes me miserable."

"Well, it's abominable."

Kitty was inclined to agree, but she was not inclined to continue the discussion, and changed the subject.

They arrived in Lambton and set off for the shops. There were very few of them, but Amy was determined to find something new that would catch the Colonel's attention. Her efforts so far in that direction had shown some promise, but were not bearing as much fruit as she had hoped, and she thought this might succeed in turning his head.

"There are a lot of lovely ribbons in this one," said Kitty, pointing in one of the display windows. "You could certainly do something remarkable with them."

They agreed to go in and have a look, and once inside they exclaimed over nearly all of the wares in the store. "There's more in here than you would expect from the outside!" Kitty said in delight. "Look, there is a whole other room back here with ribbons and lace, and a wall of bonnets to trim with them!"

"Yes but if I were to purchase a bonnet I would have to come up with a reason to wear it in his presence, and those have not been very easy to come by, of late. He has kept quite to himself and the other gentlemen, and I often see him only at dinner."

Kitty blinked in surprise; she had seen so much of Mr. Knott lately that she had assumed that Colonel Fitzwilliam had often been nearby as well, but upon reflection, she realized that she did not recall him being present nearly as frequently. "Well," she said, "I think there would be something in here that might do for you."

Amy agreed to go look, and they dove into the back room, but their tastes proved to be very different. She was immediately drawn to some lace which Kitty thought very ugly, and Kitty quickly lost interest in her exclamations over it. She wandered back toward the front, and looked for more of what she had seen in the front display. She walked to the window to remind herself what it looked like, and in doing so, glanced out the window and nearly jumped backwards into a display of fabric.

There, across the street, were Mr. and Mrs. Johns, walking arm in arm toward the shop window in which Kitty stood!

Kitty froze. Of course they would be in Lambton! Edgepark was not so very far away, and there were any number of reasons why they might need to come to Lambton—but today! Now! They were coming closer and Kitty still could not decide what to do.

Part of her wanted to run over and demand some kind of explanation, or apology, or something. He was as handsome and fashionable as ever, and she felt the old hope surge for a moment when she looked at him. Surely she deserved some kind of acknowledgement from him of what he had done to her. But Mrs. Johns hung on his arm, and she couldn't bring herself to confront her again. Besides, if word should get out to her father, he might actually kill her.

Sense prevailed, and she fled back into the room where Amy was still looking at ribbons. She couldn't bring herself to say anything. In fact, she was shaking so much, she didn't trust herself to speak without betraying something. But the bell on the shop door never rang, and after a few moments Kitty thought it might be safe to peek out. There was no sign of them in the shop, nor in the street. Wherever they had gone, Kitty was safe. She returned to Amy in utter relief.

"I think I should get this one, but this ribbon looks so much better with the lace, and I must have this lace," she was saying. "What do you think, Kitty?"

Kitty looked at them and shook her head. "I think you should get the ribbon you like and not worry about the lace." Privately, she thought it was the ugliest piece of lace in the shop, but she did not want to say that. "That ribbon is much prettier and goes better with your complexion."

"But what about the lace?"

"That ribbon doesn't need lace. It stands on its own."

Miss Pratt stared at them for a few moments longer, but eventually decided to get the ribbon she liked better and the lace, and trim two of her dresses. Kitty chose not to say anything. They were back in the carriage directly.

"Well, that didn't take long at all! Where shall we go next?" Amy said.

Kitty shook her head. She could not risk encountering Mr. Johns. "As much as it pains me to say it, we should probably return me to Pemberley and my room. I should hate for my father to come looking for me and find my room empty. I am certain that he would never forgive me."

"Why would he come looking for you? I am sure you are safe until dinner, at least."

"But if I am not, what will he say? He didn't believe that I did not return late on purpose yesterday. He would never truly believe that I have done nothing wrong today, even if I had not, and we both know that I have."

Amy rolled her eyes and looked as though she wanted to argue more, but after a moment she shrugged her shoulders. "Very well, as you wish. To Pemberley, and back to jail with you."

"Thank you." Kitty laughed and shook her head. "But if you sneak back in tomorrow, perhaps I will be able to help you trim your dresses. You know I have a knack for it."

Amy agreed halfheartedly, and they lapsed into silence. Kitty could not stop thinking about the glimpse she had seen of Mr. Johns.

Finally she decided to seek her friend's opinion. She described the scene briefly. "I did not know what to do! Should I have confronted him? Or acknowledged him?"

"I do not blame you at all for avoiding him if that miserable Camilla was with him," said Amy. "She would not have been kinder to you today than she was at Pemberley. But if you do ever encounter him by himself, I think you have every right to ask him to explain his behavior to you."

"Do you indeed? I had hoped you would say so. I don't think there is anything he could tell me that would satisfy me about his behavior, but I do think it would be right to give him the opportunity to try."

"At least he owes you an apology. But if you can avoid a very public confrontation, you ought to do it, because I cannot imagine that either of you would like to have witnesses to the conversation."

Kitty shuddered. "No, not at all." She lapsed into thought, rehearsing again what she might have done differently if she had known that Mr. Johns was married. She ignored Amy for the rest of the journey, and allowed her to lead them back through the deserted halls they'd come by.

INTERLUDE

ELIZABETH WAS NOT SURPRISED when her father appeared at her study door. Georgiana had told her enough of what had happened the previous day that she could guess the rest, and the expression on his face confirmed her suspicions. She welcomed him in and, uncomfortable being the one behind the desk after years of sitting in front of his, set her chair beside his. He sank into it with a heavy sigh.

"You overdid it." She smiled, but she meant it.

"How can she get into trouble when she doesn't leave the house? I thought it was sound enough."

"Where is she now?"

"I took her to her room. I didn't know what else to do with her, and she was clearly exhausted. She will sleep, and I can try to determine what on earth I'm supposed to do with her now."

Elizabeth shifted in her chair. She didn't know how much she could say, but she had to say something. "I'm not convinced you need to do anything. Kitty has been dealt a serious blow with the loss of Mr. Johns, and it is likely to be enough to force her to reconsider her behavior. She may no longer need your rules. You could try trusting her."

He glanced at her out of the corner of his eye. "That failed me with Lydia."

"Trusting Mrs. Forster failed. But Kitty has shown no inclination to follow Lydia's path, has she? And surely you can trust Mr. Darcy and I."

"I certainly do not trust that Pratt creature."

Sighing, Elizabeth stood up and began to pace the room. "Neither do I, but fortunately, neither does anyone else. It appears that even Kitty has cooled toward her lately. Have you not noticed? She has turned much more toward Miss Darcy, to my immense relief. It appears that Miss Pratt knows Mrs. Johns, somehow, and that seems to have set Kitty against her."

"They certainly sit and giggle together as much as they ever have."

"Kitty is not giggling, lately." She stopped before his chair, one eyebrow raised in a remarkably good approximation of his most sarcastic look. "For a man who prides himself on his observation of others, you seem to have observed very little of your own daughter."

"What is there to observe? She has not changed, and there is precious little to interest me in her folly."

Elizabeth rolled her eyes and couldn't help a slight laugh. "You might be surprised, if you would take the time to look. She is no longer Lydia's second! She is confused, certainly—she is at a confusing age. But she is learning to take responsibility for herself, and to value truth and steadfastness, and to seek more lasting qualities in her friends than momentary amusement." She paused for a moment. "I don't imagine you've noticed the way Mr. Knott watches her, either, have you?"

He shook his head. "He certainly does take her side more often than I would expect from a man of sense, yet he seems sensible enough in every other way. But I cannot judge him; he is not the first man to find that a pretty face can drive away a man's rational thought."

"Kitty is not as flighty as Mama," Elizabeth said, her voice low and tight. "Not anymore. Please, Papa. Don't do anything right now. Observe her, and try to see the young lady she is becoming, rather than the girl she was. I tried your patience well enough myself in my younger days, and I turned out all right. Give Kitty the opportunity to grow up. She is safe here, and she cannot learn without a few failures along the way. This is the best place for her to learn."

He sat in silence for a long time, and even though Elizabeth knew better than to say more yet, she was still tempted to break the silence. She held her ground, though, and at long last he rewarded her with a heavy sigh as he stood up. "I will leave it in your hands, then, for the time being." He hesitated, and Elizabeth saw in that moment a glimpse of the weight he carried. Her heart cracked. "I cannot let it happen again, Lizzy."

"Trust me," she said, her voice barely above a whisper.

He nodded and patted her shoulder as he let himself out, closing the door behind him. Elizabeth fell against the back of her chair and sighed. If this was what parenting was like, she was rather glad that she did not yet have children.

BACK IN HER ROOM, Kitty took off her outer things and flung them thoughtlessly over a chair. It had been stupid to go with Amy. Even if they hadn't actually encountered Mr. Johns, they had come far too close. And what if her father had found out that she'd left? She could have set herself back weeks in her punishment! Why had she listened to Amy? Her stomach clenched. There were too many things that could have gone wrong, and she hadn't thought of a single one of them. No wonder her father didn't trust her sense. She was beginning to see his point.

Another knock came at the door, and she hesitated. She dreaded seeing Amy again. But when she opened it, Mr. Bennet stood before her.

"Papa!"

He raised one eyebrow. "You sound surprised to see me. Were you expecting someone else?"

"I was not expecting anyone."

"Ah. You were expecting me to keep you imprisoned here until you die of old age."

"No, only until you do."

He took a step back, surprised. Then, to Kitty's astonishment, he started to laugh. "Well, it looks like your sister's wit has not escaped you entirely! Well, well, well." He had a good chuckle, but Kitty could not appreciate her success in her present mood.

"Have you decided to free me, then, sir?" she ventured at last.

"Yes, in a manner of speaking. Mr. Knott and Lizzy have conspired against me, and insisted that you would not learn the error of your ways if you were left to stew in your own thoughts. They proposed the alternative of more directed interaction with them and with Miss Darcy, to observe your behavior and modify it where necessary, under more practical conditions."

Kitty blinked at him. Did this mean she was free? Or, at least, more free than she had been? Better not to ask specifics. She would probably learn more from asking Lizzy, anyway. "Thank you, sir." She hesitated, wondering whether it was really wise to press her luck. "Sir? Might I come down to dinner with the rest of the party this evening?"

He shook his head. "Against my better judgment, you are free to move about the house as you like."

Kitty did not squeal, and she was very proud of herself for that. She thanked her father calmly, and managed to keep her composure until he left. Then she couldn't help herself. She danced around the room until she collapsed onto the bed, laughing.

CHAPTER 23

*M*r. Bennet was true to his word, and the next morning after breakfast he retreated to the library while the rest of the party gathered in the drawing room. Mr. Darcy and Colonel Fitzwilliam soon departed to inspect some place or other on Pemberley's land; Kitty did not pay much attention. She was more interested to see exactly what the morning would bring, with Mr. Knott and Lizzy (such an odd combination of personalities to have struck forth on such a mission together!) working together to observe her and modify her behavior. Whatever that meant.

It appeared to mean nothing out of the ordinary. Mr. Knott offered to read to them, and brought out another chapter of *The Absentee* when they accepted. Miss Pratt hovered near Kitty's chair, hardly attending to the story. As soon as the chapter ended, she practically pounced on Kitty.

"I am so glad you are free at last!" she cried, settling herself down as close to Kitty as she could get. "Your father has finally shown some sense."

"I believe I am indebted to my sister and Mr. Knott for that. He says that they persuaded him to take a different approach in correcting the faults in my character."

"Faults in your character? Nonsense. The only flaw *I* can find is too great a willingness to do as your father tells you to, and a perverse sort of forgetfulness when it comes to me."

Kitty had to protest. "Forget you? How have I ever done that?"

"You promised me that you would help me attract Colonel Fitzwilliam! Yet, when he announces that he will be spending the whole day away from us, and I can say nothing to him in my distress, you are silent! You have not stirred yourself on my behalf in a long time, Kitty." She picked at a pulled thread in her skirt. "Not that I wholly blame you, of course. There have been so many others who have taken your time and attention away from me. And of course you are quite desolate without Mr. Johns."

Kitty was suddenly very, very conscious of the others in the room, all of whom appeared to be very carefully not listening to her, as quietly as possible. "I would not say that I am... quite desolate," she faltered. How should she feel about him? She felt... mostly confused, particularly because everyone had such wildly varying opinions about whether she was at fault. She had liked him a great deal. She still liked him a great deal, if her reaction to his handsome figure in Lambton yesterday was any indication.

"Of course you are! I know you were very much attached to him, and for him to have pulled such a cruel trick on you would be devastating to anyone." She reached out to pat Kitty's hand, but Kitty drew it away almost unconsciously. "But he is lost to you forever, and you really must move on to new projects. Helping me would give you a renewed sense of purpose, don't you think? And it would be such fun!"

Kitty tried to gather her old enthusiasm for helping a friend find love, but she could not manage it for Amy's sake. She had gone through a bizarre ordeal, and where had Amy been through all that? If she was so worried about Colonel Fitzwilliam that she neglected her friend, well, they could have each other and Kitty would happily leave them alone. They seemed to want her to leave them alone, except when it was convenient for them. "I don't think I will be of any help to you, Amy. Truly—you've seen what a mess I can make of things."

She waved her hand. "Oh, that's nothing. None of it was your fault, anyway. And all I want is to find a way to spend some time with the Colonel alone, without Mr. Darcy always interfering. Could you not just pull your brother away and give me some space to work?"

"What on earth would I have to say to Mr. Darcy, of all people?" The very idea frightened her. He might have intimidated her less now than he had at first, but that did not mean she wished to seek him out for conversation. "Besides, he speaks to Elizabeth and Georgiana often enough. Wait until one of them has his attention."

"That doesn't work. Colonel Fitzwilliam is more often than not with him. They're thick as thieves, those two. I have no idea of how to tease them apart."

Georgiana came over at that moment, to Kitty's relief. "Forgive me, but—as it is my cousin and my brother you are discussing, would you not rather have my help?"

Amy accepted with an enthusiasm calculated to make Kitty feel guilty, and even though she knew it she still felt bad. But Georgiana would not be more helpful to her. She was interrogating Amy about her expectations regarding the Colonel, and Amy started to look rather uncomfortable. Kitty, who had no desire to witness the developing disaster, slipped away and went to join Mr. Knott and Elizabeth.

"It's good to see you freed," Elizabeth said, smiling.

"Yes," said Mr. Knott. He watched Kitty closely, but said nothing more, and Kitty shifted uncomfortably in her seat, muttering a less grateful thanks to Elizabeth than she knew she deserved.

He was certainly taking his task seriously, but did he really think that she needed such scrutiny?

She hadn't thought so. Up until this point, he had been a certain ally, but now she started to question his true allegiance. She couldn't think of anything else to say. She probably appeared more stupid than anything at that moment.

Elizabeth must have sensed her distress, because she turned the conversation away from her. "How is your mother, Mr. Knott?"

He blinked and looked over to her as if he'd forgotten about Elizabeth. But his confusion faded immediately, and then he was polite and attentive as ever. "Very poorly, I'm afraid. My father insists that I do not need to come home to her yet, but I can't help reading between the lines of his letters. I expect to need to go to her soon."

"Why do you not just go to her now? That way you can be sure to see her," Kitty said.

"If I did not have things I still need to do here, I would." His tone was mild, but it clashed strangely with the intensity with which he looked at her. How did he expect her to respond? Kitty wondered whether she would rather go back and plot with Amy over Colonel Fitzwilliam. At least there she had not worried about what they would tell her father of every word she spoke. And whether he would approve.

No one spoke for a few minutes. Kitty was unable to inquire further, and Elizabeth unwilling, so that line of conversation seemed dead, and no one introduced anything new. Kitty could hardly look at either of them. She knew they were judging her, and given her present behavior, probably not coming to any favorable conclusions about her. Worse, she still could think of nothing to say, or do, that would put her in a better light.

But a sudden recollection inspired her. Was she not trying to make Mr. Knott fall in love with Georgiana? Perhaps she could use this time to promote her friend's interest a little bit. Surely there could be nothing wrong with that, if she proceeded carefully. She glanced over to where Georgiana sat, and winced. Miss Darcy was showing the strain of her conversation with Amy—if it could be called a conversation, because it looked like Amy was doing all the talking. "Poor Miss Darcy!" she said, almost involuntarily.

Elizabeth glanced over and sighed. "I wish she did not take things so seriously as she does. I know that Miss Pratt is not the friend she remembers, but she should not feel so ashamed for not liking her as much as she'd expected to."

"It is difficult to be so disappointed in a friend, though," Mr. Knott said. "Particularly one of whom you have fond memories."

Kitty smiled a little bit. "That sounds like the voice of experience."

"Indeed it is. I know the pain of finding an old friend so altered that resuming the friendship is impossible. You mourn for the person they were, and if you are not careful, you may come to resent the person they have become."

"Perhaps you might advise Miss Darcy in handling it," Kitty said, feeling very clever about her suggestion.

But he did not take it as eagerly as she had expected. "Perhaps, if she would wish it. But my advice would be to do much what she is already doing. What else is there, but to try to love them for the sake of your old friendship, and bear with them as best you can?" He shrugged. "You are fortunate, Miss Bennet, if you have never had this experience."

Kitty never had, that she could think of, and she shook her head slowly. "It sounds painful."

"It is. But then, so much of life is painful, isn't it? Try as you might, you'll never avoid it."

He glanced over at Georgiana as he spoke, and Kitty wondered whether she had made a mistake in bringing her to his attention. Perhaps things were not progressing as well as he wanted in that area —perhaps she had made them worse by trying to interfere. She blushed and changed the subject back to him. It was safer that way. She would not make a mess of Georgiana's love life, as she had made of her own and Miss Pratt's.

THE MORNINGS BECAME MUCH BETTER. Georgiana and Mr. Knott were always ready to be her companions, and seemed to conspire together to find new ways to amuse her. Miss Pratt did not join her as often as they did, and the others almost never, but Kitty did not mind so much. They had resumed their regular morning reads of *The Absentee*, though Mr. Knott generally constrained them to about a chapter a day, insisting that his voice could not bear much more sustained reading.

To Miss Pratt, indeed, Kitty was rather colder than before. She had not wholly forgiven Amy's selfishness, and as Amy seemed perfectly unrepentant, little induced her to seek reconciliation. Kitty was sad to see a promising friendship dissolve in that way, but she reminded herself that she had Georgiana, who seemed to be a much better friend.

This morning, Kitty sat on the sofa, her work forgotten in her lap as she listened to the story, her eyes fixed on Mr. Knott. Lost in the story, she forgot about her own troubles entirely. When Mr. Knott finished the chapter, he looked up to see Kitty staring at him, and smiled at her. Kitty quickly looked away.

"It's an engaging story, is it not, Miss Bennet?"

"Yes, very. Are you sure you can only do one chapter today?"

He laughed a little. "Quite sure, unfortunately, lest I lose my voice entirely. But that means I will have a captive audience tomorrow, doesn't it?"

"And every day until the story ends," Georgiana added, smiling at Kitty. "It is a wonderfully captivating story." She turned to Mr. Knott. "And where does the rest of your morning take you, Sir?"

He placed the ribbon back in the book and set it on the table next to him. "In fact, it doesn't take me anywhere. I have absolutely no plans today, and am completely at your disposal, ladies, if you wish me to be."

"At our disposal! What shall we do with him, then, Georgiana?" Kitty asked. She saw this for the compliment to her friend that it must be, and renewed her determination to promote their mutual interest however she could.

"Our options are sadly limited, Mr. Knott. I'm afraid we can offer you no greater pleasure than our conversation and company." Georgiana smiled at him.

"You say that as though your conversation and company will be no great pleasure, and I can assure you that is not the case. But I thought, perhaps, that you had contrived some sort of plan to prove to Mr. Bennet that his daughter is not so hopeless as he seems to suspect."

Kitty blushed, remembering their conversation and the advice he had given, and which she had not followed. "I am sorry to say that I have not. I simply have no aptitude for the kinds of things he values."

"You are not as bad as you have convinced yourself you are." Georgiana shook her head reproachfully. "I fear your greatest flaw is simply that you do not think to conceal your feelings, as polite society so often demands."

"I know the frustration of not being able to express myself the way I would wish. You have my sympathy, Miss Bennet." Mr. Knott bowed to them both with exaggerated formality and they laughed. "But I would encourage you, Miss Bennet, not to abandon the pursuit of self-improvement altogether. It is my belief that we ought always to be looking for ways to improve ourselves—either learning new things, or practicing new skills, or meeting new people. It is not good to stagnate."

Kitty thought this a very pretty speech, and very much in line with what Georgiana would likely think about the matter, but she found it harder to agree. "That is very easy for a gentleman to say. You have more advantage than we have. You can improve yourself, where we are forced to wait for someone else to help us improve. I cannot simply go learn to do something new; I have to wait for someone to teach me. And there are so many fewer things that I am permitted to learn."

"There are many things a lady may teach herself, given the proper tools," Georgiana protested. "I taught myself to draw, with no formal instruction for many years, because I found pleasure in it. I copied the illustrations I found in books and pamphlets as well as drawing from life. My art improved a great deal during that time, and it was not until I was living in London that my brother engaged a master to further my skill. By then I had mastered the basics, and my master could focus on refining my technique."

"But there still came a point at which you could go no further; and besides, I have no interest in drawing."

"What does interest you, Miss Bennet?" Mr. Knott asked.

She paused. She really had no idea, the more she thought about it. She like dancing, and parties, and gossip, and pretty things. And she realized rather suddenly that she did like visiting Pemberley's tenants, which surprised her. It was hardly a skill she could refine, however. "I don't really know."

He leaned over to Georgiana, and said, "I think we have found the problem, Miss Darcy."

"The problem is not where we were stuck. What is the solution?"

"You speak as though there is something wrong with not endeavoring to learn something new each day, but I can be perfectly content with the things I already know!" Kitty said, a little embarrassed and a little resentful that they should have come together against her, however pleased she was that they were coming together over something.

"Can you? Do you not think you would tire of it, eventually?" Georgiana asked. "How many days in a row can you sit doing needlework alone before you go completely out of your mind? Variation in one's daily routine is essential."

"If my father hadn't forbade—"

"Your father can forbid you to do many things, but he cannot forbid you to learn entirely. The responsibility of seeking new occupations lies with you, in the end."

"Besides," added Georgiana, "if you intend to marry, you will want as many accomplishments as you can have. The ability to learn new things is very important when you are going to be living in a new house, with new people, and must learn a new way of life."

Kitty shook her head. "That hardly matters, as I shall never marry."

"You still haven't come around to that, have you?" Georgiana nodded in a way that made Kitty feel as though she knew better. "Well, then, I suppose there's nothing we can say to you yet."

Mr. Knott, however, was not quite so resigned. "What makes you believe that, Miss Bennet? I am certain that you are not entirely without hope."

"Then you are more certain than I am. What man would wish to risk his reputation by tying it to me? Clearly I cannot be trusted to behave myself properly, and I am not accomplished enough to attract anyone, as Miss Darcy noted." Georgiana started to protest, but Kitty would not let her interrupt. "I am well aware that I am not the kind of young lady whose attractions are sufficient to tempt any man. My sisters will all be married before me—even the plainest and most boorish of us is engaged! If even Mary can find a husband before me, I must learn to be content with the reality that I have no hope."

"You do not really believe that," Mr. Knott said. "You have let your father corrupt your thoughts about yourself until you do not see the reality of the situation any longer."

Kitty shook her head. She did not *want* to believe it, but could see no other real alternative. "I have no evidence to convince me that I am wrong."

Mr. Knott got to his feet rather suddenly, and looked as though he wanted to continue the argument, but he said nothing and walked over to the window to compose himself. Instead, Miss Darcy sat beside Kitty and took up both of her hands. "I know how you feel, Kitty. You know I do. But believe me when I say that this feeling will not last forever. You will find, one day, that you do hope for the love of a good man, and you do not think yourself entirely unworthy of it." She glanced at Mr. Knott. "And if you have been so fortunate as to earn the love of such a man, would you really turn him down for the sake of your own opinion of yourself?"

"I suppose not," Kitty said, sighing. "But it would never happen."

She raised her eyebrows. "And if you fell in love?"

"I can only strive not to."

Georgiana shook her head and patted Kitty's hand. "Don't strive too hard, dear." She looked at Mr. Knott again, but he did not turn away from the window.

CHAPTER 24

The following day, Kitty found herself too restless and irritable for company. Instead, she roamed the halls of Pemberley, hoping that by the time she encountered anybody her mood would have improved. She wandered alone for some time without seeing a soul except the formidable Darcy ancestors, watching her progress from their painted chambers. The portrait gallery was an intimidating place, indeed, and Mr. Darcy's portrait seemed to fit in very well with his fathers: tall, and stern, and fully convinced of his proper place in the world. Kitty did not like it at all.

At the end of the gallery, however, she encountered Mr. Knott, and his cheerful company soon warmed her to the idea of companionship. "Miss Bennet!" he said with a broad smile and a bow. "I was hoping to find you, when you did not join us in the breakfast room."

She returned his bow and his smile. "And found me you have, Mr. Knott; what do you propose to do with me now?" It struck her as the words left her lips that they were rather too flirtatious to be offered to a clergyman, and she wondered whether her father would have punished her if he'd heard it, but Mr. Knott did not seem to mind in the slightest.

"If you will permit me, I thought we might share in a walk about the grounds this morning. I enjoyed our last walk very much, and I have been anxious to repeat the experience without the unpleasant confrontation at the end."

Kitty laughed incredulously. "You enjoyed listening to me complain about my pitiful life? Well, I don't see why we need to wander around out of doors to replicate that experience, and I do not claim to be as strong a walker as my sister. But if you truly wish it, I will not object."

His answering smile was a little less certain. "I had not meant to suggest—that is, I truly enjoy your company, Miss Bennet, and whatever topic of conversation you choose I will entertain gladly, but I rather meant that I wished to walk about the grounds, and would like your company. We could talk about anything you like. Perhaps a happier subject might be preferable?"

She could see his awkward attempt to back the conversation up and she realized with a jolt of shame that he thought she was offended. "Forgive me; I had not meant to make you uncomfortable. I have apparently inherited too much of my sister's propensity to tease. Allow me to fetch my bonnet and my shawl, and I will happily join you for a walk." She smiled to reassure him. "Shall I meet you at the garden door in ten minutes?"

That brought the smile back to his face in full force. "Yes, of course. I will see you very shortly." He left her with a spring in his step that Kitty only half noticed as she went to find her effects.

She met him at the door a few minutes early, though he had still arrived before her. He had a small picnic basket in hand. She greeted him with a smile and took his arm when he offered it, and he led her out into the sunshine. She was immediately very glad that she had brought her parasol as well as her bonnet.

"Where shall we go, Mr. Knott?" she asked as they walked past the kitchen garden. "I have not explored very much of Pemberley's grounds, and I am quite at your mercy."

"Do you wish to see more of it than you have seen already?"

She giggled a little bit. "I have seen so very little of it that I suspect I will see more no matter what we do."

"Very well; I shall take you to my favorite place on the grounds. It is almost as long a walk as we took last time, however. Will you be able to manage it?"

"I should imagine so, if you are able to help me," she said.

"You will have my unflagging support," he said with a twinkle in his eye, and he led them off onto a much smaller path that moved directly north of the house. Mr. Knott chatted away as they walked, pointing out things that he thought would interest Kitty, or that she might not have seen before. She appreciated it, but she didn't quite understand; he had never been so uncomfortable with silence before, and now he seemed terrified of it. Had she said something wrong yesterday?

But eventually Mr. Knott trailed off and said no more, and she was perfectly content to take in the scenery as they strolled. It felt so good to give herself up to the joy of the breeze that tossed the tassels on her parasol, and the green land that stretched out around them. Eventually, however, she could not fail to notice her companion's silence, and she glanced at him questioningly. He was watching her with an earnest look in his eyes and a smile just touching the corners of his mouth, and it did not help her confusion one bit.

"Do you take this way often, then?" she asked, if only to recall herself.

"Quite often since I arrived here, yes. In fact, since I discovered it— or, rather, since Colonel Fitzwilliam showed it to me—I have come out almost every day. It is one of the most enchanting places I have ever been, even within Pemberley. I half hope that Mr. Darcy grants me that living just so that I may come out here whenever I like." He smiled at his joke and Kitty smiled back. She hoped that Mr. Darcy did give him the living. It would be so much nicer to know that Mr. Knott might become a friend whom she could look forward to meeting with whenever she came to visit her sister, someone who would not judge her for being herself and someone no one else could judge her for visiting. Perhaps she could join him on this walk again in the future. So far it was as lovely as he had claimed.

"You will have to make very good friends with Mr. Darcy so that he allows you to come visit whether or not he grants you the living," she said.

"Perhaps I might impose on your friendship."

She shrugged. "Perhaps you might indeed, though I do not know if I will live at Pemberley for ever. Mrs. Darcy and I are not particularly close." She had not meant it as more than an offhand comment of the way she saw things, but he seemed to take it as something more of an invitation.

"Are you closer to others of your sisters, then? It would be a shame if none of them saw you as a valuable companion."

"I used to be much closer to my younger sister Lydia, but she has married and moved away, even further north than this, and I do not see her much any longer. And she was never a very good correspondent, so she does not write me as often as I write her. I feel as though we have fallen away from each other since she married." She hesitated, looking out across the landscape as she decided how much to share. She was not really in the mood to open the doors she had opened on their last talk together. "I do not know how much you know about the circumstances surrounding her wedding, but they were a bit... unusual. My father was most displeased with her conduct in the matter, as were Lizzy and my sister Jane, and I'm afraid their opinions of her have altered their opinions of me."

"That seems markedly unfair."

"Doesn't it? But I suppose Lydia and I were always a unit in their minds. We were so rarely apart that they probably began to think of us as just 'Kitty and Lydia' rather than two distinct people." She did not say that sometimes she felt the same way, that she was somehow a lesser extension of Lydia, and that people loved her only in as much as they loved her younger sister. Lydia had always been the recipient of greater affection.

"Has that not changed since your sister married, and moved so far away?"

"Decidedly not," Kitty said with a strange little laugh, half strangled before it left her throat. "Otherwise I would be visiting her, instead of here at Pemberley, for she has invited me to come to her many times and I have always been denied permission."

That silenced him for a few minutes, and Kitty was grateful for the time to recompose herself. She really did not want to have this conversation right now. Finally, though, he said in a very quiet tone, "Do you regret that you were able to come to Pemberley, instead?"

She thought about that for a long while. She regretted what had happened with Mr. Johns, and to a lesser extent, Miss Pratt. But she was very glad to have made such a friend in Miss Darcy, and in her current companion. And it was not such a bad thing to know that one would never be married, and know the path of one's life. Even if it wasn't the path she would have chosen for herself. "No," she said at last. But he did not respond, and she did not know what else to say, and so they walked in silence again, this time more awkward.

Fortunately, they were not far from the destination he had in mind, which made itself inescapably clear when they rounded a corner on the path and into view came an old ruin.

"Oh!" breathed Kitty. It was a spectacular sight. The roof had almost entirely crumbled, and the walls were losing the battle with the green things that were taking over the whole place. The floor, or what had been the floor, was largely carpeted in tall grass, but in the corners which still stood there were wildflowers growing. At the north side, a large tree had grown up behind the structure, its branches reaching through empty windows and over the top of the wall, which provided a lovely, large shaded area. There was even a little stone bench along the wall, still mostly intact. Kitty could not wait to explore it all. She turned back to Mr. Knott, her admiration clear in her expression.

Mr. Knott's face lit up. "Do you like it? I had thought you would."

"It's incredible! What did it used to be?"

"It was a monastery, as I understand from Colonel Fitzwilliam. King Henry VIII had the whole thing burned to the ground when the monks defied him on some point or other—I wasn't clear on what. Apparently he then gave the land to the Darcy family after they did him some favor. Precisely what is lost to history, I'm afraid.

"The Colonel took me out here the day after we arrived. He and Mr. Darcy used to play here as boys, and it has been a favorite spot of the Darcy family for generations."

"I can see why. Can you imagine bringing a party here to explore together? What a charming afternoon that would be!"

"I would imagine that it is frequently the destination for that very thing. The ruins are convenient enough to make it a popular choice, and set off enough from everything else that you feel as though you had discovered a hidden treasure every time you come across it."

They walked all over it, poking their noses into every area they could reach. Mr. Knott explained what all the rooms used to be, if he knew, and he knew most of them.

"You sound almost as though you wish you lived here," Kitty said. "Do you really wish you had been a monk?"

He laughed. "No. But there are things about their lifestyle that appeal to me, I will admit. It would at least be a very clear way of dedicating one's life to God, to join such a place. To sit with one's brothers every day, and worship together, and serve the world around us—it could be a very good life. Just imagine this place, filled with brothers who loved each other and loved God, and tell me you do not understand the appeal just a little bit."

Kitty looked around the dining hall in which they stood, its blackened tables long left to rot into the ground. For half a moment she could see it as it must have been, centuries ago, when the monks gathered here for meals, and perhaps to sing their chants. But she shook her head. "It sounds immensely dull, to be honest."

"Dull! You are not imagining aright. Think of it this way: take the enjoyment you have in serving Pemberley's tenants, and multiply that by the time and the joy you would receive in serving a whole community for a lifetime. For you know, monasteries were not just a place to seclude oneself from the world—not all of them. Some of them were about creating safe places for people who were in trouble, and providing the people nearby with food and spiritual guidance." His eyes shone as he envisioned it. "And they were all about making the ultimate show of devotion, in giving everything up to follow God."

"I do not think I could do that," Kitty said, her voice very much softened by his sincerity.

Mr. Knott laughed, and broke the spell. "Neither could I, to be honest. I am sure I would enjoy myself immensely for about a week, and then I would become so miserably bored, and frustrated, that I would do anything to break my vow and leave. I need more variety in my service than a monastery would have been able to provide me."

"I'm sure the monks would have been very offended to hear you say that." Kitty giggled.

"Probably they would have. I'm sure they could tell me seven hundred different reasons why I ought to give up my foolish notions and join them, but there are too many joys in living in the world for me to ever really do it." He smiled a little and looked at her out of the corner of his eye. "Besides, I don't think I could vow to never marry."

"No," Kitty agreed, "it took me a very long time to get to the point that I could contemplate it. But I don't suppose I would have had much of a choice. I'm sure that if my father had the option, he would have thrown me into a monastery long ago, and had done with me." She sighed and sat down on one of the larger stones that had fallen. "In some ways, it probably would have been much easier for him."

"And much worse for you," Mr. Knott said quietly. He looked down at his shoes, and then slowly started to walk around the perimeter of the huge dining area.

She said nothing when he came back, feeling somehow that it would be rude to interrupt his thoughts. They stood and looked about themselves in silence, until Mr. Knott cleared his throat and gestured to the picnic basket. "Are you hungry? I had a few bites packed for us."

She helped Mr. Knott spread the blanket on one of the larger stones and set out the food he'd brought. It did look delicious: cold meats, fruit, and some of those delicate little rolls that Pemberley's cook made better than anyone. She complimented him on his taste, and wasted no time in starting to eat.

Mr. Knott, however, was strangely quiet. He responded to everything Kitty said, but no more, and after a little while she stopped trying to engage him in conversation. It wasn't worth continuing to try. But she couldn't help wondering, privately, what had gotten into him.

At last he stood before her and said, with some excess of breath, "Miss Bennet, I am afraid that I will have to go away tomorrow, and I do not know when I will be able to come back."

Kitty had absolutely no idea how to respond to this, and so did not respond at all. Mr. Knott did not appear to take that as an encouraging sign, as he hesitated and started pacing again. Kitty decided to try to speak instead. "I am very sorry to hear that. I have enjoyed our conversations together, Mr. Knott, very much." She still did not know what to say, and her expression must have made that plain. He stopped pacing and came to stand in front of her again.

"Thank you, Miss Bennet." His relief was palpable, and Kitty took pity on him. She stood up and took his arm, and gently led him in a slow circuit of the exterior of the ruin.

"Do you mind my asking what it is that takes you away so suddenly?"

"My mother's illness has taken a very bad turn, and my father thinks that it is best that I come home as quickly as possible."

"I am very sorry!" she said. She could not imagine what he must feel, to be away from home at such a time.

"So am I." He swallowed audibly and pressed on. "I had hoped to be able to spend more time at Pemberley. I have enjoyed the company very much. I expected to find the Darcys to be as pleasant as their cousin, and I believe they are, but I was not anticipating as many opportunities for pleasant conversation and exercise as I have found with you. I hope you will permit me to tell you how much I will miss your company, and how much I regret having to leave."

Again, Kitty had no idea how to respond. She felt as though he were expecting a response that she did not know how to provide, and she certainly did not know what it was. Still, obviously he expected some answer, and she did her best to make one. "I am sure my brother will give you the living, Mr. Knott, and if that is so, we shall surely meet again. I do not imagine that I will behave myself so terribly that my sister refuses to ever invite me to Pemberley again." She smiled encouragingly at him. "And we still plan to stay for some time yet. If you are able to return sooner than you now appear to fear, we may meet again in a month or two."

"I very much hope that is the case, Miss Bennet. Very much indeed. I had hoped—that is, I felt that you might—would you be glad to see me, if I came back?"

"Of course I would. I am always glad to see a good friend, and you have been a very good friend to me." She thought she understood now; he had not been sure whether their conversations were in the light of friendship or whether she expected him to take on the role of a clergyman to her before he had adopted a flock of his own. There, at least, she could set his mind at ease. He was the only clergyman she had ever met whom she would consider a friend.

He thanked her but could not appear to find more to say, and they finished their tour of the ruin with only the chirping of birds and the rustling of leaves to listen to. Finally, Kitty could take it no longer, and asked the only question she could think of.

"When do you plan to depart?"

"Today. I ought to have left already, but I wished to—" he glanced at her and cut himself off, shaking his head. "I had a few things left to do."

"Well, I am very glad that you chose to take some time out of your preparations to show me this place!" she said. "I will have to come back here, though I imagine it will not be the same after you are gone."

"I hope it will remind you of me." It was almost a question.

"Of course it will! I could never come here without thinking of the friend who introduced it to me."

Again, he did not respond, and eventually they made it back to the path on which they had arrived. "Should we go back?" she asked, uncertain of what he wanted.

"If you wish it."

"I am entirely at your leisure, but if you need to depart soon, perhaps we should not waste any more time. I am sure your mother will be glad of all the time you can give her."

'Yes, I am sure she will." And he lapsed into silence again. Kitty's frustration with this bizarre conversation grew with every minute. She wished he would just tell her whatever was wrong, but he did not seem so willing to open up to her as she had been willing to open up to him. Perhaps it was a good thing that he was leaving.

But he broke the silence this time, quite suddenly. "You said you lived in the south, Miss Bennet?" he asked with some urgency.

"Yes, in Hertfordshire. We live near Meryton, at Longbourn."

"Do you think I would be welcome there, if I find myself in that area someday?"

"I am certain of it," Kitty said, and she meant it. "My mother would welcome you regardless, and I am sure my father would be happy to see you there." She was less certain of that, but she could not see why her father would not like Mr. Knott, and he had certainly shown every inclination of appreciating his company, so she felt that she could at least say that with some confidence.

"And would you welcome me, if I were to come?"

"Of course, and gladly. I would be happy to show you around Meryton, if you wish it, though there is very little there which I think would interest you."

"I don't know about that; I think I could find all manner of things to captivate me." As he said this, he stopped and looked into her eyes with such solemn meaning that Kitty began to wonder whether there was something else behind his words and his silences that she had failed to understand. She did not think this expression was very congruous with what had gone before. But neither she nor Mr. Knott had any opportunity to clarify the matter, as Colonel Fitzwilliam came riding up at that moment in search of Mr. Knott. His face, on approaching, was drawn and grave.

"Knott," he said, "you must come immediately. Your mother—I have a letter. It just arrived express." He held out the document, and Mr. Knott snatched it from his hand, his face pale. It paled further as he read, and when he finished, he sprang into action immediately, almost mechanically.

"Will you see Miss Bennet back?" he asked.

"Yes, yes; take my horse and go. I will meet you there."

Mr. Knott nodded and turned to Kitty. "Forgive me; I would not leave you except in such circumstances, but as it is..." He shrugged helplessly, and turned and fled.

Kitty stared at him, then at Colonel Fitzwilliam. "What...?"

The colonel came around to her side. "His mother has been very ill lately, and his father has sent for him. They fear it is the end. He must move quickly if he is going to reach her in time to say good-bye." He stooped down and began to pack away the picnic things.

Kitty helped him, but her mind raced away with Mr. Knott. How terrible for him! She wondered how she would feel, if she were away from home and had to be always thinking, always worrying about whether her mother was all right, or whether her health had gotten worse. Her heart went out to Mr. Knott. What a strain he must have been living under! And to have it come to such a conclusion!

The Colonel returned her to the house and promptly left to follow his friend to town. Kitty returned to her morning's wandering, but Pemberley seemed hollow without the gentlemen who had departed, and she could not stop seeing Mr. Knott's face in every shadow.

CHAPTER 25

$\mathcal{D}$inner that evening was a sad shadow of what it had formerly been, with Mr. Knott and Colonel Fitzwilliam gone. Everyone expressed themselves very concerned for Mr. Knott and his family, but no one seemed willing to talk about it, or they simply ignored it by talking about something else. Kitty could not stop thinking of what had happened in the ruin. Was he trying to convince her that she should find another accomplishment to pursue? Perhaps he wanted Kitty's help in deciding whether to propose to Miss Darcy. That could have been it. Surely it would have been an intimidating prospect, for even if Georgiana had been completely encouraging he still would have had to approach Mr. Darcy and Colonel Fitzwilliam with his proposal, and they could not have been pleased by the connection. Kitty did not know how she could be of any help in that regard, but she felt strangely pleased that he had thought to seek her counsel, or even her sympathy.

After dinner, Miss Pratt approached her while she sat with Georgiana. It startled Kitty; she had imagined Miss Pratt to be quite as willing to let their friendship cool as she was, but the look on her face said differently.

"Kitty, can you forgive me for how terribly cruel I acted toward you that day?" She sank onto the chair next to Kitty and clutched her hand. "I have been perfectly desolate without you ever since, but I have been too afraid to seek reconciliation till now. But with so much of our party gone, what will we do if we do not have each other?"

For a brief moment, Kitty considered denying her. She had, after all, been very hurt by what Amy had said and done, and she was not at all convinced that she had been "perfectly desolate" without Kitty's company, when she had her Colonel Fitzwilliam to make love to. What did it mean that she had not come forward with her apologies until now?

But it would be miserable to be trapped in so limited a company with two people whom she wished to avoid, and Miss Pratt did have her good qualities, as long as Kitty stayed within the boundaries of what she would not mock. There were a great many things, Kitty thought bitterly, about which she had to be much more careful than she would like, for fear of making her life more miserable than it had to be.

"Well, all right—I can forgive you," she said. But she pulled her hand away.

"Perhaps she would like to join us for *The Absentee* tomorrow morning?" Georgiana asked Kitty.

"Mr. Knott is gone," Kitty reminded her. "We will have to take turns reading to each other, and I am not half as good a reader as he."

"I can read," Amy said eagerly. "I am not as good as Mr. Knott either, but I can certainly manage a chapter of a novel."

Georgiana looked skeptical, but Kitty, eager to find out how the story would end, agreed to let her.

Mr. Darcy and Mr. Bennet soon joined them, having exhausted, Kitty supposed, the few things they had to say to each other in a very brief span. This limited the ladies' planning for the following morning, but Kitty did not find that she minded. A more general conversation would better benefit her state of mind at the moment, as it would allow her to return to her own thoughts without so readily being noticed. But Georgiana saw that she looked pensive.

"Is something the matter, Kitty?" she asked.

"No..." Kitty said slowly, but she knew it wasn't quite the truth. Something was the matter, only she couldn't quite place what.

"I thought, perhaps, that your father might like to talk to you tonight."

Kitty started. "What? Why?" Had she done something else wrong?

For a moment, Georgiana looked confused, but she covered it quickly. "Only that, as there are no more unmarried gentlemen in the house, and there have been no more disasters, perhaps you might be allowed back into some further society. You know, to dinner parties and the like. Elizabeth received an invitation to a dinner party at the Dawson's for next week, and meant to accept, but she had hoped that you would be able to go with us by then. Has your father not mentioned anything?"

"Nothing," Kitty said, shaking her head miserably. "I suppose he means for me to stay out of society altogether for my whole stay here."

"Well, he has conceded much so far. Perhaps we can talk him out of this, as well." Georgiana patted her hand gently. "It is not entirely hopeless."

"No, only mostly so," Kitty amended.

"Well, if it is, I shall not go either, and remain here with you. I don't love the Dawsons so well that I am not willing to give up their company for an evening in favor of yours."

Miss Pratt overheard this and interjected, "Do you mean the Dawsons who live at North Lavender? Their daughter is such a darling thing. I quite love her."

"Miss Dawson is a very friendly person," Georgiana admitted. "But if Kitty is not allowed to go to their dinner party, I do not feel inclined to go either. I should be far happier to show my support for her and remain here."

"Should you?" Amy looked askance at this. "I think it would be more pleasant for Kitty to let us go, so we can bring her back a description of everything and every one there. If we exercise our powers of description well, we could make her feel as if she had been there."

"Would it not only make it the more painful that she could not be there?" Georgiana asked. Kitty was inclined to agree with her, but more than that, she was inclined to keep peace between the two of them. She did not want to find herself trapped between two friends at war with each other.

"If it comes to that," Kitty said, "I will send Amy, and keep Georgiana, and then both of you are satisfied, and I have the joy of company for the evening and a description of what I missed."

Neither Amy nor Georgiana seemed perfectly satisfied with this answer but they allowed the subject to be dropped.

THE NEXT MORNING brought Kitty no further understanding of the events that had transpired with Mr. Knott, but she couldn't stop thinking about it. She had concluded that he must have been looking for help in proposing to Georgiana, but that explanation simply did not satisfy her. Why would he turn to Kitty for such a thing? Even Elizabeth would have been better. And if that was the case, why did he have so much trouble speaking? Clearly, he had been very nervous about whatever he wanted to say, but it is not generally quite that stressful for a man to indicate to a woman that he is thinking of marrying one of her friends, even if she would tease him about not going directly to that friend.

She could not even keep her thoughts focused while Amy was reading to the ladies, who were all gathered together in Mrs. Darcy's sitting room. Much as she tried to keep her mind on the story and her gaze on her work, she still had to force her attention back to both every few moments.

Georgiana noticed her preoccupation. "Kitty, is there something you are not telling us? Perhaps about Mr. Knott?" She looked slyly at Elizabeth, who briefly lifted her eyes to the ceiling.

"You... know about that?" Kitty stammered.

"We know that he took you for a walk yesterday, and that you have been quiet and preoccupied ever since," Elizabeth said. "I hoped that you would have confided in Georgiana or me by this time, but it appears that you have not. Perhaps you might do so now."

Kitty hesitated. "There... I don't know what there is to confide, exactly." She explained briefly what had happened. "I don't know what to make of it. Do you?" The other ladies exchanged glances, and Kitty began to worry. "What have I missed?"

"So, he didn't propose?" Elizabeth asked.

"Propose?" Kitty dropped her work and it tumbled to the floor, unheeded. "Why on earth would he be proposing to me? I'm not the one he was in love with!"

They laughed. "Who did you think he was in love with, silly—me?" Georgiana said. Kitty said nothing, too stunned to answer.

Amy said, "Of course he's in love with you. All the rest of us have seen it for weeks, and we were wondering when he would finally get around to proposing, and whether you would accept him."

Kitty's thoughts raced through the last few weeks... she had been so wrapped up in Mr. Johns, and her own conduct, that she hadn't noticed anything else. And lately she had found it next to impossible to believe that anyone could care about her. And she had thought his affection, whatever it was, belonged to Georgiana. So had Amy, come to that, or at least she had early on. How long had she known? Why didn't she say anything?

But if he had really been in love with her! Ready to propose to her! Suddenly the whole of yesterday rang with clarity.

"What do I do?" she whispered. She hadn't meant the others to hear it, exactly, and it startled her a bit to hear them respond.

"Well, you had better decide whether you like him well enough to marry him," Amy said, "and you'd be smart to do it before he gets back, because if he does come back and you aren't able to give him a straight answer, you might well find yourself leading apes after all."

Elizabeth gave her a warning look for that, but Amy blithely ignored it.

"Do you love him, Kitty?" Georgiana asked gently.

"I... I don't know." Kitty had never been more bewildered. She had never given Mr. Knott more than two seconds of thought in her life, before yesterday. He was pleasant, and he read very well, and he was always kind to her, and helped her learn to walk again, and defended

189

her to her father, and singled her out to spend time with her... Lord, what a fool she had been to believe that he was indifferent to her!

"That might not be the best place to start." Elizabeth set aside her work and leaned forward. "Instead, Kitty, consider: do you think you could learn to love him well enough to be happy with him? You needn't be madly in love right now. But love can grow slowly, some-times—so slowly that we are not always aware of it."

"And you don't have to decide this very moment," Georgiana put in. "He has gone to London, and will probably be there for a week or two at least. You have at least that long to determine what your answer will be, if he asks you."

"What do you mean, *if* he asks her?" Amy said. "He has been making sheep's eyes at her since before Mr. Johns left. I can't imagine that a few days in town will overcome his feelings."

Kitty's eyes went wide and again her whole time at Pemberley raced through her memory. Now that she knew what she was looking for, the evidence shone from every moment. "So long! And not one of you thought to mention to me that the whole time I was losing my head over a married man, there was another in this very house who was developing an affection for me—you just let me believe that I am entirely unloveable!"

"We tried to convince you that you are not, but until a gentleman declares himself, there is not much use in speculating on his affec-tions," Georgiana said.

"And when Mr. Johns was here, you wouldn't have cared one jot for the love of Mr. Knott, you know you wouldn't. If he had been stupid enough to propose, you would have turned him down in hopes of getting Mr. Johns, and that would have turned out worse." Amy sniffed. "Really, it's probably only after Mr. Johns left that Mr. Knott believed he had a chance."

It did not make any sense. There could be no reason that Mr. Knott should be in love with her. He was a man of God, who thought deeply about things and cared about people, and she was... someone who threw herself after a married man. She felt as though they were toying with her for their own amusement, and though she would believe that of Amy, she never could of Georgiana, or Elizabeth—not for something of this magnitude. Lizzy teased, but she could restrain herself when she needed to be serious.

"Poor girl—I think we've driven her to madness," Amy murmured to Elizabeth.

"No." Kitty shook her head. "I'm not mad... only very surprised... and I haven't quite determined what to make of all this, yet. I need to think more." She stood up and started pacing the room, not even seeing the ladies watching her. Mr. Knott's every feature, every expression, every movement, were constantly before her. It seemed that she could not be still. That if she walked long enough, or fast enough, she'd arrive at some kind of a resolution. Her voice matched the pace of her feet. "I don't know how I missed it before. Now that you have made it clear to me, it seems so obvious. But I have no concept for how to feel! I am grateful to him, for how he has tried to protect me from Papa, when he felt it was necessary. I think of him as a friend, I suppose—which is its own surprise, for I never imagined I could be friends with a clergyman."

"What do you think of his tastes? Do they align with yours?" Georgiana asked.

"They... sometimes, I suppose, but not always. He is far more inclined toward retirement and quiet pursuits, and does not prefer company as much as I do. But when he is in company, he is very engaging, and has no difficulty in expressing himself well, usually." She blushed, thinking of how poorly he expressed himself to her when she had last seen him. "He is not a great dancer."

"But he enjoyed going to visit with us, and was very encouraging of you when you wished to go."

"And you like his reading."

"Do you think he is handsome?" interrupted Amy.

Kitty thought about it for a moment, trying to draw forth his image in her mind. His thin face and straw-colored hair did little to recommend him, but his eyes were warm and twinkling, and he had a strong arm for her to lean on when they walked together. "I don't think he is handsome, exactly," she said slowly. "But I do not find his looks disagreeable. He is pleasant to look at, but not handsome." She dropped into her chair and had to laugh at herself. "That is not a very promising foundation for a marriage, is it."

"It is more foundation than some people have," Elizabeth said.

"At any rate, you do not need to make up your mind this morning. You have at least a week to think about it, and I am sure we are all happy to help you think through it." Georgiana smiled broadly. "I have to admit, I hoped he had proposed already. I tried to put the two of you forward whenever I could, but it was not easy. You kept trying to bring me back in!"

Kitty blushed, and did not mention what her intent in doing that had been. "Well, it is probably a good thing he did not. I clearly would not have had any idea of what to say."

At that moment, Mr. Bennet walked into the room, and the conversation ceased. "Ah! Kitty, I had hoped to find you in here," he said. "May I have a word? Lizzy, I would like for you to remain as well."

The sisters exchanged glances as Georgiana and Amy excused themselves, but neither spoke as Mr. Bennet settled into a chair.

"Did Mr. Knott speak with you before he left, Kitty?" he asked.

Kitty blushed. She was very grateful that she knew what he meant, now—if he had asked her this before the conversation with the others, she would not have been even marginally prepared to respond. She spoke slowly, choosing her words carefully. "He did, Papa, but he was interrupted before he could say what he wanted to. We... we have no understanding."

To her surprise, her father seemed pleased. "Good! Clearly you know his purpose."

"Yes." She glanced at Lizzy, a little bit ashamed, but received an encouraging smile.

"I suppose you mean to accept him, if he returns for you?"

"I... don't know..."

Lizzy came to her rescue. "Papa, she has plenty of time to determine her feelings while he is away. It has all come rather suddenly for Kitty."

He looked at Lizzy for a few minutes, almost as though searching for something. But he must not have found it, because he looked back to Kitty with no change of expression. "I will not require that you give me the answer you will give to him. But I will tell you what he told me, so that you have some idea of what to expect from him."

He paused and seemed to be waiting for a response, so Kitty nodded.

"Mr. Knott came to me about a week ago, hoping that I might give him some insight as to whether it was worth his time to try to win your heart. He feared, it seemed, that you were so hurt over the loss of Mr. Johns that you might not be ready to entertain the thought of other suitors."

He wasn't entirely wrong, Kitty thought. How perceptive he had always been!

"When I asked him to explain to me what had led him to form an attachment to you, he regaled me with such a portrait of your playfulness, affections, and good nature that I could scarcely believe he was speaking of the same daughter I thought I knew." He bowed his head and glanced at Lizzy again, who smiled at them both and squeezed Kitty's hand.

"Papa..." Kitty whispered. She wasn't sure how to respond. Had Mr. Knott worked the magic in her father's heart that she had never managed on her own?

He sighed. "I owe you an apology, Kitty. I treated you the way I ought to have treated your sister, without taking the time to consider that you are no longer following Lydia into trouble at every turn. Mr. Knott has seen in you a woman worth pursuing, and Lizzy has been trying to convince me of your great improvement from the start. I have only been too willfully blind to see anything but what I expected, and in doing so I have done you a great disservice. Can you forgive me?"

"Of course I can." The relief and gratitude that welled up in her heart would probably have led her to forgive much more than that! She slid out of her chair and knelt down before her father, picking up his hand and kissing it. "Thank you, Papa."

Elizabeth, too, got up to join them, and sat next to her father so she could embrace them both. "I am so pleased that you've reconciled at last!"

Kitty laughed and leaned back. "Yes, I'm sure that having us constantly at odds under your roof has not been pleasant! I'm sorry, Lizzy, for my part."

"So am I," said Mr. Bennet. He chuckled and shook his head. "It is not a pleasant thing, to be so wrong about two of one's daughters. But I am much happier to have been wrong about you, Kitty."

Kitty decided that she would not take the offense that lurked in the corners of his statement. Instead, she smiled and went back to her chair. "So am I."

CHAPTER 26

*C*olonel Fitzwilliam returned from London a week later. The party had gathered in the music room late one morning, listening to Miss Darcy play a new piece she had been practicing, when he walked in unannounced. Miss Darcy noticed him first. In her surprise, she stopped mid-chord and jumped up to greet him. "We did not expect you back for another week at least!"

He looked quite pleased with himself. "Then I have succeeded in catching you all off guard, which was precisely my object." He shook hands with Mr. Darcy and Elizabeth, and greeted the rest of them warmly. But his happy manner soon dimmed with his succeeding announcement. "My return is hastened by an unfortunate circumstance, though not at all unexpected: Mr. Knott's mother passed away four days ago."

Murmurs of concern came from the party gathered, but Kitty felt as though someone struck her. Of course she had known it was coming, but that did not make her feel any better about it. Poor Mr. Knott! He had been so affected by her illness; surely he had suffered at her death.

"Mr. Knott means to remain in London for at least a week to come. His father is not in particularly good health, either, and so he has agreed to stay until her affairs are settled. I do not anticipate that he will be willing to leave his father until he can assure himself of his father's good health, and that he will be well cared for."

"Are you planning to return to London as well, Colonel?" asked Miss Pratt.

He shook his head. "No, I can be of no further use to him, and I have no other reason to return. Since Darcy was so kind as to extend me a standing invitation to Pemberley, I thought I might as well come back and see how you were all getting along." Turning to Georgiana, he added, "I believe I interrupted your playing, my dear. Do you mind starting the piece over so I can hear the whole thing? Your brother commissioned me with acquiring the piece and having it sent here, so I think I have a right to it."

Georgiana resumed her concert with pleasure, while the Colonel took his seat between Miss Pratt and Kitty. Kitty had lost all ability to focus on the music. She could think of nothing but Mr. Knott, and how soon he would return. It never occurred to her to question whether or not he was going to return—of course he was, and if he really meant to propose to her, he would come back for her sake if nothing else.

That thought warmed her heart, but it did not help her decide whether she would actually accept his proposal. Could she live married to a clergyman? Granted, he was not as tedious or as stupid as Mr. Collins, nor as ancient and sleepy as the rector at Longbourn. But it was hardly the life she had envisioned for herself. She had really expected a wealthier man, like she had believed Mr. Johns to be, who would be a good friend of Mr. Darcy's and keep her in fine style for the rest of her life.

Then again, Mr. Knott might well be the only man who would ever love her. She had made it this far in her life without finding any man who showed her the smallest bit of interest. All of her sisters were married or engaged already, and she could hardly bear to think that she would be obliged to go home to her mother without having anything to show for her time away.

She knew it ought to come down to how well she loved him. He was not handsome, of course, but he was so pleasant, and he was a good friend to her. Perhaps—

"So, Colonel, how long do you mean to stay at Pemberley this time?" Amy spoke over the sound of Georgiana's playing, startling Kitty out of her thoughts.

He did not take his eyes off of Georgiana, and he lowered his voice pointedly. "As long as Darcy will allow it, I suppose."

"So your plans are not fixed, then?"

"Not at present, no." Still he did not look at her, and Kitty wondered that Amy did not notice his clear disinterest in the conversation.

"I do hope you will remain through Michaelmas. I plan to stay that long myself, you know, although my mother has written that she is still much engaged with preparations to bring my sister out into society this winter."

"I did not know that."

"Yes; I am very glad to have escaped the preparations myself, for I remember my mother's preparations for my own coming out, and I pity my sister for having to endure them. I do hope I can be present for her first ball, however. She will need someone a little more acquainted with society than my mother is, to ease her transition."

He nodded but Kitty had the distinct impression that he had no idea what he was agreeing with.

"I am sure my mother has done her best for us, of course, but she is not able to keep up with the latest fashions the way I am, and of course her understanding is so old-fashioned, that she cannot quite see the necessity of going out as often as one really must, to keep up with society. I don't know what she would do without me, to be perfectly honest. I really think, sometimes, that I am the only one that keeps that family in any kind of fashion whatsoever."

Kitty looked around the room in wonder. Did any of the others notice what was happening? They were watching Miss Darcy intently... but she could see the twinkling glances shared between Elizabeth and her father, or Mr. Darcy. They were not entirely ignorant. They just did not care to say anything. Well, she could ignore it too.

"Do you go to many parties and balls when you are in London, Colonel?"

"There are not many held at this time of year."

"That is true, and a great tragedy, to my mind. There are some parts of town which are very pleasant at this time of year; the parks are never lovelier, I am sure."

"Most green places are greatly improved by the presence of vegetation," he admitted.

"Yes, and strolling about them with a few intimate friends is such fun. Of course, there aren't really any shows worth speaking of in the summer, and there is hardly anybody there, which does make it a bit harder to keep oneself entertained. But you gentlemen are to be envied above all creatures, for you have at your disposal many more sources of entertainment than we have."

"That is unfortunately true. But there are some ladies who are able to find sufficient entertainment in the avenues they have available to them; for example, Miss Bennet has been greatly entertained by Georgiana's performance this morning, have you not, Miss Bennet?"

Kitty could not help herself. "Oh yes, Colonel, very much so. It would have been very vexing to have missed it." She fought to contain her smile, but when even her father's shoulders shook with suppressed laughter, she couldn't keep a broad smile from spreading across her face.

KITTY WAS NOT to see how much Miss Pratt had deluded herself about the Colonel until after dinner, when she outlined her ideas in secret.

"You were sitting on his other side, of course. Did you not see how easily we conversed together this morning? I learned ever so much about him, too; his preferences when in town, for one, and that is very important for a lady to know."

"Forgive me, I must not have heard that part. What did he say he preferred doing while in town?"

"Oh, only exploring the parks and enjoying the theater, which are two of *my* favorite London activities as well," Amy said with a proud smile. "I really do think that he is beginning to like me very well indeed."

Kitty did not know what to say. It had been quite clear to her that Colonel Fitzwilliam did not care for Miss Pratt, so how could Amy be so confident that he did?

She recollected that she had seen no symptom of Mr. Knott's affection for her, either. Of course, now that she knew to look for it, she saw the evidence she had missed before, but perhaps even knowing to look for the Colonel's feelings did not mean that he would express them in a way which she could perceive.

Fortunately for Kitty, Amy required no answer. "My only concern is that one of us will be forced to leave before he can finish the business and propose to me. He does seem to be taking his time about it! I thought for sure he would propose to me before he left last time, but of course that was so sudden, that perhaps he meant to and did not have the chance. I must be sure to give him every chance of proposing that I can arrange." She hesitated, and frowned. "But why has he not sought me out yet? Perhaps I have not given him enough encouragement."

"I don't think that is the trouble," Kitty said, trying to keep her confusion out of her tone.

"No? Well, I didn't really think so either. But I really cannot account for it. Unless his family tried to discourage him while he stayed with them! I am sure they will not think that I am good enough for him. How will I ever convince them that I am the right choice?"

"That may not be it either." When Amy looked searchingly at her, she had to come up with some elaboration. After a moment of panic, she said (too loudly), "What if he is only waiting to be sure that he can offer you a stable situation? He might not have enough money to be secure of offering for you, either."

Amy waved that away. "Oh, I do not think that will be a problem; I have plenty of money. Goodness! If he does not think that five thousand pounds is enough to marry on, what will satisfy him? I know it's nothing to Miss Darcy's fortune, of course, but it ought to be enough for him. It's certainly enough for me."

"You don't know whether any of these scenarios is the right one," Kitty pointed out.

"I know." She sighed, and her shoulders slumped forward a little bit. "I am running out of options, Kitty. I have to find a way to make him propose!"

"That isn't in your power. You have the right to refuse him or accept him if he does offer, but until he does, you are at his leisure. And what if he doesn't mean to propose at all? What if he does not like you well enough to be willing to marry you?"

"Of course he does! What do you think I have devoted myself to while I've been here? I am very good at making men like me, Kitty. There is really no chance that he does not want to marry me... I just cannot see how to bring it about. Unless..."

There was something in her tone that set Kitty on edge. "Unless?"

"Well, what if I did just what Camilla did?"

"Camilla Johns?" If Kitty had expected anything, she couldn't have told what, but it was not that. Who in their right mind would do anything the way Mrs. Johns had done it? That she had done something served as proof, in Kitty's mind, that it ought not to be done. It didn't take a long acquaintance with that woman to know that anything she thought right was probably far from the mark.

"It worked wonders on Mr. Johns, you know. Why not? I'll just trick him in to compromising me, and I shouldn't have any trouble convincing him to marry me after that. If his honor is not up to the task, Mr. Darcy's extreme sense of protection for his guests will do it. I have never seen a man more beholden to the minutiae of honor as he is."

"You cannot be serious. What if he still will not have you? You would be compromised and have no husband to show for it!"

"Well I can't imagine that would actually happen. I know he loves me, after all—he just needs to be convinced that marriage to me is the right choice, and if the best way to do that is to seduce him into doing a little bit more than a gentleman ought, well, that's what it takes. I won't mind, as long as we marry in the end."

Kitty had a sudden vision of Lydia's letters from Brighton, with so many of the same sentiments expressed therein. She shook her head. "It will not end well. Besides, I would not like to live with someone I tricked."

"Oh, you're being ridiculous now," Amy said, waving her hand. "I don't see any reason why I should not have as good a marriage as any woman. Besides, I would only be tricking him to get him to realize something he should have known all along. That's not the same as forcing him to do something against his will. I just need to persuade him." She paused, and lowered her voice even more, in what seemed to Kitty to be a ridiculous precaution, as no one was near enough to hear her anyway. "I might need your help to do it, though."

Disgust welled in her stomach, but Kitty only shook her head and said, "I cannot. Can you imagine what my father would do to me if he found out? I would be risking far too much."

"Don't be such a coward, Kitty! Your father would not find out. I only want you to help me get him alone, if you need to, and keep anyone out until I give the signal. For we must be found out, you know. I think I would need to start small, and build to something truly compromising. It might take several days, or weeks. So it would only be a matter of keeping people away until I'm ready. I wonder if we could use your bedroom?"

That really was too far. Kitty stood up. "If he is the sort of man to join you in another woman's bedroom, he is not the sort of man any lady should think of marrying," she said quietly. "I will have no part in it." She marched away without a backward glance.

CHAPTER 27

*M*iss Pratt's plan weighed on Kitty for the whole evening. Half the time, she couldn't bring herself to believe that anyone could be so deluded about reality—Kitty did not honestly think that Colonel Fitzwilliam thought about Miss Pratt as anything other than a friend of his ward, if he thought of her at all. But she couldn't help wondering if she should warn him of what might be in the works. She would hate to see him entrapped by a young lady who had so far proven herself to be entirely insensible to the kind of man he was, and the kinds of signals he was giving.

She tossed and turned through the night, wondering what to do, but by morning she had decided on a course of action: she would tell Elizabeth, and let her decide whether to warn the Colonel or allow events to play out how they would. That would ease her conscience and absolve her from the responsibility of deciding what to do about the situation herself.

The next morning answered her wishes when she arrived in the breakfast room and only Elizabeth and Georgiana were there. "Where is everyone?"

"I believe the gentlemen ate early; they were planning to ride out to the south fields today and wanted an earlier start," Elizabeth said.

"And Miss Pratt has gone to Lambton."

Kitty frowned. "Again? Forgive me, but I cannot see why she is so enthralled with Lambton. There is little enough there, and the shops have so little variety that she must have seen it all by now."

"Yes," said Georgiana, "but I think she is used to a greater variety of company than we have at Pemberley, and Lambton does at least offer a new group of people to talk to."

"No one in our social circle, surely," Elizabeth said.

Georgiana could only shrug, and Kitty had no answer either. But since Miss Pratt's convenient absence gave her the opportunity she was looking for, she was not inclined to press the issue. She gave them a brief summary of the conversation she'd had with Amy the night before.

"I don't know whether I believe her," she concluded, "and I don't know if Colonel Fitzwilliam ought to be warned so he might be put on his guard. I can hardly believe that Miss Pratt would be capable of such things, but at the same time..." She shook her head helplessly.

"I do not even know what to say," Georgiana said, her hand clenched around her knife.

Elizabeth laughed. "I do. Don't worry about the Colonel, Kitty. He is not naive enough to fall for that kind of thing, even if Miss Pratt does try to do something."

"But if she does succeed..."

"She won't! Colonel Fitzwilliam has been in the world long enough to understand that some women do not play by the rules of propriety. And I don't believe that Miss Pratt would really do that. She might talk of it, to shock you and persuade you to help her find other ways to attract him, but she would never act on it."

"I cannot believe that," Kitty said firmly. Of all that she knew about Amelia Pratt, she had never seen anything to make her suspect that she might not do something improper that she'd threatened to do. She had certainly encouraged Kitty to do enough!

Of course, Elizabeth didn't know that. "She is not a very well-bred young woman, I'm afraid, but I have no reason to believe her that bad," she said.

"I have been wondering whether we should write to her mother and see if we can send her home early," Georgiana said.

"Georgiana! That's a little too far for what amounts to nothing more than an idle threat, even if it is against your cousin."

"It's not just that, Lizzy. It's... she's not the girl I grew up with. She is coarse, and selfish, and no great companion. If I had known, or even suspected, I never would have asked her here." She looked ashamed of herself to be saying such things, but Kitty could not help agreeing with her. She would have regretted extending the invitation, too.

"You could not have known how this visit would turn out; do not blame yourself. She is misguided, I am sure, but that is no reason for us to evict her from our house. If she were to violate our trust in such a way as Kitty says she proposed, then we might be able to justify asking her to leave, but until then, it is absolutely unthinkable that she should be sent home."

"I know. But I suppose..." Her shoulders slumped as she sighed and she shook her head. "I'm sorry. I was only giving vent to my frustrations."

Kitty smiled at her. She understood that very well. "So what can we do?" she asked. "You must at least tell the Colonel of what I've told you, so he can decide how to act. I don't think it would be right to come from me, but from you, he might take heed enough to do something about it. He can at least be more vigilant."

Elizabeth sighed. "I'll tell him to keep a watch for what Miss Pratt may do, but honestly, Kitty, I don't think it will matter."

"Please, just tell him. I will feel so much better about it if you do."

"If you would rather not tell him, Lizzy, I would be happy to. I think Kitty is right; he deserves to know, so he can decide how to act."

"It will not change his behavior toward Miss Pratt or anyone else. He is always on his guard," Elizabeth said. But she promised that she would mention it, and with that Kitty had to be content. "Now, let's say no more of it. Kitty, have you given any more thought to what you might say to Mr. Knott?"

"Yes, and I still have no idea whether I should accept him or not," Kitty said miserably. She was not pleased to be forced to admit it. She felt like a failure for her continued uncertainty; her mother would be furious, if she knew of it.

But Elizabeth was not angry. If anything, she looked pleased, though surprised. "It is good to hear that you are considering it so carefully," she said. "But you will not be able to remain uncertain forever. At some point, you will be required to decide how you feel."

"I might not," Kitty insisted. "He might not propose."

Elizabeth and Georgiana exchanged smiles. "I highly doubt that!" Elizabeth said.

Kitty didn't know whether she found that comforting or not.

A FEW DAYS LATER, Kitty found an opportunity to slip out of the house for a solitary stroll through the gardens. She wanted a chance to think through the matter of Mr. Knott, but she kept wondering what would become of her when she returned to Longbourn. She had hoped that she might join the Bingleys at their new house, but her mother, judging by her letters, was not willing to allow that to happen; she wanted Kitty home for Mary's wedding. Kitty scowled at that thought, skirting around a bush that had grown out of its place and was encroaching on the path. Mr. Warde, it seemed, had nearly scraped together enough money to keep himself and Mary comfortably in Meryton, so they planned on having the banns read soon.

Kitty was not excited at the idea of going to Mary's wedding at all, but her mother insisted that she be there to act as bridesmaid, and she could not find a good enough reason to object. The question that weighed on her mind was whether Mr. Knott would return to Pemberley in time, and if he did not, whether she would be able to receive him at Longbourn. She tugged at a climbing vine absently as she walked past, and one of the leaves came off in her hand. As she walked, she rolled it between her fingers, the stem pressing into her fingertips. She had decided to act as though Mr. Knott certainly meant to propose, but she still had not decided whether or not to accept him.

If she went home, however, she realized that Mrs. Bennet would not allow her to decline. It would be Lizzy and Mr. Collins all over again, and Kitty had neither her sister's strength nor her father's support. If she wished to decline Mr. Knott's proposal, she would have to do so at Pemberley.

Under the shade of a large tree, she paused, dropping the leaf she'd been twirling to run her fingers along the tree's trunk. She was, for the most part, resigned to accepting him. But she worried that it was merely out of the quiet certainty that she would never receive another offer. She believed that she could be reasonably happy with him, but she was not so in love with him that she felt she could live with no other, and a small, vocal part of her mind insisted that she was betraying herself for not being willing to wait and trust that a true, passionate love would come to her in time. When that voice spoke, she believed she could not allow herself to marry Mr. Knott, no matter how kindly he treated her, for kindness did not equal love, and how miserable must it be to be married to a man one only likes!

Someone ran up behind her, distracting her from her thoughts; she turned and found Miss Pratt, smiling broadly. "Kitty! You will never believe who is coming up the drive right now!"

Her stomach clenched. Mr. Knott! And she had not at all settled how she would answer him.

"It is Mr. Johns," Amy continued, "and he is actually coming up to Pemberley's front door!"

"Mr. Johns?" Kitty repeated dumbly. What—how—why on earth would he dare coming back? "Well, Mr. Darcy will soon set him straight, I imagine." She said it with conviction but inwardly she was not at all certain that he would. It would be very difficult for a gentleman to cast out someone who was not only a prominent neighbor, but one whom the neighborhood particularly wished to retain.

"That's what Mrs. Darcy said. And I think he will; Mr. Darcy is going out to the front to meet him, and I imagine he means to tell him off. Come watch with me! It will be such fun to see him set Mr. Johns down." She grabbed Kitty's arm and tried to pull her along, but Kitty snatched it back. She did not at all feel equal to seeing him—not when the mere mention of his name was enough to send her reeling back into the confusion she'd felt when she first found out about his wife.

"You go on," she stammered. "You can tell me all about it after he leaves."

"Don't be ridiculous. What are you afraid of? He won't even see you."

"I hope he does not! But I have no desire to see him."

Miss Pratt rolled her eyes. "You are being ridiculous. The last time you almost saw him in a shop you wanted to go talk to him. Nothing has changed in so short a time, has it?"

"Perhaps it has; I only want to forget him."

Miss Pratt stared at her, and Kitty met her gaze without flinching, however uncomfortable it made her. Finally, Miss Pratt shrugged. "Have it your way, then. I'm going to go listen in."

Kitty shook her head and watched her run away. She wondered if she was feeling a fraction of what Georgiana felt, on finding Amy so different a friend than what she had first thought. She did not want to dwell on it.

Instead she walked out away from the house, toward a path that would give her enough of a view of the lane that she could see when Mr. Johns left and know it was safe to go back. She tried to go back to her former train of thought, but Miss Pratt had effectively destroyed it. All she could think of now was how glad she was to have missed Mr. Johns, and she wondered what he might be saying to Mr. Darcy.

Could he have come to offer an apology? What apology might he have to give? On behalf of his wife, perhaps—though, without her there to say it, it would ring rather flat. And for himself, all he was really guilty of was concealing the existence of his wife, and letting Kitty make a fool of herself with him. She could accuse him of nothing other than thoughtlessness, and that sin was not generally condemned in such cases. She resented his deception, and the loss of his attentions hurt her, but that merited little from him.

She wandered for some time with these thoughts, without any satisfaction at all, and without any sign that he had left. After a while, she began to suspect that she must have missed him. Should she just go back? If she came in through the kitchen, she would certainly avoid any chance of meeting him. And if she saw Miss Pratt after, she would know it was over and she was safe. She turned to go back—and Mr. Johns himself stepped onto the path in front of her.

"Miss Bennet." He bowed deeply, sweeping his hat from his head in a cunning display of grace and gallantry. Kitty cursed her stomach for the betraying flutter it gave. She had no right to be pleased by his attentions.

"Mr. Johns?" She fought to keep her expression neutral, but she didn't think she'd been very successful. "What are you doing here?" That definitely did not sound neutral, and he looked wounded at her tone.

"I came to apologize to you, and Mr. Darcy would not even allow me in the house. I have been given to understand—that is, I suspect— you see, I had no idea of ever making myself anything more than a friend to you, and I'm very sorry to learn that you came to believe anything else of me. I thought only to enjoy your company while I stayed here, not to engage your expectations."

The sincerity with which he uttered this did not convince her of its truthfulness. She couldn't quite keep her tone from showing her hurt and growing anger. "Why did you not just tell us that you were married? Surely that would have resolved any uncertainty on my part." There could be no good excuse for *that*, certainly.

He sighed and tugged at the little finger of his glove. "I came here wishing to forget that fact myself. You see, my wife and I do not get on very well—to own the truth, I believe she despises me as much as I do her. I had hoped that, by coming to Edgepark and improving it, I would have a retreat from her. She prefers to live in Town, you see, and was quite opposed to any mention of living in the country some day. But I quite underestimated her determination to make me miserable. She followed me here when she heard a rumor that I was making love to some other girl, and when she arrived, she fixed on my mention of you as evidence that you were the girl in question. I had intended to come and warn you, that day and explain myself then, but before I could summon the courage to speak, she came sweeping in.

She has a habit of doing that—of descending upon people precisely when they do not want her."

His evident misery softened her heart a little bit, but only strengthened the sternness of her response. "Had you only mentioned it beforehand, it would not have been a problem, and I would not—we would not be in this situation."

"I know," he moaned. "If I were not such a coward—if I had not so wholly deluded myself into believing that I had control of the situation—but you must understand, Miss Bennet that if I were free, you would have been my choice. I enjoyed nothing so much as the time I spent in your company. And when I contrast your company to that of Mrs. Johns, I am completely miserable."

"Well," Kitty said, her voice barely above a whisper, "I have always found 'if' to be a very unsatisfactory word. Pray excuse me; I am certain to be wanted at the house." She hurried past him and did not slow when she heard him calling her name behind her. It felt good to leave *him* bewildered this time.

CHAPTER 28

*T*wo weeks passed before Kitty felt comfortable telling anyone that she had seen Mr. Johns, but she confessed it to Georgiana when they were out in the garden, cutting flowers to make an arrangement Georgiana had read about and wanted to try.

Georgiana was more angry about it than Kitty had been. "I can't believe that he came and sought you out after my brother specifically told him not to! What right did he have? How could he dare do such a thing when you are under our protection? Has he no honor?"

Kitty shook her head and knelt to see whether she could find anything worth cutting from the lower side of the bush, and to conceal her emotions. "I cannot account for it, except that he told me that he had come to Pemberley to apologize to me particularly. He was very repentant, or at least he seemed so."

"I think he has proven himself untrustworthy enough that you can easily disbelieve him." She jerked a flower toward her and swiped at its stem with her knife.

"Yes, and I do, largely. That is, I believe the outline of his story is true; I have no reason to doubt that he came here wishing to forget that he was married. He did an exceptionally good job of it. But I do not believe he regrets it as much as he claims to; I think he is rather pleased that he was able to inspire as much esteem in me as he did." She paused, and placed the posey she'd been gathering into the basket at Georgiana's feet. She did not let herself dwell on how much esteem he truly had inspired. She still could not decide how much she'd really liked him, and his return had stirred up feeling in her that she would have rather forgotten. "I wish I could believe him when he told me that, had he been free to engage his heart, he would have given it to me. But I suspect that is nothing but flattery."

"You are probably better off without his heart or his hand, for that matter. Even if he had been free to bestow it, he has betrayed an insensibility to the feelings and impressions of others that cannot recommend him. I do not wonder that his marriage is not a happy one, but I do not place all the blame for that at his wife's feet."

"No; although considering the way she flew at me, a complete stranger, I cannot place it all at his, either." Kitty shuddered at the memory. "I believe I pity him, for having to live with such a creature."

"It is his own fault; he had to make her an offer in the first place," Georgiana said.

Kitty looked at her, dropping her hand in her lap. "Georgiana, do you mean to tell me that you do not remember?"

"Remember what?"

"All those stories that Miss Pratt told us about her wild friend—Miss Camilla Irons—who forced a gentleman to compromise her and then offer for her? And Mr. Johns, introducing his wife as Mrs. Camilla Johns? Miss Pratt told me she recognized her. I am surprised that she did not also mention it to you."

Georgiana stopped what she was doing and put her scissors in the basket. "She did not say a word, and I never realized—my goodness, what a terrible woman! I believe I begin to see why you feel sorry for him." She shook her head. "But, Kitty, do not feel *too* sorry for him. No matter how bad his situation is, that does not give him the right to do what he did to you."

"I know." She picked up the scissors and handed them back to Georgiana. "That big pink rose back there looks promising for the centerpiece; can you reach it? Anyway, I do not suppose it matters at this point. I do not expect to ever see him again, except possibly in passing, so he will never have the chance to cause me more pain."

"I certainly hope not, for all our sakes." She pulled the rose out carefully, avoiding the thorns, and added it to her basket.

Kitty, for all her talk to the contrary, was not entirely pleased with the likelihood of her never seeing Mr. Johns again. Part of her wanted to meet him again just so she could feel her power over him again, and restore her confidence that she was attractive to more men than only Mr. Knott. And to torment herself by wondering about his final words: *if I were free, you would have been my choice.*

"Oh! Here is Elizabeth!" Kitty looked up at Georgiana's words to see her sister hurrying across the lawn toward them. She put down her scissors and stood up.

"Mr. Knott has just returned from London," she said, watching Kitty closely. "He means to join the party for dinner tonight."

Kitty felt that she ought to say something, but did not know what. "Ah. Mr. Knott?" Stupid!

"Yes; will you be all right, dear?" Elizabeth put her hand on Kitty's arm. "You look a bit unwell."

"I..." She shook her head slowly; she was beginning to panic and she felt stupid for succumbing to it. "I still don't know how I'm going to answer him! I'm not ready!"

"He isn't very likely to ask you today," Georgiana pointed out. "He has only just returned; you still have a day or two before he is likely to try."

"I can't decide in a day or two! What am I going to do?"

Elizabeth laughed. "Don't borrow trouble, Kitty! He has not yet asked you anything, and if he does, there is no harm in telling him that you would like time to think it over before giving your answer. That may be the time to panic, if it comes. Until then, be calm. Perhaps something may have occurred in London to make him unable to make you an offer anyway, and then it won't matter."

Kitty bit back the protest that rose to her lips. "You won't leave me alone with him, will you? Even if he hints?"

"Of course not, Kitty. Mama is not here to embarrass you the way she did to Jane, and neither of us would think of doing such a thing to you."

Kitty could not help a sigh of relief. "Thank you! I will decide something... I will... somehow, I will make up my mind."

"It is not as hard as you are making it out to be," Elizabeth said gently. "Observe how he interacts with you tonight, and take your time to know your own heart. If you are going to spend the rest of your life with him, a few more days at this end will not do any harm."

Kitty tried to be reassured by these things, but she was in agony all day until dinner. She continually alternated between excitement at seeing him again, and fear of seeing him again. What would she say? What would *he* say? She changed her dress three times, trying to find a balance between looking well, and not looking as though she had gone to extra trouble for his sake, and she was still not satisfied with the result when she finished. But it was too late to undress again; she would already be the last one there.

Her fears in that regard were unfounded. On her arrival in the drawing room she saw that Mr. Knott was not there yet, either, which gave her more time to steady her nerves as she greeted the others. She wondered, for one wild second, whether he'd had the same difficulty in deciding how much care to put into his appearance as she had, but she dismissed the thought as soon as she had it. He didn't seem like that kind of man, and she knew that he had more likely taken more time because he had just arrived and his trunks had not yet been fully unpacked. He was probably just searching for a missing shoe.

When he did arrive, her mental state was not much more collected than it had been when she came down; certainly she was not prepared for the anticipation and concern that unconsciously drove her greeting. But she was too shy to say anything else to him, and he did not seek her out for conversation either. The others were doing a fine job of keeping his attention, anyway, expressing their regrets about his mother and hoping that his affairs in town were resolved to his satisfaction. He gave all the correct answers to these questions, but Kitty thought she sensed that his mind was not fully engaged in them.

She did not know, when they went in to dinner, whether she

wanted to be seated near him or not; and so when she found herself not remotely close to him, she did not know whether to be relieved or regretful. But she could not attend to any of the conversation around her, as every thought and feeling focused on him: confusion, concern, pleasure, pain, all were wrapped up in what he said, or might have said, at that moment. She was a very stupid dinner companion, but as she sat between her father and Miss Pratt, she did not imagine that anyone noticed much.

Elizabeth led them to withdraw far before she felt herself ready, but she dutifully followed the others out of the dining room and waited in silence for the gentlemen to join them. Georgiana sat loyally by her, saying nothing but remaining close, and Kitty tried to be grateful. But she wasn't grateful at all. What if he wanted to talk to her? Did she want to talk to him?

Never before had she spent half an hour in such strange terror. She longed to see him—she had missed his friendship, and he had been so constantly on her mind. And she wanted to assure herself that he really was all right after his mother's passing. But what would she say to him? How could she converse with anything approaching composure when her mind refused to be still?

Her heart leapt when the gentlemen joined them at last, and even more when Georgiana left to help Elizabeth by serving the coffee, leaving the seat beside her open. But her father soon occupied it; he wanted Kitty to pass him the book on the table at her side, so he could point out a passage to Mr. Darcy. By the time he departed, Mr. Knott had started a conversation with Colonel Fitzwilliam. Georgiana returned to her side before they were finished talking, and Kitty wondered if she ought to go interject herself into his conversation, just to be sure of a chance to speak to him. But she could not be so rude, and she had no idea what she would say, anyway.

Finally, when the tea and coffee things were cleared away and Elizabeth wondered whether anyone wanted to play cards, Kitty saw her opportunity, and volunteered for whist in hopes that Mr. Knott would offer to partner her. She was terrible at whist—she had a dreadful time trying to keep track of her trumps and she always seemed to give them up too soon—but if it meant that she might be able to speak to him, she would gladly lose at anything. But Elizabeth was, apparently, determined to make good her promise to keep them apart until Kitty declared herself ready, because she made up the table with Colonel Fitzwilliam and Mr. Darcy. Kitty did not scowl, and was grimly proud of herself for this accomplishment.

In the end, the only conversation she had with him was in the few minutes before they retired for the night. He asked how her ankle did, and she could at least report that it was very much healed; that was all. Kitty could not settle with herself whether she thought the question signaled his continued affection, or merely a polite inquiry. She did, however, stay awake half the night puzzling it over, for all the good it did her.

CHAPTER 29

*P*art of her problem, Kitty decided, was that she simply did not know how long she would have to make up her mind. She could not very well go to Mr. Knott and insist that he inform her of when he intended to propose so that she could be prepared. For a couple of days, she worried about it to the point that she could hardly think of anything else.

At last, she had an idea. She could ask her father how long he meant to remain in the country. So she found herself in the library, curtseying to Colonel Fitzwilliam and daring to interrupt her father in his reading. He looked up from his book and gestured to the chair facing the door, and Kitty had only begun to articulate her request when Miss Pratt walked in. She was clearly on the hunt, and she had finally found her prey. Kitty watched out of the side of her eye as she sidled up to the Colonel, completely ignoring the other two at the fireplace, and asked him what he was looking for. Kitty trailed off and looked at her father, half amused and half alarmed. He arched an eyebrow, and she sat down, but she couldn't help overhearing Miss Pratt.

"Perhaps I can help you find something. I am quite a reader myself, you know."

Kitty heard her father exhale the smallest whisper of a chuckle, and stopped even pretending to talk to him. They were both clearly determined to hear this.

"I do not doubt that, but you and I do not appear to have similar taste in books. I doubt that you could suggest anything in which I am truly interested."

"What do you think of Gilpin?"

"I suppose it's amusing enough, but it's absolutely ridiculous to expect something as sublime as artistic taste to be capable of description, even in a book as long as his. Did I need him to inform me that three cows standing on a hillside is pleasant to view? Though I suspect that the gentleman has not spent much time in the presence of actual cows, or he would know that it is next to impossible to expect them to be always grouped as charmingly as he argues is ideal, unless one owns precisely three of them."

"Yes, that is precisely what I think."

"Oh? Have you spent much time in the company of cows?"

"What? No, of course not. I meant..." She looked around the room but the books and drapes offered her no help, and certainly neither Kitty nor her father leapt to her aid.

Colonel Fitzwilliam smiled. "You see. Thank you for your offer of assistance, but I am sure I will be able to find something that interests me without help. Do not let me keep you from your object in coming here."

Kitty, who knew Miss Pratt's object in coming there, smirked. Miss Pratt squared her shoulders and puffed out her chest a little, then wandered to the Colonel's other side so she stood between him and the door. She looked at the books in front of her for a minute, or, rather, pretended to. Her eyes rarely turned any direction but his. It was not long before she spoke again.

"We were quite desolate without you here. I am so happy that you chose to come back."

"I am glad to have been able to return, but I am happier that I could go and be of service to my friend, and open my father's house to him. I hope my support benefitted him a little as he dealt with his family crisis."

"Are your parents not at home at present, to have hosted him?"

"They are at home; for them, home is in Lancashire. They usually only go to town for the season."

"Oh! Do you visit them often?"

"Tolerably often."

"I have never been to Lancashire, myself."

"Indeed? It is not so far from here."

"Yes, but when we travel, we travel south. We have no family any further north, nor any friends that direction." She picked a book off the shelf, thumbed through it quickly, and put it back. "I hope, however, that you do not plan to leave us very soon. We will not easily endure another reduction in our party."

"I am sure that Mr. and Mrs. Darcy are not so negligent in their hosting that they would permit you to be without any entertainment."

"Of course they are not; but a large party is always to be preferred to a smaller one, is it not?"

"I find unique charms in each."

"Well... that is true, I suppose..."

He picked up a book off the shelf and bowed to her. "It appears that I have found what I was looking for," he said. "Thank you for a... fascinating conversation. I will leave you with the hope of equal success in your search."

Kitty could see Miss Pratt's panic rising. "But—one moment—do you think—I cannot *quite* reach the one I want—that one there, you see?" She pointed to one only slightly out of her reach. "Can you help me?"

Without speaking, he took three steps past her and picked up a small folding ladder kept in the library for that purpose. He unfolded it, placed it before her, and bowed again.

"Thank you!" She climbed onto the ladder but intentionally missed the top step and started to fall toward him. "W—oh!"

The colonel, shaking his head, steadied her by taking her arm, and brought her safely back to earth. He arrested her attempt to lean on him by grasping her other arm, and released her the moment he could. He sighed. "Miss Pratt, it seems that I can no longer hope that subtlety will be effective. Do not believe me ignorant of what you are trying to do. If I were of a mind to make you an offer, believe me, I would have done so already. This manner of behavior is not at all calculated to increase its likelihood. You will not succeed in this object and for both our sakes, I ask that you stop trying. It pains me to be compelled to be so blunt, but you have been entirely deaf to more polite hints. I hope that in this case, my breach of propriety will at least ensure that I may be spared these insulting manipulations in the future." He left without even bowing, except toward Kitty and her father.

Mr Bennet bowed back and Kitty looked away quickly, but Miss Pratt hurried out soon after, and said nothing to either of them.

Kitty looked at her father, unable to disguise her amusement, and at his suppressed smile and shaking shoulders, she couldn't help giggling. Then he started to laugh, and she burst into loud laughter with him. Poor Miss Pratt! That had to be the end of her quest to seduce Colonel Fitzwilliam—and what an end!

CHAPTER 30

*K*itty stared out the window of the Lambton shop and sighed. Somehow Miss Pratt had talked Kitty, Georgiana and Elizabeth all into coming with her to town, and then disappeared without a word. Kitty had not even noticed that Miss Pratt was gone until she turned around to make some comment and couldn't find her.

Elizabeth and Georgiana were browsing the ribbons in the back room and did not seem concerned at all about Miss Pratt's absence, but Kitty had no interest in joining them; the ribbons had not changed since she had been here last. Besides, the shop was increasingly crowded, and increasingly stuffy, and the more she thought about it, the more she wondered where Miss Pratt had gone. She glanced back at her sisters but when they did not so much as look at her, she decided she'd step outside to see if she could find Miss Pratt on the street.

Outside the air was fresher and there were certainly fewer people, but no Miss Pratt. She walked down the street a little way, although she made sure to stay close to the shop so she wouldn't lose the others. She took a deep breath. This was a little better.

"Miss Bennet?"

She turned and took a couple of steps back, her stomach clenching into complicated knots as her heart leapt. Mr. Johns! Why was he here now? She did not feel prepared to face him at all. Not as long as her insides betrayed her every time she saw him. She turned down the first street she saw, a little side alley that was entirely deserted, but he followed her there. Realizing that she would not be able to avoid him, she closed her eyes and offered up a brief prayer for strength, then turned to face him.

He was as handsome as ever, and looked dashing and regal in his tan coat. He bowed to her and said, "I am so glad I encountered you. I had thought, at our last meeting, that you were not best pleased with me—that my apology had not quite accomplished what I wished it to. You are not still angry with me, are you?"

She did not know how to respond to him, but he kept talking without giving her the chance. "Because I know you have a right to. Would to God I had not been so stupid! But you are so easy to talk to —I hardly knew what I was doing. You must understand what I suffer at home; you have met my wife. She does not improve on further acquaintance. It is so refreshing to be in company with a woman who is gentle, and graceful, and everything that Camilla is not. Can you blame me for wishing to spend more time with you?" He stepped closer to her with every sentence, until Kitty had to back up a few paces.

"I do not think that excuses you from allowing me to believe you available and interested in me for so long." She did not mention that she, too, would probably have been anxious to forget about Mrs. Johns. But how different things might have turned out if he had really been single! And how much worse for her!

"I may not be available, but you cannot believe me disinterested!" He moved closer again, and Kitty took another step back. "Never disinterested. Miss Bennet, you are... you are so damned beautiful." He let out a deep, shaking breath. "Your company eases my mind. Even now, when I can see your resentment shining out of those lovely eyes of yours—good God, you do not know what you do to a man, do you? I know I behaved wrongly. But I only wished to delude myself into believing, for a short time, that things could be different. That I could be happy. You must know that if I had not been married already, I would have married you. Yes! If I had any chance to change any part of my wretched life, I would have cast Camilla off—risked death rather than marry her! If only I had known that I should later meet you, and could have married you! It would have given me enough courage to do anything, I believe."

His flattery was perfectly calculated to make her warm to him, and even though she knew it, she could not entirely stop it from having that effect. He did look miserable enough, poor man! Kitty did not doubt that she would have been a better wife than his. She stood up a little straighter to hide her feelings. "But there is nothing you can do about it now; you cannot change what you have done, and only control what your behavior must be in the future."

"I know," he whispered. "But all my future holds for me is dreams of what might have been." He lowered his head and stared at his boots. "Do you know, Miss Bennet, what I would have done, if I could? I'd have proposed as soon as Edgepark was complete—nay, before! You and I could move in as soon as the repairs were finished, and you could have full control of decorating every room. I'd have devoted myself to seeing you smile. I would kiss you always." He looked up abruptly, his eyes wide and dark. "Kiss you! What I wouldn't give to kiss you now!"

Every possible objection to this rose up in her mind at once, and the one she voiced was not the strongest of them. "Mr. Johns, we are in a public road!" It was one thing to acknowledge that he wished things had turned out differently. It was quite another to suggest *that*! She couldn't help blushing at the idea of it, and tried very hard to ignore how much it flattered her.

He looked around, and Kitty noticed for the first time that they were standing in a wide doorway. "There is no one here to listen or hear me," he said quietly. "I can dream as much as I wish." His eyes slid closed and he lowered his voice even more. "I would be free to love you as I wish, by now. I could hold you whenever I liked; I could kiss you at any point of the night or day; I could look at you whenever I liked... your milky skin... your bright eyes... your beautiful hair..." He groaned, and opened his eyes. "And now I can only stand before you and torment myself with what will never be. When only to hear you say my name is the sweetest gift any woman could bestow!"

He painted the very picture for her that she had painted for herself, back when she had believed that it was possible. Her heart beat wildly, thrashing between fear and desire. She was angry with him. But no angrier than he was with himself. And she regretted the circumstances as much as he could do. If he had only been single, how happy she could have been with him! She shook her head, but without as much of the conviction that she had displayed before. "Mr. Johns..."

"Call me Gregory," he pleaded, and took another step closer to her. She blinked. "What?"

"Just once... please... I can have nothing. All pleasure is forever denied me. But this—there is no one here—you can give me this one gift—call me by my name. Give me something that I may cherish when I must go back to her."

She did not speak for several moments. What he asked was nothing, really. Just a name. A name that no one would ever hear, except him. A gift that he might cherish, as he said. So why did she hesitate?

"Gregory," she whispered.

He slid his eyes closed and moaned. "Kitty. Yes."

She did not know what to do, so she repeated his name.

"Kitty. Say it again, Kitty," he whispered, stepping closer to her again. She leaned back and found a doorpost there.

"Gregory..." She barely got the word out before he crushed his mouth against her, his lips working insistently.

She froze. What on earth was he doing? What should she do? She should push him away. She tried, but he only stepped closer and deepened the kiss. And most confusing of all, a part of her enjoyed it.

"My darling Kitty!" He grabbed her shoulders, kissing her again.

She could not speak, even when his lips weren't on her mouth. His hands started to move, caressing her. Chills ran down her spine and she trembled, half afraid and half thrilled. One of his hands ran up the back of her neck, knocked her bonnet loose, and tangled itself in her hair, and she had to bite back a moan. She liked it! If they could only have married, this could have been hers by right, not stolen in hiding. Curse Camilla Johns!

He grabbed one of her arms and put it on his waist and she put the other one there too; he pressed his body against hers and she leaned heavily against the brick behind her. His mouth left hers and she gasped, and gasped again when he moved to her neck, her jawline, and her ears—her ears! Sparks of delight shot down her neck. Could anything feel better than this! Her entire body awoke at his touch.

Her breath came in shorter and shorter gasps, and she could not keep her eyes open, particularly when his hands began to move again, caressing and stroking everywhere they could reach. She hardly noticed when he began to tug at her skirts; she could only think that anything he could want to do would be delightful; she must help him do it. She fumbled with his hands, hindering as much as she helped.

"Good God! Miss Bennet!"

Everything shattered.

Kitty opened her eyes, the spell quite broken. Terror and disgust overwhelmed her, at herself and at Mr. Johns. He backed away, his eyes locked on her chest, and all she could do was shake her head. What had he done? What had *she* done? And who had stopped them? Her body felt dull and slow as she fumbled with the ribbons of her bonnet. She tore her eyes away from Mr. Johns and looked to see who had discovered them.

Mr. Knott stood at the entryway of the alley, looking as though it was he who had been assaulted, his ears redder than she had ever seen them. Their eyes met, and Kitty could not look away.

In that moment, the clarity for which she had long searched came to her with crushing finality. Staring at Mr. Knott, whose fists were clenched at his sides, whose jaw was set in lines of ferocity she had never seen before, she knew. Her heart shouted it to her: this man, whose heart she had just torn out, was the kindest, sweetest, most thoughtful man she had ever met, and she loved him with a ferocity and longing that shook her to her core.

She loved and wished to marry Mr. Knott and him alone. And now she never could.

CHAPTER 31

$\mathcal{M}$r. Johns fled. She did not see where he went; she only knew that he was gone. She still leaned against the wall, the enormity, the shame of what she had done crashing over her again and again. Why had she done that? What had come over her? What could she have been thinking? She didn't even like Mr. Johns! She covered her face with her hands and shook her head again and again but nothing would remove the awful memory of Mr. Knott's face. The betrayal, the hurt, the destruction of all she had not known she wanted until it was gone! She sank to the ground, her knees close to her chest, and cried.

"Miss Bennet, what happened? Why did he attack you? Are you all right?" Mr. Knott's voice was quiet but came from very nearby, and she looked up to find him kneeling in the dirt beside her.

"I'm so sorry," she whispered, again and again. She could never say it enough. "I'm so sorry. I'm so, so sorry." She put her head back down. It hurt too much to look at him.

"Kitty." God, it was her father. Well! He had been right about her all along. She was worse than Lydia! Mr. Wickham had at least been able to marry her! "Can you stand, child? We ought to get you home."

The dirt scraped as Mr. Knott stood up. She could not look up. How could she bear to look at either of them? She wished the door behind her would open for a moment, and allow her to fall into whatever lay behind it. Hopefully into somewhere she could curl up and be left alone to die. "Did you see where he went?" Mr. Knott asked.

"Johns? No. Did you?" A pause. Kitty trembled. "Well, we know where he lives, and I shall have to call him out over this, I suppose. Come, Kitty." He sighed heavily. "And here I thought I'd managed to avoid dueling." His arms came under hers, and he brought her to her feet. Her hands trembled as she tried again to straighten her bonnet. She kept her eyes on the ground in front of her.

"If you will take her back to Pemberley, I will tell the other ladies where she has gone," Mr. Knott said, his voice low and sad.

If her heart could break again, it did. She had done this to him! She gave a shuddering gasp through her tears. "I'm so sorry!"

"Come along, child. The carriage is waiting for us."

Kitty allowed him to lead her to it and tried to control her sobs. But she had just ruined her entire life, and this time there was no hope for her. How could she help crying?

They were in the carriage and probably quite out of town before Mr. Bennet spoke again. "What happened, Kitty?" His voice was more gentle than she expected, but she could hear the anger underneath it, and she couldn't find the words to answer.

"I'm sorry," she whispered again.

He exhaled sharply. "I gathered that much. What I have not yet determined is how my daughter found herself in a back alley kissing another woman's husband."

She shook her head and cried harder. She hardly knew what happened, let alone how to explain it. "He... kissed me."

"I saw that! How in the world did you even get into a position where he could kiss you?"

"I don't know," she said, shaking her head again. She honestly didn't. Everything seemed unreal, and she could not focus on anything. "Everything is ruined."

Her father leaned back in the seat. "Well, that is certain. Have you any other insights?"

"I only want to go to my room." And curl into a little ball of all-consuming regret, forever.

He huffed and folded his arms over his chest. "How lucky for you that your wishes should coincide with your fate so exactly. I'm sure that will make it much easier to bear."

What could she say? She deserved worse. Only that morning, her life had been on a path to a happy establishment with a man she loved, whose engagement to her would have secured his living from Mr. Darcy and answered all her hopes. Now, it all lay shattered before her. What a difference one morning could make! Kitty ached, deep in her heart, to somehow go back, to re-do the morning—never to enter the shop, and never to see Mr. Johns. What cared she for Mr. Johns when she could have had Mr. Knott? One man held all the joy her life could give her, and the other only disaster, and she had somehow tricked herself into falling under the spell of the wrong one. How could she have allowed Mr. Johns to flatter her into believing him again? She knew better!

She hardly noticed her father escorting her to her bedroom. She barely took the time to yank off her bonnet and shoes, and throw them angrily into the corner of the room. Then she sank onto the bed and screamed her despair into her pillow.

SHE ONLY HAD a few minutes to wallow in her pain, though, for the lock clicked in the door again and Elizabeth peeked her head inside. "Kitty?"

"Go away, Lizzy," she whispered.

But Elizabeth stepped through the door and closed it behind her. "Papa has sent me up to help you pack. He means to depart for Longbourn as soon as you are ready."

Kitty sat up and tried to sniff back her tears. Of course he would waste no time, and neither could she... she should want nothing more than to leave the country as quickly as possible... but the thought of actually leaving made her feel even worse. "I can't," she whispered.

"I know it's hard, dear, but if we're to preserve your reputation we need to move quickly." She pulled out Kitty's trunk, but Kitty did not move. Who could think about clothes at a time like this? Throw them in the trunks however they would fit; wrinkle and destroy them; what would it matter? She would have no need of them ever again. She would never leave her room.

"Can you tell me what happened?" Elizabeth asked. She came over and sat on the bed beside Kitty, and started to rub her back gently. The motherly gesture sent Kitty into sobs all over again, but she tried to tell her story. It came out disjointed and confused, but Elizabeth did not ask any questions until she lapsed into silence.

"So he forced himself on you?"

Kitty nodded, then shook her head, and then shrugged. "I did nothing much to stop him. I—I didn't know what to do. It all happened so quickly, and I thought he was just going to apologize, and that's what he did, and then he was kissing me." She swallowed hard but she couldn't stop herself from adding, in the smallest whisper, "I actually enjoyed it... for a moment."

"Oh, Kitty." The disappointment in her voice made Kitty flinch.

"Only until I came to my senses! It... he... I don't know what he did to me! I knew he should stop, I knew I should stop him, but I couldn't. Until..." Until Mr. Knott found them. She couldn't acknowledge it out loud. She only cried more.

Elizabeth hugged her awkwardly with one arm, and let her control herself again. When her sobs had turned back to sniffles, she said quietly, "Fortunately, I do not think anyone knows of this except Papa, Mr. Knott, Georgiana, and me. So your reputation is secure, provided that Mr. Johns does not speak. And Mr. Darcy will ensure that he does not, when I tell him of it."

"Must you tell him?" Kitty asked, shuddering. She had got over some of her fear of Mr. Darcy since living in his house, but she could not imagine how she would spend three seconds in his presence ever again, if he knew.

"If he is to help protect your reputation, he must know of the threat to it, dear," Elizabeth said. "He did the same for Lydia, you know." Kitty sniffed. She did not know that story, exactly, but now was not the time to ask. Elizabeth continued, "He fiercely defends those he loves, and as you are now his family, that includes you." She smiled sadly, and patted Kitty's arm. "We must begin packing. Papa wants no delays."

Kitty allowed her to help her stand up and walk over to the wardrobe. She packed mechanically, hardly even seeing the things she was putting away, and more than once Elizabeth had to ask her what she had intended to do with some article that had been poorly placed. Kitty always answered with a shrug—intent had no part in her actions. Lizzy would sigh and find a way to pack it without her sister's help.

They were not halfway finished when the door banged open and Mr. Bennet stood in the doorway. "What is taking so long? I had intended to be on the road by now."

Elizabeth glanced at Kitty, who was silent and avoiding even looking at her father, and answered. "We are still packing, Sir. I promise to send her down as soon as we are finished."

"Does she have enough to get her through the journey to Longbourn?"

"What?"

"Close up that trunk and send it down. The rest can be sent to Longbourn after it is packed; if the expense troubles you, I shall pay for it myself."

"Papa, you know that the expense does not matter, but for Kitty's sake, give her enough time to finish packing her things the way she wants them. You will be on your way soon enough."

But Mr. Bennet would not hear of further delay, and when Kitty did not answer Elizabeth's plea for support, carried his point. Within ten minutes, Kitty found herself back in the carriage, ready to begin the journey home. At the last possible moment Elizabeth pressed a letter into her hand, Kitty's name hastily scribbled in Georgiana's handwriting. Kitty could not muster more than a whispered thanks before the carriage door shut behind her and they were on their way.

At first, Mr. Bennet was silent, and as Kitty had no inclination to say anything either, the only sound was the creaking of the carriage and clanging of the horses' tack. However, Mr. Bennet could not hold his fury back forever.

"How could you do such a thing?"

Kitty said nothing; she did not know how.

"You had to have known that nothing good could come of it! What did you expect from him? Did you hope that he might set you up as his mistress? A fine situation for a gentleman's daughter! Or did you suppose that no one would ever notice? Had you met so often in private that it no longer mattered whether anyone knew? Or were your private indiscretions no longer exciting enough for you? You met together often enough that the risk of discovery in the house was no longer enough for you. You had to seek more thrills by taking your dishonor public—like a common whore!"

That insult elicited a choked "No! Never!" from her, but Mr. Bennet hardly noticed.

"Couldn't bear to be outdone by your younger sister, I suppose. Why should Lydia have all the scandal? You must have your share, and more besides. What would have happened if someone with less discretion than Mr. Knott had found you? You were not exactly well hidden back there. Anyone could easily have seen you!"

Kitty stared out the window, resolved only to never think of Mr. Knott again—it would destroy her to dwell on him. What he must think of her!

Mr. Bennet threw up his hands and said no more for the present, but he was never silent long. He alternated between icy silence and fiery rage for the entire trip home. It was, Kitty thought, the longest journey anyone had ever undertaken. Never had she been more relieved than when she came home and could flee to her own room. Her father would have to deal with her mother's confusion. She would let him tell her anything he wished; he would say nothing that she did not deserve, and if he valued keeping Kitty's disgrace quiet, he would tell her very little indeed.

Kitty was exhausted, but too despondent to sleep, and so she acted on her resolution to never think of Mr. Knott by wondering, every ten minutes or so, what he might be doing, and who he would marry now that he would not marry her.

CHAPTER 32

itty kept herself to her room, and would speak to no one. Her father summoned her to his library at least once a day, but she could not bear to go. She insisted that they deflect curious visitors with vague answers, and so she remained "in poor health" and "indisposed" to everyone, and not even Mrs. Bennet knew much better. She knew only that Kitty did not wish to leave her room; that this was Kitty's decision and that Mr. Bennet was not inclined to argue it; and that Kitty expected to remain there indefinitely. This, of course, did not please Mrs. Bennet in the slightest, but as neither Kitty nor Mr. Bennet were willing to say more, she had little choice but to keep pressing them both in the vain expectation of information.

Since her arrival home, Kitty had been failing to compose the letter of thanks to Elizabeth which custom made essential and which circumstances made abhorrent. She had started this letter at least a dozen times, and again sat staring at her paper, but so far she could only think of saying what she had already said and rejected.

Thank you for inviting me to Pemberley. I'm so sorry I made such a mess of it.

No.

I enjoyed my stay very much, for the most part.

Definitely not.

I was glad for the opportunity to meet

She couldn't even finish that one.

I hope that I left everyone in good health. Please express my apologies for not being able to take my leave in person—though of course you have done so already, I am sure—but I should very much like to say to Mr. Knott especially

She threw down her pen in frustration. *He* was the problem. If Mr. Knott weren't lurking at the corners of every sentence she wrote, the letter would be written and in Elizabeth's hands by this point. But she wanted desperately to know how he was doing, and did not know how to ask. Had she driven him to despair? Did he ever ask after her? Was he—had he moved on to some other young lady?

For, of course, he would. The only question about it was when the news would reach Kitty and break her again. She tried to steel herself against it, by believing that he had moved on already, that he really had been in love with Georgiana all that time and meant to propose to her after all. But she could not fool herself, and she wanted more than anything to know whether he had forgotten her yet.

She did not dare to hope that he had forgiven her, but she wished she could be certain that he didn't hate her. In her better moments she reminded herself that he was a clergyman and therefore bound to uphold such holy practices as forgiveness. In her worst moments she believed that he hated her so much that he would go out of his way to warn every person he ever met against her, taking the shards of her shattered respectability and flinging them into the dirt.

Thank you for the hospitality you showed to our father and to me while we stayed there. I know that we were a trial to you but you were always gracious with us.

That may have been true, but she could hardly send it.

She looked up at Georgiana's letter, the one Elizabeth had pressed into her hand as they departed Pemberley. It sat, pristine, on top of her writing desk, though she did not know why she kept it there. She had not read it, nor even opened it. She wasn't sure that she could. It must contain either pity and sympathy, or blame, and she did not think that she had the stomach for either one. But she could not help thinking that Georgiana had seen Mr. Knott—had he not said he was going to tell Lizzy and Georgiana what happened when he left the alley? If she knew something that would give Kitty some idea of his state of mind... She would never say it, and Kitty knew that. But the possibility still existed, right up until she opened the letter and proved that it did not.

THE DOOR OPENED, and Mrs. Bennet walked in with arms full of "little things" for Kitty to do. Even when all others were barred from entry, Mrs. Bennet felt it her duty to encroach upon Kitty's privacy as much as possible, and Kitty hardly knew how to dissuade her, so she bore it. Kitty shoved her poor excuse for a letter under her prayer-book and stood up.

"Kitty, my dear! I heard from Hill that you sent your breakfast back untouched. Are you sure that you do not wish us to send for the apothecary?"

Kitty sighed. "Yes Mama. I was not very hungry."

"Well, you must not make a habit of it, for once you are feeling well enough to join society again, you will have to look your best! I can tell you, every person I know is dying to know whether you are all right. And you really do look as though you were quite healthy, if you would only eat more."

"I eat enough to keep me from being hungry, Mama, but I do so little in my room that I do not require much." She did not say, again, that she had no intention of ever rejoining society.

"Well, if you are certain..."

"Yes, Mama." To change the subject, she gestured to the work in her mother's arms. "What have you brought me today?" Over the past week and a half, her mother had brought countless things to make, mend, or decorate for Mary's wedding. Mr. Warde had, apparently, some distant relative or other who had died and left him just enough money that he felt he could support her sister adequately, and so their nuptials were proceeding without further delay. The banns had been read once since Kitty came home, and she thought her mother had been quite as full of pride on that occasion as she was for either Jane or Lizzy's marriage.

As Mrs. Bennet explained what she wanted done with each article she'd brought, Kitty's mind drifted in and out of attentiveness, always drawn away by the thought of Mr. Knott. The more she resolved never to think of him again, the more surely he would remain in her thoughts, and keeping her attention elsewhere for any length of time proved difficult. Kitty wondered often whether she would spend the rest of her life thinking of him: wondering how he did, tracing his smiles in her memory, and recalling all the times he stepped in to take care of her without her ever noticing. She tormented herself with thoughts of how differently she would behave now, if she had the chance to go back and relive those mornings when he was helping her walk again, or when he was visiting tenants with her. She dwelt in memories of those mornings when she had sat listening to him read *The Absentee,* and at last correctly interpreted the little smiles and glances he sent her way. And she envisioned him doing the same for another lady, who would not be so ignorant of his motives, who would encourage him and not disgrace him, and displace Kitty in his mind forever.

Perhaps after a few years, she might persuade Lizzy to tell her what had become of him. By then, she might be better able to bear the news she would receive. But of course, in order to keep that correspondence going, she had to finish writing that letter! She shot a dark look toward her writing desk.

"...And so I thought you and I might sit and work for a little while together and have a chat," Mrs. Bennet concluded. Kitty realized with a guilty start that she'd missed most of what she should have been doing with the pile of work her mother had brought.

"Just tell me what you want me to do first," she said, hoping it would be clear from context what to do with whatever her mother handed her. Thankfully, it was a nightgown that needed mending.

"It must be so difficult on you not to know anything that your friends are doing; not even to see them! You have been at home two weeks and the most of any person you have seen is at church."

Kitty smiled. "I have seen you every day, Mama, and Mary and Papa most days." The arrangement did not thrill her, but it was true.

"Yes but your family counts for nothing! I was talking to Mrs. Lucas yesterday and she said that Maria met the most charming gentleman at a picnic held by the Bells last Monday, and she is very hopeful of its becoming a match, if she can find out how to get them in company together again. Can you imagine, even Maria Lucas! I had not thought you would be the last to marry, Kitty." This was said, as always, reproachfully.

"Nor had I, Mama, but I suppose I cannot help it if no gentleman wishes to propose to me."

"No, poor dear." She reached forward and patted Kitty's hand. "But I am sure someone will be along some day; though not if you insist on remaining here forever! Can you not receive at least a few close friends? It has been two weeks; people are beginning to talk."

"I cannot, Mama." Kitty cringed inwardly. She hated this part of the conversation, and it had been coming more and more frequently, lately.

"I wish you would tell me why not, for your father never will."

"I am not well, Mama."

"You say that, but nothing about you seems the least bit unwell! Except that you do not eat as much as you used to." Mrs. Bennet sighed and shook her head. "There was a time, you know, when you girls used to tell me what was going on in your lives. Lord knows, I have precious little else to concern myself with, and why should I not know the nearest concerns of my own daughters?"

Kitty shook her head. She did not know whether telling her mother would have ended in sympathy or condemnation, but she did not imagine that she could withstand either. Her mother's emotions were too violent for the quiet, desperate ache that pervaded her life at the moment. "I'm sorry, Mama," she whispered. It usually was all she could think to say to anybody. It was starting to sound like nonsense even to her ears.

Mrs. Bennet could, and did, wax eloquent on the matter of her waning intimacy with her daughters, but she left eventually, like she always did. Kitty put aside her work as soon as she was alone again, and returned to the letter. This time, she told herself firmly, she would stay in her chair until she finished it, and if it took her until the break-fast-tray was sent up tomorrow, so be it.

She crossed out as many sentences as she left in, but she saw it through, and managed to mention Mr. Knott only once. If Elizabeth wanted to understand, she would send word. If she did not, Kitty would endeavor to forget about him. Again.

She glanced at Georgiana's letter. Might it mention him?

If Elizabeth never answered her, it would be her only information about him, perhaps ever. Could she bear that?

Kitty snatched up the letter and broke the seal, but before she could read anything more than her own name, a knock came at her door.

"Excuse me, Miss Kitty, but you have a letter." In Hill's outstretched hand was another letter, addressed in Miss Darcy's elegant writing.

CHAPTER 33

*K*itty accepted the letter with a trembling hand. A second one! And she hadn't read the first! She stared at the new letter for a few moments, but realized she had better start at the beginning. So she took up the first one and began to read.

Dear K—

Haven't much time. Sorry so short. But don't despair.

I know how you feel. I wished never to speak to or see anyone after W. You likely feel similar.

I do not believe you are beyond hope or repair. I know how persuasive a man can be even if you know what he is asking is wrong.

He is at fault. You can only move forward, and do not allow him to defeat you. Mr. J will only become more bitter and miserable but that won't be your fate.

E tells me you are leaving now. Write to me as soon as you can.

Love,

Georgie

Kitty folded the letter back up with tears in her eyes. She had repaid her friends' unflagging support and affection by ignoring her and casting her aside! She started back to her writing desk to add something to Georgiana to her letter, but the thought of the second letter stopped her short. She had not written back, as Georgiana had requested, and it had been over two weeks since she'd departed. Likely enough this second letter was only to say that as she had received no response, she must believe that Kitty did not wish for her friendship, and she would end the acquaintance. And she would have every right to do so, but the idea of it stabbed her bruised heart.

Kitty nearly dove for the second letter. It must not say any such thing. It could not!

Dear Kitty,

I begin to suspect that your father has forbidden you to correspond with me, and though the idea pains me, I can imagine that he is overly upset right now with anything or anyone connected to Pemberley. I hope for your sake that I am mistaken, and that you have only been unable to write because you have been busy elsewhere.

Now that I have more leisure, I can tell you more of what is going on here. I am sorry if any of what I have to report might pain you, but Elizabeth and I both feel that it would be best that you know now, lest you receive other, less accurate information. Miss Pratt has left us. In fact, she departed the same morning you did. It seems that she has gone to stay with—of all people —Mrs. Johns! Now we know what she was doing in Lambton all those mornings!

Before you think too ill of her, let me ease your mind. She did not, as far as we can tell, know of Mr. Johns's intent toward you, if she even saw him that morning. However, I believe that her meeting with his wife was what provided him with the time he needed to slip away and find you. Given what we know of Camilla Johns, I find it difficult to believe that she would know- ingly assist him in seducing another young woman. Her extreme jealousy toward you cannot have abated so quickly. Miss Pratt said nothing of the matter, and I do not believe that she thought of you at all. Her only thought was of her old friend, and the society she found with her.

She did not say that was her reason for leaving of course, but I think I know better. I cannot say that I am sorry to see her go. I have learned that a person with whom one used to be intimate when one was seven is not there- fore a good candidate for intimacy when one is seventeen. And, after all, what have children of seven to do with intimacy, anyway?

My cousin has also been called away, and as Mr. Knott has left us as well, we are quite unexpectedly bereft of all our company at once. But I suspect I know which part of that communication will interest you most.

Mr. Knott has, indeed, gone back to London, though I do not know precisely why. I can gather, from things my brother has said, that he did offer the vicarage to Mr. Knott, although there is some point about the particulars of the arrangement that I do not quite understand from the veiled conversations I have heard.

All I know is that he has not yet accepted it, and that my brother has agreed to hold it for him for the time being, until whatever conditions exist can be met.

I wish I could tell you more, but I know nothing further of him. He missed you terribly, I believe. Does that give you peace or pain? I wish I knew whether such news hurt you or not.

The letter went on about other things but Kitty could not bring herself to read them yet. So, Mr. Knott had left—gone from Pemberley, and possibly never to return, if he could not meet Mr. Darcy's conditions! She realized then how foolish she had been to expect that he would remain there always, or at least always close enough to the family that she might get news of him. This could easily be the last she would ever hear of him. He had gone to London... and there to stay for ever, as far as she might ever know.

She set the letter onto her writing desk, all thoughts of replying having quite vanished, and went over to her window to stare out at the garden. She hardly knew what she saw. All she knew, all she could think, was that she would probably never know what became of him. The thought made her numb, the kind of numbness that reached out to every other sensation and dulled them all.

One sensation, however, soon began to burrow its way out of the numbness: worry. Why had he not accepted that living? It was a good living, she knew—and his reason for coming to Pemberley in the first place had been to seek it. Had he decided that he could not live so near the place where he had met her? Had something else come up related to his mother's demise? Had his father fallen ill as well?

There were too many questions and too few answers, and Kitty would never know the rest. Yet if she had not been such a fool, she might now be entitled to know his nearest concerns! She would be able to write him and encourage him. She would, perhaps, even have been able to go with him, or at least follow him there.

As it was, she was trapped in her bedroom with nothing but speculation, and no way to offer him, or herself, any comfort.

LITTLE INDUCED Kitty to leave her room in the following two weeks. She posted her reply to Georgiana without really knowing what it said. She knew she did not hide her desire for news of Mr. Knott very well, and she could only hope that her friend would forgive her preoccupation.

To find ways to pass the tedious days, she tried all manner of distractions. She discovered that she could not abide drawing; she had no ear for music, and less for languages. The usual accomplishments with which women occupied their time held no interest for her—even those she had formerly enjoyed. It did not help, she supposed, that she could focus for no more than ten minutes on anything before thoughts of what she had lost intruded and she could no longer think of anything else. She was beginning to believe that her entire life would be lived in misery and regret. She knew she deserved nothing less, but she refused to give in. If she was destined to live alone, she had to find a way to do it without so much wretchedness.

She took to reading every book she could find. Losing herself in someone else's world, however dry it might be, was preferable to dwelling in her own. This had the somewhat curious consequence of sending her to her father's library more often than she had ever entered it before, but he did not say much to her when she was there, and she said nothing to him.

The only other thing that could distract her from her misery was her mother's daily intrusion into her room. These visits were not exactly pleasant, but they gave Kitty something to think of besides her own ruined life, and almost always gave her some piece of work to do for the rest of the day. She tried, as she sewed, to occupy herself with thoughts of what Mary would be doing while she used or wore whatever Kitty was mending or making. It provided, at least, a different kind of pain. But she could hardly bear to watch Mary preparing for her wedding, and how smug she was about it. What kind of bride showed so little joy and so much self-satisfaction? Kitty longed for the day when it was all over, and she could hide in her room in peace.

CHAPTER 34

$\mathcal{M}$ ary's wedding came at last, and Mrs. Bennet had successfully conscripted Kitty to attend her sister as bridesmaid. Kitty had no real interest in the post, but her mother insisted, and she did not have the energy to argue.

Accordingly, one crisp morning, Kitty found herself out of her room and dressed in her best gown, attending Mary as she pledged herself to Mr. Frederick Warde. She looked happier than Kitty had ever seen her. Gone were Kitty's vicious thoughts about her sister's lack of joy. Mary had never smiled more or looked more content. Really, today, she was as beautiful as any of her sisters. And Kitty tried very hard not to hate her for her happiness.

Watching them standing at the altar exchanging vows was its own kind of torment. Kitty tried to focus on the ceremony—or, rather, tried not to focus on anything except surviving the ordeal. But her heart would not be quiet, and kept casting up before her visions of what could have been. Rather than a glowing Mr. Warde standing before the altar, it would be Mr. Knott, probably quoting along under his breath with the minister as he read the service. He would be smiling at her the way Mr. Warde smiled at Mary—the kind of smile that said, "This is the most thrilling thing that I have ever done"— a smile that belonged to his lady alone.

Had Mary and he talked about what they planned to do with their house together? Was he looking forward to evenings spent reading aloud to her? Mr. Knott would have read her novels, if she wished it; Mr. Warde would probably just read Fordyce and extracts from the duller parts of the Bible. Of course, Mr. Knott would read the Bible to her also. But Kitty would have loved it, because he would have chosen only the more interesting parts to read to her. And he would practice giving his sermons to her, and she would love to hear it. They would visit parishioners together just as they'd visited Pemberley's tenants, and he would pray with them as Kitty set their homes in order for them...

Kitty had to inhale deeply and tried to focus on her sister. It could never happen! She would never be as happy as Mary—she would never stand before the altar and say those words—Mr. Knott would marry someone else and read to *her* in the evenings—

In that moment she could see her life stretching out before her, a formless void save for the visions of what might have been, and the weight of it caused her knees to buckle and tears to flood down her cheeks. She was gasping and shaking and only kept herself upright by grabbing the railing beside her.

Bride and groom stopped to stare at her. So did everyone else. But she could not help herself and she could not stop. How could it have gotten to this point? Mr. Johns had ruined everything for her, and she had just *let* him. And for that she would pay with a lifetime of loneliness and frustration! And this aching jealousy toward every other woman who was fortunate enough to marry.

Mr. Bennet appeared beside her, and whispered loudly, "Kitty! What is the matter with you?"

She tried to control herself but she couldn't—she couldn't breathe. Her father grabbed her elbow and pulled her out of the church.

The moment she was outside she leaned against the church wall and screamed her grief into the air.

"For heaven's sake, Catherine, will you hush? Let me get you back to the house and you may lose your mind all you wish without disturbing everyone else." He grabbed her arm again and dragged her away, albeit more gently than his words suggested he wanted to. He took her back to the house and sent her inside. "Keep out of the way of the wedding breakfast if you haven't found a way to calm yourself by then," he said, and left.

Kitty would not have needed his instructions for that. She fled to her bedroom and allowed herself a good long cry, screaming at herself, and Mr. Johns, and her own hateful foolishness. Why had she gone outside the shop? Why had she not just remained inside, in safety? Why did he have to be there? Why did she have to speak to him, instead of turning right around and marching back inside as soon as she saw him?

The loss of Mr. Knott would torment her forever. She would be better served trying to forget her own name than to forget him. This was her punishment for her behavior with Mr. Johns, and not even her father could have devised a more fitting one.

SHE HAD NEARLY CALMED herself by the time the others arrived for the breakfast, but she had no intention of joining them. Surely they would not wish to see her, and the last thing she wanted was to go down to join them and pretend that nothing had happened.

She did not at all expect to see a furious, red-faced Mary standing at her door.

"How could you?" she snarled.

Kitty sniffed. "I'm sorry," she said. She thought, *Do I even remember how to say anything else?*

"You're sorry? Don't you think 'sorry' rings a little hollow after all this? Mr. Warde is dreadfully offended by your behavior, and I am completely lost as to what to tell him. What should I say, Kitty? That my sister, so far from having forgotten her silly attempt at flirtation with him, is still stupid enough to want him for herself, instead of wishing us well at our wedding?"

"What?" Mary's accusation was at least enough to startle her out of her own misery for a second, and into indignation. "You cannot be serious. I want nothing to do with Mr. Warde! You are welcome to him, and I wish you both very happy."

"Oh? It certainly didn't seem that way. When you started sobbing and screaming when he said 'I take thee, Mary' it appeared rather different! How else am I to understand it?"

"I wasn't crying over *him*! I am only miserable because I met someone else—at Pemberley—and I love him, and I want to marry him, and I never will. He hates me. Is that not a good reason to cry? To see my sister so happy and know that I will never have any part in that happiness, in a marriage of my own?" Which speech plunged her right back into the misery she'd so briefly escaped.

"It may be good reason to mourn," Mary said, her tone not much softened, "but it is no good reason to make a spectacle of yourself at my wedding. I am sure that no one will talk of anything else for weeks! What a beginning to our marriage! Why do you have to make everything about you? Life is not one of your novels, Kitty. It isn't romantic to cry for your lost lover at your sister's wedding; it's just rude, and embarrassing."

"Well, at least you *had* a wedding," Kitty said. "I never shall."

"I am sure it is your own fault if you do not." She turned and stormed out of the room.

The truth of that final blow hit Kitty harder than she could bear, but she had no tears left. All that she could do was sit on her bed and clutch at her stomach. But nothing could stop the agonizing ache that threatened to overtake her entirely. She felt as though she simply could not go on living—that she would suffocate in her own regret.

"I can't do this," she whispered. "I have to do something to keep me distracted or I will die—or go mad—and I don't know which I would prefer."

CHAPTER 35

That evening, Mr. Bennet summoned Kitty into his library again. She did not have the energy to keep resisting him after such a day, and she knew that she would well deserve whatever punishment he could think of. It would be better to have it over with.

She appeared on his threshold, and when he invited her in, stepped through and closed the door behind her.

"Come and sit."

She obeyed. He stood up and began pacing the circumference of the room. He made several false starts before he settled on what to say, and she sank further into her seat with each one. What he did say, though, startled her to speechlessness. "Clearly, I have failed you in every way. I have done everything I could to keep you from following Lydia's path, and at every turn I have accomplished nothing but driving you further down that very road."

Kitty stared at him in mute astonishment.

"I am going to try something new, and ask you exactly what is the matter, and what you propose I do about it."

Kitty stared at her hands, folded in her lap. "I don't know what is the matter with me," she said. She couldn't manage to speak louder than a near-whisper. "I don't mean to do anything wrong, but somehow I always seem to manage it anyway."

"You certainly have developed quite a knack for it. I had hoped that you would begin to come into your own when Lydia left. I had not anticipated you choosing this."

"I did not choose it!" she said with sudden fury. "Do you think I would have chosen any of this? If I had my way, I would never have seen Mr. Johns again—I would have married Mr. Knott and settled down with him and been happy! What person would choose this anguish? Who would rather be ostracized, and misunderstood, and hated, and laughed at? All I have ever wanted was someone to love me —me, not Lydia, not one of the Bennet girls, but ME, Kitty. And now nobody ever will, and I cannot find out where I went so terribly wrong as to ruin forever every chance I might have had in finding it! Mr. Knott—" But even his name nearly choked her, and she could not say more.

Mr. Bennet's pacing had slowed, and finally stopped during this tirade. Now he stared at her, arms folded across his chest. "I was not aware that you cared for Mr. Knott at all," he said.

"Well, I do," she said, as passionate as she was bitter, "and I can never love another man the way I love him, and he will want nothing to do with me. Did you see his face when—when—Papa, he hates me!"

Almost in spite of himself, Mr. Bennet's lips twitched a half-hidden smile. "Well you certainly gave him plenty of reason to."

"God! I know it!" She put her face in her hands and waited for the tears to come again, but she couldn't cry any more. She just couldn't bear to look at him. "I just want everything to go away. I never want to see anyone again."

He sighed heavily. "Well. I see you have repented of your behavior, at least, and I believe your heartbreak is sufficient punishment that I don't feel it necessary to add anything else to your tribulation." He chuckled, though the sound held no mirth. "You seem quite miserable enough to satisfy even me."

If he meant that to be a relief to her, it missed its mark. What did she care if he punished her as severely as he wished? There was nothing for her in her room, and there was nothing for her anywhere else, either. Her misery was not of a sort that he could touch.

"So my question is, what shall we do with you now?"

Kitty shook her head. How should she know?

"Well, I shall have to think of something, since I can't very well have you moping around here for the rest of your life. Do you have any suggestions?"

"No, Sir."

"I thought you might not."

But no sooner had she said she did not have an idea, when she thought of something. "Wait. Papa... what if I were to take care of Longbourn's tenants the way Miss Darcy takes care of Pemberley's? I think... it might be good for me to be able to worry about someone else's troubles sometimes."

He sighed again, shaking his head. "You hardly seem in a fit state to think of anyone but yourself, troubled or otherwise."

"Well, I don't want to think of myself any longer," she said, her anger returning. "Or ever again. There's nothing of myself worth thinking of. I've ruined my own life. The least I can do is keep someone else from ruining theirs."

For a few moments, he said nothing, only looked at her closely. She raised her chin. She did not know whether it would actually help relieve her misery, but it was more than she'd had since she returned to Longbourn. She would not give it up easily.

He must have sensed it, or decided that her idea had enough merit to warrant a trial. "Your mother has been the one to care for the few that need it, since your elder sisters left. You will have to see what she wants you to do."

Kitty did not think she would have a difficult time convincing her mother to give up the task. Mrs. Bennet had never been particularly attentive to anyone outside of her immediate family. And this gave her something to think and plan for. Tomorrow, she decided, she would go out and talk to everyone, and see what might be needed. Then she could make a plan to bring it to them. Her spirits lifted a bit just thinking about it—and the best part, though she hardly allowed herself to think it, was that Mr. Knott would certainly approve. She intended to conduct herself in a manner that was worthy of him. She would never make up for her failure, but she might avoid adding to her reproachfulness.

She was on the threshold when her father called her name, and she stopped, still facing the hallway. His voice was quiet. "I am very sorry, Kitty."

She did not know how to respond. She nodded once, and left.

KITTY HAD no trouble with Mrs. Bennet, as expected. Her mother was so happy to see her asking to leave the house that she probably would have agreed to anything. For, as she said to anyone who would listen, who knows what might happen while a young lady is out walking in the country? So, Kitty went out the next morning, with very little idea of what to do except see what help she might offer.

She spent most of the morning going about to as many of the tenants as she could, and compiling a mental list of things she might do to be helpful.

And, indeed, one boy showed an interest and aptitude with horses beyond what Kitty had ever seen before. His response, when she complimented him on it, provided her with her first sense of the real difference she might make.

"Thank you, Miss! I been working hard as can be. Uncle Tim says if I keep on this way, I might find a post at a real stable."

"I imagine that would be just the place for you," Kitty agreed. "Have you any prospects? You're old enough to find some situation of that sort, surely."

"No, Miss, but Uncle says to keep on anyway, and promised to keep an ear out for something that would suit."

Kitty knew her father's needs were too small to justify hiring a stableboy, but she promised him that she would talk to Mr. Fields about allowing him to come to her father's stables and learn, if he could spare a morning per week. "I do not know whether there would be much in the way of payment, but he could at least supply a good reference for you, if you do well, and I am sure he would hear of more eligible situations than your uncle might."

"Would you really, Miss? If Uncle Tim allows..." The excitement on his face as he calculated the opportunities that might await him lifted Kitty's spirits as nothing else had done. Here, at least, was one positive accomplishment she could point to, and say that whatever mess she had made of her own life, she had improved someone else's. She promised him faithfully that she would send Mr. Fields to talk to his uncle as soon as may be. And, when she returned to the house, that's exactly what she did.

OVER THE COURSE of the next week, Kitty went out every day to visit her father's tenants and attend to the list she had made for herself. She got to know most of the tenants fairly well, and started to look forward to seeing them. She was so relieved to have something to worry about other than her own troubles. By the end of that week, she was starting to believe that she might not die of despair, after all.

She returned from her visits later and later each day. It wasn't exactly on purpose, but she so much preferred visiting with them, working with them, and seeing what they were up to, to anything else she could do, that she found it harder and harder to go back home. At home she only had despair, and a constant reminder of what she had lost. When she was visiting, she could focus on other problems, ones that had solutions that she could provide, or at least that indicated a need she could meet. Life lost some of its bleakness.

By Thursday afternoon, she had to run home to be sure that she would be back in time to dress for dinner. It was not very ladylike of her, but she made it to the front hall in good time, breathing heavily.

Hill stopped her almost as soon as she came in the door. "You have a caller, Miss Bennet; he has been in the parlor for an hour at least. Your mother is frantic for you. Will you not go in?"

Kitty frowned, still trying to catch her breath. "A caller?" A caller, moreover, who was apparently male? She could think of no one who would call on her, much less a gentleman, but her spirits were still high enough that she felt equal to some company. "Let me change out of these filthy clothes, at least."

But Mrs. Bennet came into the hall at that moment and would not hear of Kitty leaving for even a moment to change. "You look well enough! He has been waiting too long as it is. How could you be so irresponsible as to vanish for the whole morning? Go, go!" She nearly yanked off Kitty's bonnet and gloves as she spoke, and gave her a little push toward the parlor door.

Kitty was more confused than ever by her mother's urgency, but she did as she was told and entered the parlor. She did not notice when her mother closed the door behind her. She saw only one thing, and it was the last thing in the world she expected.

Before the fireplace, one long finger tracing the carvings on the mantle, stood Mr. Knott.

CHAPTER 36

*K*itty could not move, or breathe, or think. She could not bear to look at him. How could she withstand the disappointment that would surely show in his manner toward her? And if he had come to tell her that he was engaged to someone else, how much worse would that be!

She started, turned, and was halfway to fleeing out of the room without so much as another glance at him, when he spoke and froze her in place again. "Miss Bennet, please, don't go." His voice was so quiet that she might have missed it if she had not been so keenly attuned to him already.

She stood beside the pianoforte, her heart doing everything within its power to flee her chest entirely. He brushed past the sofa and came close enough to her to touch her arm. Still, she could not look at him. She had to force herself to swallow, which did nothing to relieve the thickness of her throat. "Please, I can't bear it," she managed to say.

Mr. Knott, as gentle as she had ever known a man to be, pulled her over to the sofa and somehow contrived to convince her to sit on it. She stared resolutely at his boots. They were scuffed and plain, and dusty from the roads. She started to tremble, and cursed herself for it.

Why could she not say anything? Why could she not meet his eye? Why, oh, why had he come?

"Are you all right?" he asked. "What is the matter?"

"How... why... what are you doing here?" The words would not come out right. Nothing came out right. Why could she not stop shaking! She pressed her hands into her stomach. It helped neither her hands nor her stomach return to normal.

"I came to see you. I thought... you said I might, did you not?"

She nodded. She had said that. Why had she said that? She hadn't known then what torment it would be if he came.

"Perhaps you have changed your mind?"

She finally looked into his eyes, startled.

"You have not changed your mind," he said, and smiled a little. "I wish you would tell me what is the matter. You seem terribly unwell. Are you still suffering from Mr. Johns's assault?" His eyes flashed with contempt as he said the name, and Kitty flinched. "I am sorry, Miss Bennet..." He took one of her hands and extracted it from the tight grip she held against her stomach. Gently, he pressed it between both of his own and turned a little on the sofa so he faced her better. "I did not come here to distress you. Please forgive me."

When she did not move, he let her hand drop, but kept his fingers resting on it, and did not move farther away. His persistent gentleness was too much. "Oh, I am a stupid little fool and I have never been sorrier for it than I am in this moment!" She took a deep, shaky breath. "I am utterly, completely ruined, and it is all my fault, and I regret it so bitterly!"

"Kitty, I do not understand..."

"Mr. Johns!" He could not be so cruel as to expect her to explain it.

"He imposed himself on you. I know how the world views such things, but I saw the look in your eyes when you... when he..." He shook his head, his hand tightening over hers. "I am a clergyman, Miss Bennet, and as such it is my duty to forgive as our Lord does. I have quite forgiven you for whatever small role you played in it."

Somehow his belief in her innocence hurt more. "He did not... I let him do what he did... I thought... oh, I thought he only wanted my pity, and I was so stupid, and so wrong, and all the time I did not even know I was in love with—" She stopped abruptly. She could not tell him how much she loved him. It was too late to do anything about it. She sniffed back her tears and clutched after the handkerchief he offered her.

He didn't say anything, but he took her hand up again, and traced little circles across her knuckles. It was enough to break what little self-control she had left, and she began to cry: great, harrowing, choking sobs that only made her feel worse about how he must think of her.

Finally, after what seemed to Kitty to be a very long time, but not nearly long enough, she managed to stop crying and merely sniffled a lot instead, and swiped angrily at her face with the handkerchief. "I am so, so, very sorry," she whispered. "It is a very frightening prospect, having ruined one's life before one is even twenty years old. I have not fully adjusted to the idea yet."

"Is your life ruined?" he asked.

She shrugged a little. "I cannot see how it could not be. Everyone who knows about it must say so."

"They know nothing." The venom in his voice surprised her, enough that she looked up at him and could finally meet his eyes. "They do not know you the way I know you, or they would never say such things about you. You are not yet twenty? Miss Bennet, your whole life is before you, and you are not bound by the mistakes that you have made no matter how much any of the old ladies of the world might like to screech at you. You made mistakes; well, so does every other living person, and they aren't any better than you are. If they have made you feel like this, I would say they are quite a bit worse."

"But my reputation..."

"Your reputation is a little bit tarnished, I suppose, and you are the object of pity to those few of Lambton who have heard vague rumors, but that is all. Your sister and her husband have already forgiven you, and their concern for you is only that you are well." He hesitated. "Mr. Darcy has awarded me the living, provided that I can help to protect your reputation."

She stiffened. Of course, Mr. Darcy had promised to protect her, and he probably thought that he was doing her a favor in this. But it sounded so dreadful when he put it like that, and she could just imagine the gossip that must be spreading about her, and about how she forced her brother to impose on a clergyman he hardly knew. Her eyes burned uncomfortably, but she was too exhausted to cry again.

He paused and lifted his hand from hers. His fingers traced the line of her chin ever so gently. Kitty closed her eyes, ashamed at herself for how desperately she wished for him to continue. He could not possibly still want to marry her. Could she bear being married to a man who'd agreed to have her only because it secured him a living? She would release him, and allow him to take the living without the smear to his honor that marrying her would bring him. She could sacrifice that for his sake. She had to.

"I told them that I would be honored." Again he paused, and Kitty opened her eyes to stare at him. He was smiling. "I believe Mr. and Mrs. Darcy were expecting this, for they were halfway to bundling me up and sending me out after you that very afternoon. But I was there to accept the living and Colonel Fitzwilliam called us to task."

"I am sure they will give you the living either way. I do not imagine that my brother could be so cruel as to deny it to you, when you are such a worthy candidate."

This show of her good opinion of him elicited a broad smile, which spread across his face like the dawn. Kitty felt it was perhaps the handsomest thing she had ever seen. He was such a good man, such a kind man, such a wonderful friend and she determined right then and there that she would go live with Lizzy at Pemberley as soon as she could, so that she could always be near him. The scandal at Lambton was nothing if it meant that she could maintain this precious friendship. Even if she had ruined all chance at it becoming anything more than a precious friendship, Kitty knew that she could not deny herself this, too. Her life would be bearable after all. They could go on walks together and she would hear him preach every Sunday. That had to be acceptable.

"I am glad that you approve of his choice," Mr. Knott said. "Do you think you should like it there?"

"Pemberley is a beautiful house, and I would be happy to go back to Derbyshire," she said, wondering how he had guessed at her thoughts.

The agitation from that long ago day in the ruins of the monastery reappeared in his manner, and he dropped his hand to her side. The other hand still clutched hers, though, and Kitty did not wish to take it back. A wild, mad little hope fluttered up from the rubble of her twisted stomach, and she fought to smash it down. She could not ruin his life by marrying him.

"Miss Bennet, I..." He stopped, coughed, and tried again. And failed again. He threw up his hands, finally dropping hers, and Kitty pushed it back against her stomach. "I am such a coward!" he finally managed to say, and stood up and started pacing the room.

Kitty stood as well, though she did not know how she could help him. "You are not a coward," she said.

"But I am! Miss Bennet, do you know, I have been longing to speak to you for months; I have regretted not saying to you what was on my heart so long ago, when I last took my leave of you, and yet when I am here, and you are before me at last, all the pretty speeches and declarations that I had thought up for this very moment have fled me entirely." He shook his head and laughed a little, a bitter sound which Kitty had never heard from him before. "I am entirely undone and I have no idea how to proceed. Please; you cannot mistake my meaning, my intent, only I am too lost to know how to say it."

She was trembling again and she felt her share of his terror, but she could not let him leave her again without knowing; if there was some small hope; if she could have the desire of her heart after all... "Do you mean to tell me, Mr. Knott, that you love me?" she said in a very small whisper.

"Love you! Good God, Catherine Bennet, if I loved you any more I think I would die of it."

Though she had begun to hope, hearing it was an entirely different matter. Suddenly the tears that had abandoned her before returned in full force.

He came to her side in an instant, apologizing for everything, and through her tears and the hysterics she could feel threatening to rise, she forced herself to respond. "Do not apologize; never apologize; for heaven's sake, Mr. Knott, you have nothing to be sorry for!" She managed to push him away and composed herself a little, but her overwhelming emotions were fighting to take control again and none of them knew which should express itself first. "Please, don't be sorry. I am not angry or sad or distressed over that, it is only that I thought..." She took a deep, shuddering breath. "I thought there was no chance of you loving me after everything I had done. I thought it must be impossible. I am only overcome with my own relief." She still had his handkerchief, and she scrubbed her eyes with it in a rather unladylike manner. "I did not know my feelings the last time; I would not have been able to answer you the way you wished, had you been able to say it then. But I know now that a world in which I do not have your friendship, at least, is a world in which I do not wish to live."

"You have my heart entirely," he said, still standing a few paces away from her. "Whether or not you want it, it is yours."

"But I do want it!" The dawn rose again on his face, stronger than before. Kitty had to look away. "Only I should not take it."

"Why not?" Each word was tight and clipped.

She pushed aside her feelings. This was for his sake. But it was hard, oh, it was hard to say the words! "Because it would destroy your living! Think, Mr. Knott! If you and I were to marry, and to go back to Watercress Hill, where I am suspected to be, if not known to be, a loose woman of no morals, how could they respect you? How could they treat you as a congregation should when you have married a woman that they cannot respect? How could I do that to you?" She shook her head. "What frightens me most is that there was a time when I would have done it without thinking of it, and in the process I very probably would have ruined your happiness forever. I know better now and I will not make that mistake."

"Kitty..." He took a step forward, his look as pleading as his tone, but she shook her head again.

"I have decided that, when I am of age and can make my home where I choose, I will ask to live with the Darcys at Pemberley. I could be your friend, Mr. Knott. That would not be so very improper, would it? We could go on our long walks together like we used to, and it would not be improper for a ruined woman to seek the counsel of the rector, would it?"

His ears started to turn pink. "It would be miserably improper for a man to maintain a friendship of that sort with a woman he loves and never marry her," he said, his voice quiet and severe. "And I will have no part of it."

Kitty sank back onto the sofa behind her. The entire world was once again bleak and colorless, and so much the worse for the brief moments of hope that had illuminated it. "Then, there is no hope for us. I shall remain at Longbourn forever."

"There is every hope for us if you will stop being so foolish and agree to marry me!"

"I can't! You haven't asked me!" she said. The absurdity of it all hit her at once and she giggled.

He raised both eyebrows and came and stood before her. "Very well, since you insist on mistaking my meaning, I will be plain. Miss Catherine Bennet, will you do me the honor of becoming my wife, no matter what a couple of stupid old women in Watercress, or Lambton, or Meryton, or anywhere else stupid old women can be found, might say about it?"

Kitty still did not know if she would be able to bear it, if she was the reason that the world did not respect him. She hesitated, toying with the fringe on the pillow beside her. In front of her, Mr. Knott still stood, and she could hear his breathing grow harsher as he waited for her answer. She finally looked up at him, and took a deep breath. "Yes," she whispered.

CHAPTER 37

The stiffness in Mr. Knott's posture vanished as he settled on the sofa beside her and claimed her hands in his again. Kitty, still clutching his handkerchief, bowed her head and stared at his fingers. They were long, and wrapped all the way around her hands. He was here! He was here, and he loved her, and they were engaged. She could hardly believe that she had not imagined it all. And should she be terrified? Because the strongest emotion she felt just then was stomach-churning fear.

He seemed to sense her feelings. "We will marry from here, if you wish," he said quietly. But she could hear the joy bubbling under every word. "In a month, or a little more, we could be at Watercress Hill together."

"A month!" It was both too soon and not nearly soon enough. "I... would like that," she said. She realized as she said it that she would like it very much. She still had one objection, however. "But my father may not consent..."

"He's already given his consent, my dear. Unless he sees fit to retract it now, and I don't believe he will." He squeezed her hands. "But if you wish to wait longer, we could..."

"No! —no, there's no need." She frowned. "I suppose I should have guessed that you would have spoken with him while I was out. I am sorry to have kept you waiting. But I could not know that you would be here."

"I know. And I do not mind having waited. I've waited this long. What's another day?" He smiled, squeezing her hands. "But I haven't seen your father today. He gave me his consent when we were at Pemberley."

"What? So long ago!" Of course. Now she remembered—rather too late—that her father had hinted as much, shortly after Mr. Knott left to be with his mother. So much had happened since then that she'd completely forgotten how much her father knew, and didn't know.

Mr. Knott blushed. "I needed a reason to persuade your father to lighten your punishment. So I told him I wanted to marry you, but I wanted more time with you to ensure that you would give a favorable answer, first." He hesitated, and his thumbs tracked circles on her hands. "I—I'm sorry if that offends you. But, I thought you were still in love with Mr. Johns, and wouldn't have accepted me..."

"So did I, at the time." She shook her head, smiling a little. "But I did not understand what it felt like, to love."

"And do you, now?" He raised his eyebrows, but smiled at her.

"Of course I do!" This kind of teasing made her strangely happy. It was as affectionate as it was provoking. "It feels like... like life is more precious, when you're in it. Your affection means I'm safe to learn to be myself. And because I love you, I want to be the best self I can, for your sake, if not my own." She shook her head. "I don't know. It's difficult to describe."

His voice, when he spoke, was low and rough. "I think you did an excellent job." One of his hands lifted from hers, reached halfway to her face, and stopped. He glanced down at it, and back up at her. "Kitty... may... may I kiss you?"

The fear and nervousness returned to the pit of her stomach, but she looked into his eyes and nodded. *You love him. It will be nothing like with Mr. Johns.*

He placed his hand alongside her cheek and leaned in. Kitty closed her eyes, and his lips, soft and moist, brushed against hers in more of a question than a kiss. She smiled. It was nothing like Mr. Johns, in the best possible way. Leaning forward, she kissed him back. Then she turned her head and kissed his palm.

He leaned back and dropped his hand, and Kitty opened her eyes. He was looking at her with such a mix of affection and pleasure and pride that she couldn't meet his gaze for very long, but she couldn't stop smiling.

"Thank you," he whispered. Kitty only smiled more.

MR. BENNET WAS NOT NEARLY AS ANGERED, upon walking in on this scene, as Kitty had reason to believe he would be. Then again, he had barely so much as crossed the threshold before Mr. Knott was there, apologizing for the somewhat unexpected nature of it all, and the lack of propriety he had shown in allowing them to be together unescorted for so long. In his hesitant way, he explained that Kitty had agreed to marry him, and that he wished Mr. Bennet to keep his word and permit them to marry, all in one long, rambling sentence.

Mr. Bennet looked between the young man standing before him and his daughter, who stood behind Mr. Knott with her tear-streaked face shining and all of her attention fixed on the man she'd agreed to marry. Her smile was incredulous, but delighted.

There was one lingering doubt that he still needed to address, however. "Will you be content to live so near to Mr. Johns, Kitty? Edgepark is not far from Watercress."

She glanced at Mr. Knott, but when he did not say anything, she looked down at her feet. "I hope I will not need to see much of him." With a start, she looked back to her betrothed. "He does not attend service at Watercress, does he?"

Mr. Knott shook his head. "When he attends service at all, he goes to a church much closer to Edgepark." He took her hand. "I will not let him hurt you again."

"I know." She smiled and turned back to her father. "If the chance of meeting him is the price I pay for marrying Mr. Knott, I will gladly pay it. Besides, his punishment will be to live the rest of his life with

Mrs. Johns, and endure far too much of Amy Pratt's company. For that, I can almost pity him. I'm not afraid of him any longer. Besides, I have no intention of ever putting myself in a position where he could do that again. He, or anyone else."

"I will see that she is protected from him, Mr. Bennet." Mr. Knott stepped forward and held out his hand to shake. "You have my word."

Mr. Bennet raised an eyebrow and shook the hand. "In that case, you have my blessing."

From the other side of the door, Mrs. Bennet squealed.

PREPARATIONS for the wedding moved as quickly as they could, and the wedding was set for as close to exactly three weeks as they could manage. Unlike Mary, Kitty spent the entire time in raptures. The work she had bemoaned doing for Mary she delighted to do for herself. She received congratulatory callers with a thrill that never diminished, and could hardly contain her excitement each time the banns were read.

The morning of her wedding, Kitty snuck out of the house and ran out to the stables in all her wedding finery to remind Mr. Fields that he had an appointment the next day with Timothy Barnes to see about establishing his nephew in the stable. Mr. Knott, she knew, would be proud of her for remembering. And, come to that, she was proud of herself.

Kitty and Mr. Knott were married quietly, with enough fashion to satisfy Mrs. Bennet and enough economy to satisfy her husband. Mary threatened to come to their wedding and cry as uproariously as Kitty had cried at hers, but it was an empty threat; neither of the Wardes were in attendance.

Mr. Knott surprised his bride with a journey to the seaside at Lyme, courtesy of his wealthy cousin. There, for a full week, they had no concerns beyond whatever struck their fancy at the moment, and nothing could have suited them more. They planned their entire future together in that week, and if it came to pass, in the years to come, that things did not work out quite as they had foreseen, at least they were confident that they should never be apart. Kitty was never happier than when in his company, never more content than when settled as his wife.

Mr. Knott had, as it turned out, taken some precautions before they were wed, to ensure that his wife would not suffer in her marriage to him. He took great pains to introduce her to the neighborhood and requested that the most venerable and wise ladies of that community take her in, for his sake if not for her own (though he assured them that they would come to love her as quickly as he had), and ease her way into the neighborhood. Watercress seemed to regard the whole affair with Mr. Johns as, if not a scandalous falsehood, at least a misinterpreted tale, the blame of which was assigned entirely to Mr. Johns himself. Kitty, for her part, felt herself obligated to insist that she had her share of blame in the matter, but the society of Watercress saw it as her natural modesty. Kitty was so determined to make her husband proud of her that the improvements in her character surprised even Elizabeth.

Her intimacy with Amy Pratt was now quite as far gone as her intimacy with Lydia. Amy had no trouble with moving on to more accommodating company, and remained with Camilla Johns for some months. Kitty avoided them, and they seemed content to avoid her.

With her older siblings—even with Mary—Kitty became better friends, and her friendship with Georgiana supplied all that could have been missing in Lydia's affection. And even when her father came to visit Pemberley, he visited Mr. and Mrs. Knott with a small, surprised sort of pride in this daughter of his, formerly one of the silliest girls in the country.

THE END

Like what you read?

The most helpful thing you can do for an author is leave a review and share the love. The more reviews a book has, the more likely someone else is to pick it up and give it a try.

It would be the greatest gift you could give me if you took a minute and let the world know how you feel about *Learnt To Be Cautious*. Thank you!

-Jaina

Want to learn more about Kitty and Mr. Knott?

Want to hear more from Jaina Kirke?

Visit jainakirke.com to join my reader's group! You'll be the first to know about new book releases and special sales, and receive progress updates, juicy historical details, and even exclusive short stories starring characters from my books.

ACKNOWLEDGMENTS

First, to **Troy**, my amazing husband: you believed in me when I did not know how to believe in myself. You bent over backwards to make sure I had whatever I needed to write this book. Without you, not only is there no *Learnt To Be Cautious*, there is no Jaina Kirke. Thank you, my love.

To **my parents**, for being willing to believe that my crazy ambition to write a book might actually be worth following, and to **my siblings** for making less fun of me than siblings have the right to do.

To my beta readers, **Sarah T.**, **Yael**, **Katrina**, **Emily**, and **Sarah H.**: thank you for suffering through this book's toddler years. I know they weren't pretty, but your feedback was exactly what I needed to bring it up into something worth sending out into the world.

To my editor, **Sarah Yepishin**: thank you for reminding me of what I did right along with what I needed to change. Anything that's still messed up is entirely my fault, and anything that shines is entirely yours.

And finally, to **Jane Austen**: your peerless characters and your perfect stories are an inspiration to so many writers like me. I know nothing I have written can match your mastery, but thank you for letting me play with your toys for a spell. I hope I returned them not too much worse for the wear.

ABOUT THE AUTHOR

I have been writing stories since I knew what a story was, and eventually they became good enough to be worth sharing with other people.

My favorite kind of tales are the ones about girls discovering who they are and what they're doing in the world, through a ton of exciting adventures.

From Catherine Sutton in *The Perilous Gard* to Celia Bowen in *The Night Circus*, from Hermione Granger in *Harry Potter* to Ani Isilee in *The Goose Girl*, the legacy of such writers as Jane Austen and Charlotte Brontë is strong indeed, and it is a privilege to add my own humble offering.

When I'm not writing, you can probably find me exploring my new Pacific Northwest home with my husband and our two dogs. (The cat prefers to stay at home.)

I love hearing from my readers! Please get in touch:
www.jainakirke.com
jaina@jainakirke.com

Made in the USA
San Bernardino, CA
19 July 2017